THE HAUNTING OF GABRIEL ASHE

DAN POBLOCKI

SCHOLASTIC INC.

Copyright © 2013 by Dan Poblocki

This book was originally published in hardcover by Scholastic Press in 2013.

All rights reserved. Published by Scholastic Inc., *Publishers since 1920.* SCHOLASTIC and associated logos are trademarks and/or registered trademarks of Scholastic Inc.

The publisher does not have any control over and does not assume any responsibility for author or third-party websites or their content.

No part of this publication may be reproduced, stored in a retrieval system, or transmitted in any form or by any means, electronic, mechanical, photocopying, recording, or otherwise, without written permission of the publisher. For information regarding permission, write to Scholastic Inc., Attention: Permissions Department, 557 Broadway, New York, NY 10012.

This book is a work of fiction. Names, characters, places, and incidents are either the product of the author's imagination or are used fictitiously, and any resemblance to actual persons, living or dead, business establishments, events, or locales is entirely coincidental.

ISBN 978-0-545-40271-2

10 9 8 7 6 5 4 3 2 1   15 16 17 18 19

Printed in the U.S.A. 40
First printing 2015

The text type was set in Adobe Caslon Pro.
Book design by Christopher Stengel

*This book is dedicated to the memory of
John Bellairs and Edward Gorey,
my lifelong literary inspirations.*

PART ONE

❖

STICKS

IN THE DARK FOREST OF HOWLER'S NOTCH

THE TWO ROBBER PRINCES FOLLOWED the trail of blood deeper into the thicket. Ahead, in the shadow of towering trees, the child's cries grew faint. A pale violet mist seeped from the damp earth as the late hour secreted daylight away.

The boys knew that in the coming night, the small splashes of red at their feet would blend entirely with the leaf-plastered ground. If the child ceased her panicked wailing, they would lose not only her, but also the monster — a hulking sort of man whom the people of the two kingdoms referred to as the Hunter. He had stolen the girl from her parents' cabin, where the forest met the plains of Haliath.

"Hurry," whispered Prince Wraithen, dashing forth, careful to avoid each stone and dip.

But Prince Meatpie continued to lag behind. Distracted.

Wraithen turned to find Meatpie tucking his cell phone discreetly into his jacket pocket. "What are you doing?" said Wraithen with a forced calm, trying, as if it were possible, to keep his face from burning red with fury.

Prince Wraithen, of the kingdom Haliath, refused to call Prince Meatpie by his chosen name. He'd told his partner several times that he thought it was impossibly stupid. Wraithen also claimed that Meatpie's home, Castle Chicken Guts, sitting atop the slope of green meadow on the opposite side of the forest, might also benefit from a different nomenclature. Wraithen knew it was not his place to make such a suggestion — these were ancient lands with rich histories, and he was not a god but a mere Robber Prince. Still . . .

Meatpie of the Kingdom Chicken Guts? he'd asked when first they met. *Really? That's what you're going with?*

"Just checking the time," said Meatpie. "It's getting late. My parents —"

"Forget *time*," interrupted Wraithen. "The Hunter will not take hiatus from his offense simply because the sun has begun to set. And neither should we. The girl is in danger. Come."

Meatpie sighed, but jogged forward. The two scoured the ground, trying to find further evidence of the trail. Meatpie was about ready to give up when Wraithen pointed ahead and cried out, "There!"

In a small clearing, upon a barren square of earth, thick blood glistened red through the mist and the dimming light. A good and bad sign, both. The boys dashed forward.

The Dark Forest of Howler's Notch was a no-man's-land, populated with rogues and outsiders who found neither solace nor support in the peaceable domains of the nobles. The villains among them sought sustenance by stealing from farmers and families, mostly crops and livestock, but the worst of the folk — the mutated humanoid-beast they were currently tracking — found pleasure in taking human young, boiling them up for stew, and after the meal, as if in a mock gesture of good will, returning the bones to the family for burial.

At the age of twelve, the princes had become ordained Robbers — a long-standing tradition of the two kingdoms. Their job was to steal back what had been stolen from the people, and they had trained for this purpose since birth. Their parents, allied kings and queens, believed that this noble role would prepare them to become great rulers, inheritors of future thrones.

Following the trail past the clearing, the boys came upon an ancient wall, the stones of which were encased in leathery lichens and feather-soft mosses. The trail of blood appeared to stop here. Long ago, someone had built the seemingly endless barrier for reasons still mysterious. This waist-high wall was only one of many that had been raised like jagged scribble-marks across a map of the wooded hillside. People whispered rumors that the stones were magicked.

The princes paused, listening carefully to the forest for a clue. Crickets sang and pheasants fluttered between low branches. The wind scattered dry leaves across the ground. But that one sound they needed to hear — the cry of the injured babe — had gone silent.

"Fiend!" Wraithen shouted.

"Look," Meatpie whispered. He nodded at a patch of ground a stone's throw beyond the wall. A pale arm wiggled out from underneath a shallow pile of leaves. Wraithen moved toward the wall, but Meatpie grabbed his friend's shoulder. "Wait."

Wraithen spun, his eyes wild. "The child is there! We must save her."

Meatpie raised an eyebrow. "Umm. Duh? Trap."

Wraithen's confidence crumpled. "Really? You think?"

Meatpie answered by glancing around the small clearing. "He must be watching."

Wraithen sighed. "We can't just leave her there. She's hurt. We can worry later what the beast is up to."

"Okay," Meatpie said uncertainly.

The Robber Princes ran at the wall, placed their hands on the topmost stones, leapt up and over, then landed silently on the other side. The pale arm was a few feet away now. Wraithen rushed forward and gently lifted a small figure from the ground. Blonde hair and blue eyes sparkled in the indigo light. Delicate fingers pressed into the prince's neck. She seemed uninjured. She stayed quiet, as if she knew that any sound might bring back the thing that had snatched her from her crib.

Meatpie's mouth dropped open and he shook his head. "That is *so* creepy, Seth. Did you really plant a doll out here for us to find?"

Wraithen spun on his friend, disappointment filling his eyes. "My name is Wraithen! And no. I didn't *plant* her. The Hunter *stole* her from —" He turned toward the wall. "He's here!"

Meatpie glanced over his shoulder. At first he saw nothing, but then he forced himself to recognize a large shadow rising from the ground near the mossy boulders. The night had come up quickly, so the Hunter's features were difficult to discern. The silhouette stood nearly seven feet tall. Its broad shoulders made its small, neckless head appear to melt into its torso. When it reached for them, the boys ducked away from enormous hands that looked strong enough to crush a throat with a simple reflexive clutch.

The Robber Princes raced alongside the wall, back down the hill toward the child's home in Haliath. Wraithen cradled the girl inside his coat. A great rushing sound came up behind them as the Hunter gave chase. "You were right," Wraithen said, his voice shaking with every footfall. "It *was* a trap. What is the worth of a stew made from a single child when he can have the two of us as well?"

"Shut up and run!" Meatpie cried. He could feel the presence of the Hunter coming closer, could hear the rattle of quiver arrows in its pack, the jostle of the sharpened machete tucked into its belt. A warmth caressed the back of his neck. The monster's breath. Gooseflesh puckered Meatpie's skin. The Hunter was upon them.

In the distance back up the hill, a voice called to them.

"*Gabriel! Dinner!*"

"Shoot," said Prince Meatpie — who was not actually a prince at all, but a boy named Gabe. Gabriel Ashe. He stumbled and slowed. The trees seemed to shrink. The light grew slightly brighter. His companion kept running. "Seth!" Gabe said. "Stop! It's my mom."

Ahead, Prince Wraithen — also an ordinary boy, whose name was Seth Hopper — skidded to a halt. His shoulders seemed to deflate, and he turned. The eyes of the baby doll in his arms rolled into its head as if in disgust.

"Shoot," said Seth. "Just when things were getting good."

The woods were not actually enchanted nor filled with villains. This tree-covered slope was, in fact, an ordinary forest in a small town in eastern Massachusetts. Gabe's family, the Ashes, had only moved there several weeks earlier. They were staying with his grandmother in her big house up the hill. "We can keep going tomorrow," he suggested, feeling bad for ruining the game. "Pick up everything right here."

"It won't be the same."

"*Gabriel!*"

"Coming!" Gabe shouted. Seth looked crushed. "I'm free in the morning. I'll give you a call. Promise."

"You're not around in the afternoon?"

Gabe felt his cheeks flush. His other new friend, Mazzy Lerman, had asked him not to mention the pool party to Seth. "I-I'm busy," he stammered.

"Oh." For a moment, Seth looked confused, hurt even. But then he sighed and gave a slight smile. "Okay."

"You can find your way home?" The shadows had deepened, tinting the landscape indigo.

"Just down the hill." But Seth didn't move. He only clutched the doll tighter. The thing was bald, dirty, and naked — nothing like the golden babe Gabe had imagined during the game.

"*Gabriel! Now!*"

Gabe rolled his eyes and Seth turned to go. "Hey!" Gabe

called. Seth paused, glanced over his shoulder. "You *really* didn't plant that doll out here for us to find during the game?"

Seth smiled fully now. "I really didn't."

"That's so bizarre," said Gabe, shaking his head. "We were *pretending* to look for a missing kid, and we actually ended up sort of finding one."

"These woods are weird," said Seth, holding the doll up above his head. "You'll see."

A House of Brick

THE TRAIL OPENED onto an upwardly sloping meadow. Gabe continued on, listening to the chirping of frogs and the wind through the trees.

His grandmother's house was a brick building, over a hundred years old, that sat at the crest of the hill. It had been built by Gabe's great-great-great-grandfather Mordecai Temple. The gabled roof rose sharply from the walls like the bent wings of blackbirds, the many pieces of dark slate overlapping like armored feathers. A white wooden extension grew from the right side of the house — two stories high and full of windows. Those rooms contained art supplies and canvases, and had a view that overlooked the town. The sky was almost entirely dark. At this hour, it was a disappointing sign; summer was packing her bags and getting ready to go.

Gabe recognized the tall, trim silhouette standing halfway up the meadow. It was his mother, Dolores. Her dark brown hair lifted in the breeze. Her skin was several shades lighter than the shadows and a touch more olive-toned than Gabe's, who'd inherited some of his father's European paleness. "It's almost eight, young man," she said, her accent barely detectable. Since she'd moved to New England for college, her Spanish had taken on hints of Bostonian.

"I'm sorry," Gabe answered, running now to meet her. "We got stuck in our game."

She wrapped her arm around his shoulder. "And what game is this?"

"Just something Seth came up with a few days ago. We're princes who've formed a sort of special-ops task force." He blushed as the words came from his mouth. It suddenly sounded so childish. "Today we were looking for a cannibalistic baby snatcher called the Hunter."

Dolores shivered dramatically. "I don't like that. Creepy."

"You'd rather have me sit inside and stare at the wall all day?" Gabe asked with a teasing smile.

"It's not my fault that your father's mother doesn't have a cable connection —"

"*Or* the Internet —"

"Or the Internet," Dolores conceded. "But *I* didn't have the Internet when I was your age. Do you know what I used to do when I was little?"

Gabe sighed. "Eighth grade is not little."

"You've got a few days left before school starts," she went on. "Until then, you're *little*. Do you know what I used to do?"

"No. What did you used to do?"

"I would read books. You've heard of those, right?"

Gabe laughed, his voice echoing out into the calm of the evening. "Nice try."

She sniffed, disappointed. "You promised: just *one* book before the end of summer." And quickly, glossing over how Gabe's books had been lost in the fire, his mother went on, "You know your grandmother has a whole library." They came closer to the house. Light glowed from the dining room window, spilling out onto the grass below. Silhouettes moved behind the sheer curtains — Glen, Gabe's dad, and Elyse, his grandmother. Gabe's baby sister, Miriam, was most likely perched in her high chair, sucking on Cheerios and smearing banana on her face. "She'd be happy to lend you a book. Especially the ones she illustrated the covers for."

Dolores climbed the few stairs up to the house's rear patio. "She's a pretty famous artist, you know."

"I know, I know. That's what everyone in this town keeps telling me. Famous. Just like Dad."

Dolores was quiet for a few seconds, and Gabe immediately regretted bringing up his father's work. Like the books Gabe had owned, his father's workshop had been destroyed. She cleared her throat, dispelling bad thoughts. "Like mother, like son, I suppose," she chirped as she reached for the screen door.

Elyse wouldn't allow Gabe to sit at her dinner table until he'd scrubbed his arms all the way up to his elbows. He didn't blame her — he'd been crawling through the forest floor all afternoon. "Were you in those woods again?" she asked him before he'd had a chance to pull out his chair. She squinted at him intently from her place at the head of the table, her eyes like X-rays. His father sat beside her, fiddling with his cloth napkin.

As far back as Gabe could remember, his grandmother had dressed in dark colors, even before her husband passed away. She still dyed her hair a shimmering raven color. Gabe had never seen her without bright red lips and high-arched eyebrows, with a cat's-eye wick of black that lifted off from the edge of her eyelid.

Gabe felt his face flush without even knowing why. No going into the woods behind the house? Was this a new decree? "It's really pretty out there," he said, hoping that his nonchalance would put a cap on the subject. "You should walk with me some time."

"Oh, I don't know if that's a good idea," she said with a small shudder, as if someone had splattered something disgusting onto her nose and she was trying to shake it off.

"Why not?" asked Dolores, drying her hands on her jeans. She was a pro at pretending Elyse didn't frighten her. She slid her chair out from the table to be next to Miri, who offered her mother a slobber-covered piece of cereal.

Elyse licked her lips and glanced at the ceiling, considering the answer as if she had several to choose from. "The woods are dangerous," she said after a long moment.

Gabe sighed. He knew Elyse was right, in a way. On his first day in Slade, he'd discovered how for himself.

After the movers had left, Glen and Dolores had begun organizing their new bedroom. They'd asked Gabe for space, and the shadowed forest at the bottom of the sloping meadow had called to him. At the edge of trees, Gabe happened upon several wide and mysteriously well-worn paths that seemed to circle in upon themselves, echoing the stone walls that also crisscrossed the forest. He'd followed one of these trails down the hill, deeper into the woods, and found himself surrounded by a stillness that was unique to this place. No wind. No sound. The feeling of isolation made his heart race. In his old town outside of Boston, there was a constant whine of traffic, of children playing, of neighbors' televisions blasting from open windows. But the woods were so peaceful that when he closed his eyes, his pulse slowed and the memory of the past few weeks disappeared. Through this simple act, he'd traveled to another world — a world where he had never been the *Puppet Boy*, a world where he'd never wished for everything bad to fall away.

"Watch out!" called a voice. Startled, Gabe tripped on a tree root and snagged his T-shirt on a prickly bush. A skinny blond-haired boy with a sharp nose and wide eyes, who looked even more panicked than Gabe felt, emerged from behind a cluster of small trees. "I'm *so* sorry," the boy said, reaching out to help Gabe untangle himself from the thorns. "I didn't mean to scare you. It's just . . . You were about to step into my trap." The boy nodded at the ground a few feet away where a patchwork of leaves, sticks, and mud lay like a dirty welcome mat. "I covered up a hole to see if I could catch a rabbit." Sheepishly, he added, "I wasn't expecting anyone to come by. Mrs. Ashe doesn't usually let people wander around on her land."

Gabe managed to release his shirt and brush himself off. "She's my grandmother. I didn't think she'd mind."

The boy looked surprised. "I didn't know she had any family," he said. "Me and my mom live in the cottage at the bottom of the hill, on the other side of this forest." He wagged his thumb over his shoulder.

"I'm Gabe. We're staying with her for a little while."

"Seth Hopper," said the boy, with a wry smile.

Dangerous, his grandmother had said.

"I wouldn't go that far, Mother," Glen replied. "The woods behind Temple House are no different from anywhere else around here."

"The trails are great," Gabe offered. "It's like a park."

"I know what it's like," Elyse said. "I was born in this house, remember?" She wore a look of disdain. The rest of them sat at the dinner table watching her quizzically. Silence bounced around the dining room for a moment. Then Miri laughed and slapped at the high-chair tray.

The sudden sound broke whatever spell had fallen upon the family. Everyone jumped. Gabe slowly released his breath, unaware that he'd been holding it. Elyse shook her head and glanced at him, flustered. "I'm sorry," she said with an apologetic grin. "I just don't want you to get lost out there. That's all."

"I won't."

"Very good." Elyse folded her hands and lowered her head, but she couldn't hide the groove of tension between her eyebrows. "Now say grace, Gabriel."

"*Grace, Gabriel,*" Gabe whispered as his mother smiled and his father threw him a dirty look.

WHEN GABE AWOKE from a dream of the fire, he found himself tangled in sweaty sheets. He kicked them off.

A breeze blew in from the open window, and he caught his breath. Even after weeks of sleeping nightly in his new bedroom, he still sometimes woke in a panic, wondering where he was.

His previous room didn't even exist anymore, but his brain continued to hold on to the image of his superhero figurine collection that had stood on the shelf over his old bed board, his *abuelita*'s quilt that he'd hung on the back of his desk chair in case he got chilly at night, his father's bullfighter marionette that had dangled from a hook above his dresser.

Sometimes when he awoke in this new house, his pillow was damp with tears. He thought of what Father Gideon had said to him afterward — a quote from the Bible about leaving childish things behind. *We still have one another*, his mother had added. But Gabe wondered, if you have nothing left besides your family to remind you of your childhood, did it mean you had grown up?

In his new room, the breeze cooled his damp skin, and Gabe was chilled. He knew if he tried to sleep, embers would drift up once more into the darkness behind his eyelids, arms of molten plastic reaching for him, marionette strings blazing. A chorus of voices whispering, *This is your fault*.

Gabe needed a distraction. He kicked at the mattress, annoyed that his parents insisted on charging his phone in their bedroom so he wouldn't stay up late playing with it. He grabbed his T-shirt from the floor at the side of his bed.

Downstairs, Gabe crept toward the back of the house through the labyrinth of dark halls. He found the door he'd been searching for and pushed it open. Inside was a small room. Moonlight shone through a paned window at his left, throwing a strange prison-bar pattern onto the Persian rug at his feet. Outside, the leafy tops of the trees glistened in the silver light. High above, the moon was nearly full.

Down the meadow slope, something caught his eye. Standing a few yards from the edge of the forest was a tall, broad-shouldered man. The figure was a mere shade lighter than the deepest shadows, but Gabe could see the silhouette clearly. The shape stood unmoving. Was it a tree? A large shrub? The idea that someone was watching him from the darkness outside made his stomach squirm. *The woods are dangerous. . . .* But there had to be an explanation. Wasn't there always? Gabe blinked and the silhouette was gone. Must have been a trick of the light, he thought. Or of the dark.

He switched on a table lamp, and the world outside the house disappeared. Now, reflected in the window glass were the shelves that lined the walls of the small library. But not every shelf held books.

From the moment Gabe had stepped through his grandmother's front door, he understood that her house was like a museum, crammed with odd objects and strange artifacts. In this room sat tribal-looking sculptures and masks made of wood and bone. There were tiny framed pictures of odd circus performers, dangerous plants pressed behind glass, postcards from places that no longer existed. A taxidermy display of small rodents dressed in children's clothing stood beside a collection of old tin robots. There was a darkness to the selection — an indication of what lived inside his grandmother's mind. Gabe focused on the strange books instead. *Decoding the Pyramids*, *The Secrets of Practical Mysticism*, *Abandoned Mansions of the Hudson Valley*. And more. Much more. He didn't know where to begin.

In the corner of his eye, something moved. When Gabe turned toward the window, he realized that he'd seen the reflection of something in the room with him. He froze. A shadow shifted near the office door. There was a small creaking sound. A thump. The long feet of a rocking chair hit the floor as the person who'd been watching him finally stood up.

THE LOST FIGURINE

"CAUGHT YOU." A shadow slithered forward onto the carpet.

Gabe backed against a bookcase, jostling it hard enough to topple a few books off the shelves. They hit the floor with a *whoomp*. He heard his grandmother's chuckle and felt his face burn. The moonlight illuminated Elyse with a ghostly phosphorescence. Her floor-length black satin robe was tied tightly at her waist. The rocking chair continued to sway, brushing at the backs of her thin legs. She'd been sitting alone in the dark.

"I couldn't sleep," Gabe managed to say after a moment.

"So you thought you'd do some snooping?" she teased, raising an eyebrow.

"Mom said you have a lot of books." He nodded at the shelves.

"To say the least." His grandmother stared at him. She looked different — softer than usual. At first he thought it was the strange light, but then Gabe realized that her face was clean of makeup.

"May I borrow one?" he asked.

"Of course. That's what they're here for."

Surprised, Gabe turned to the closest shelf. "Mom said you might have a few of the ones whose covers you illustrated?"

"You don't have them already?"

"Dad got me copies when I was younger. But the fire . . ."

"Of course," she said. "The fire." Elyse motioned for him to follow her toward the window. "Here they are." She nodded at another bookcase. Gabe examined the books' spines. One name leapt out again and again.

"Wow, that's a lot of Nathaniel Olmstead."

Elyse raised an eyebrow. She pulled a thin volume from a shelf and brushed off the cover. "Yes. The creepiest author of the past thirty or so years." A smile spread across her face. "I always tell people that, since he was my bread and butter. I illustrated almost all of Nathaniel's covers. At one time, his stories made us both pretty famous." She handed the book to Gabe. He ran his hand across the title. *The Revenge of the Nightmarys.* "The publisher asked me to create a set of trading cards for this one, way back when kids still cared about that sort of thing. I hear that now you're all collecting and trading electronic things. 'Stuff' doesn't even exist anymore. *That*, to me, is spooky."

The illustration on the cover was a sketchy pen-and-ink image of a shadowy attic room. A group of girls clothed in tattered dresses stood in a line, reaching out with clawlike fingernails. He thought it was pretty cool that his grandmother had been able to come up with something so macabre.

"Go on. Read it. I dare you."

"Thanks," said Gabe, tucking it under his arm. "I think." He wasn't sure it was the sort of book that would help him get back to sleep, but he didn't want to offend her.

Elyse moved toward the window and stared out at the moonlit meadow, turning her back on him.

He realized that this was the first real conversation they'd had since he'd come to stay at Temple House. She'd been so busy helping with the baby, with the organizing, with the stress. "Why were you sitting down here in the dark?" he asked.

"You weren't the only one who couldn't sleep," she said, glancing at him from over her shoulder. "When I'm up late, I come in here and watch the night." She sighed. "Sometimes it watches me back."

Gabe shuddered. "And that doesn't, like, freak you out?"

She glanced over her shoulder. *"Freak me out?"* She smiled, nodding at the collection of oddities that filled her shelves. "In case you can't tell, it takes quite a lot to 'freak me out,' Gabriel."

"Where did you get all of it?" Gabe picked up a stone figurine from a small collection. The humanoid figures all wore long cloaks. Their postures were static, erect, almost monklike.

"Here and there," said Elyse. "New York thrift stores. Massachusetts junk shops. Flea markets and yard sales all over New England."

Gabe held up the figurine. "I think Seth Hopper has one just like this," he said. "I saw it at his house the other day. Standing on a shelf in the spare bedroom."

Elyse was silent for a moment, then said, "How funny." She deliberately took the object from him and placed it back on the shelf. Gabe felt like he'd made a mistake by mentioning it. "A couple years ago, I remember purchasing five of these little men at a comic book store where I was doing a signing. But now, there are only four. Apparently, one simply walked off." She gazed directly into Gabe's eyes. "Isn't that the strangest thing?"

"Yeah," said Gabe. Was she implying that Seth had somehow taken it from this room? How was that possible? Seth had never mentioned entering Temple House. "Really strange."

Elyse nodded at the book under Gabe's arm. "You found what you were looking for. Better hurry back to bed, before the monsters under your mattress realize you're still awake."

THE ALTAR OF THE CROOKED TREE

AFTER THE ROBBER PRINCES RETURNED the blonde baby to her parents, the kingdom of Haliath rejoiced, but Wraithen and Meatpie only allowed themselves to feel a fleeting victory. They were certain that the Hunter was still out there in the dark forest of Howler's Notch, watching, waiting, plotting to lure them into the shadows once again.

And so, early the next day, they met at the forest edge, where Wraithen's territory gave way to wilderness. The morning air was warm and damp. A canopy of silvery leaves towered high above, providing a cool, if temporary, shade. The boys listened to the woods. Critters scurried through ground brush. Birds called playfully to one another from across the rocky cradle of land beyond which stood the Kingdom of Chicken Guts. That the forest was so vocal was a good sign. No animals were hiding from predators.

"I received a tip," said Wraithen, shouldering his pack and starting into the forest, "from an archer who went to retrieve a lost arrow."

Meatpie followed reluctantly. "Why would an archer risk entering these woods for a stupid old arrow?"

Wraithen threw him a dirty look. "I don't know *why*. He just did. He said he found an altar of some sort — a pile of rocks next to a tree with a crooked trunk. He thinks the altar might be where the monster works his magic."

"So the Hunter is *magic* now?"

Wraithen stiffened, but continued onward. "If we destroy the altar, we may destroy some of his power."

"Okay," said Meatpie. "So you're suggesting we take apart his pile of rocks."

"His *altar*. Yes. We destroy it." Wraithen stopped and pointed. "There."

Ahead, a small tree stood upon an upraised mound that jutted slightly from the hillside. Its trunk grew from the ground at a sharp angle, leaning dramatically to the right. And just as Wraithen had described, a mound of stones — stacked at least five high — stood directly beside it, looking as though it were preventing the tree from tipping over. In a way, the site looked holy.

At the crest of the slope, Meatpie placed his palm on the crooked tree. It released a faint vibration. He instinctively pulled away. Standing unaware beside him, Wraithen reached out and lifted a stone from the top of the pile. "Hunter, be gone!" he cried, and tossed the stone. It spun like a discus down the hill, hit the ground, and rolled, coming to rest at the edge of a small brook.

Meatpie grabbed a stone too, but as he swung his arm back to throw, a harsh voice whispered in his ear, *DON'T!*

Gabe spun. No one was there. Seth stood on the opposite side of the tree — not nearly close enough to whisper like that. Had he been so lost in the game that he'd imagined it? He felt someone watching them. He glanced up the hill, then down. As far as he could tell, no one else was around, just him and Seth . . . well, Meatpie and Wraithen.

Seth continued to examine the rock mound, his shoulders pulled back in a regal stance.

"You knew this tree was out here, right?" asked Gabe.

"Only because the archer told me."

"Stop," said Gabe. "Just for a second. Stop." Seth blinked at him and Wraithen was gone. "Did *you* build this thing?" he asked.

Seth sighed, frustrated. "You can't keep doing that!" he said.

"Doing what?"

"Quitting the game."

"I didn't quit," said Gabe. "I hit pause for a second. But seriously. What *is* this?" He gestured at the makeshift altar. "It's creepy."

Seth shrugged. "I told you. These woods are weird."

"You keep saying that," said Gabe, planting his feet in the soft ground, even as it seemed to shift beneath his sneakers. "But it's not an answer." He remembered hearing heavy boots cross the path when he and Seth had been alone, and later, seeing that shadow at the edge of the forest from the library window. He sensed that his grandmother had seen it too, and worse, that she might have been seeing it for a while. *The woods are dangerous.* And now, a voice had whispered in his ear. Loudly. "Someone built this 'altar' from pieces of the old walls. It must have taken a lot of work. Who would do that? Why?"

"Who cares? *We* can use it for our game." The game. Right. Of course. Seth added, "I noticed the altar from the path over there about a year ago. I remembered it this morning and thought exploring it would be fun." Gabe stared uncertainly at the rocks. "High school kids mess around back here sometimes. Maybe *they* piled them." Gabe raised an eyebrow skeptically. "Does it really matter?"

"I guess not," said Gabe. "It's just . . . I thought I heard something."

He touched the crooked tree again and realized that the vibration he'd felt earlier had simply been the breeze echoing down the trunk from the top branches.

"What kind of something?"

"A voice. It whispered, '*Don't.*'"

"Don't?" Seth laughed. "Don't *what*?"

Before he'd fallen asleep the previous night, Gabe had managed to read a few pages of the book his grandmother had lent him. In the morning, when he remembered the vivid imagery of the ghost girls, his stomach felt tight. He hadn't been able to shake it. He'd had no idea that books could do that: dare him to finish reading. "I'm being a weirdo," said Gabe, if only to stop Seth from staring. "I slept funny last night."

Seth smiled slightly. "You want to take a break?" Gabe nodded. "Come on. I'll make us some peanut butter sandwiches."

Gabe checked the time on his phone. "Yeah, but I can't stay too long." He had to be back by noon if he was to make it to the pool party on time — the one Mazzy Lerman had said Seth wasn't invited to.

A HOUSE OF STICKS

THE HOPPERS' COTTAGE STOOD in a wide meadow at the bottom of the slope. It was a dingy white box of a building. A wide porch drooped from the front. Tall grass and weeds grew around its foundation. A gravel driveway stretched off into the woods on the opposite side of the wide yard, leading to the road that wound back up the hill toward Temple House. A ramshackle barn loomed over the driveway, and beyond it stood a small, empty stable. A large portion of the nearby yard was fenced in. Seth had told Gabe that they'd once owned a horse, that he'd learned to ride it through the trails in the woods. But they'd sold it a few years back. He didn't say why.

When the boys stepped onto the porch, Seth froze. "Shoot," he whispered, glancing around the side of the house at a small blue Honda parked in the driveway. "My mom's still home." Gabe hadn't met Mrs. Hopper yet. Seth had made her out to be a real weirdo: sleeping all day, accidentally putting her clothes on backward, staring into space for hours at a time.

Inside the house, Seth practically dashed down the short hall to his bedroom. When Gabe slipped through the doorway behind him, Seth closed the door.

"Seth! Is that you, honey?" a soft voice called.

"Yeah!" Seth shouted out.

Footsteps padded down the hall. "I called in sick today," Mrs. Hopper said through the closed door. "I thought we could —"

"Again?" Seth interrupted.

Gabe backed himself against Seth's bed, suddenly uncomfortable.

The door creaked open slightly. Seth's mother was a dim shape visible through the crack between the door and the jamb. "I wasn't up for it," she said.

"Hopefully they won't fire you this time," said Seth, plopping down in a chair beside his desk. "Helen's probably tired of covering your tables for you."

Gabe's face burned with embarrassment. He couldn't imagine talking to his own mother that way.

The door swung wider. "Oh. I didn't realize you had someone here." Mrs. Hopper held on to the doorknob as she peered in at the boys. She wore thick glasses that made her eyes look enormous. She was dressed in a faded purple sweat suit, and her gray-streaked hair was rumpled. She looked like she'd just gotten out of bed.

Gabe glanced at Seth, expecting him to make introductions, but as Seth stared at the desk, he realized that wasn't going to happen. "Hi," Gabe said, waving from his spot near the bed. "I'm Gabe."

"I-I'm Sharon," she said, touching her hair, apparently realizing how she must look. "Seth's mom."

"Yeah, he gets it," Seth mumbled, looking up. "Gabe's grandmother is Mrs. Ashe. His family moved in with her last month."

Sharon's face lit up. "Oh . . . yes." Then she shook her head, morphing her mouth into a serious expression. "I'm so sorry to hear about the fire."

"It's okay," said Gabe. "At least we're all alive." His mother's words. "That's what's important."

"We're kind of busy, Mom," said Seth.

"Oh. I apologize. Didn't mean to intrude. Let me know if you boys need anything."

After Sharon shut the door, Seth turned to Gabe and said, "Sorry about that."

"About what?"

"*Sharon*," said Seth with a sneer.

"She's your mom," said Gabe. "Why . . . why do you talk to her like that?"

Seth sighed. "Because she's trying to ruin my life." He was silent for a moment. "She's lost three jobs in the past three years. Thank goodness my dad's parents left us this house, or I'm sure we'd have been kicked out by some bank by now."

"She said she was feeling sick."

"She's been saying that ever since my older brother, David, ran away. She's *sick*" — Seth made air quotes with his fingers — "which means she won't stop thinking about him. Like, ever."

Gabe didn't know what to say. This was the first time Seth had mentioned having a brother, never mind the fact that he'd run away. "So no one knows where David is?"

"He might be with my dad," said Seth, carelessly moving objects around on his desk. Pens, paper, books. Back and forth. "But we don't know where *he* is either, so I guess that doesn't really matter." Seth stopped what he was doing and stared at his hands, wearing a strange smile. "My family's screwed up."

"So's mine," said Gabe quietly, knowing that wasn't quite true. Things weren't nearly as bad for him as they seemed to be for Seth. In fact, right now, they didn't seem bad at all.

Seth nodded. "That's why we're friends," he said, looking up from his desk. "We get each other."

"Yeah . . . sure." Gabe sat down on the bed. "So the spare bedroom, the door next to this one, that was David's?"

"Uh-huh."

"And all the stuff in it?"

Seth squinted at Gabe. "Why are you asking?"

Gabe hesitated. "Well . . . the last time I came over, I noticed a little figurine on a shelf in there. A black stone carved in the shape of a man in a hooded cloak."

"What about it?"

"My grandmother has a collection of them. The same exact kind."

Seth's face flushed red. "Oh, really? That's funny."

Gabe didn't want to press the issue, but he was curious. "The figurine in the other room belonged to your brother?"

Seth turned back to his desk. "I guess so," he said.

"My grandmother said that she's missing one of them. From her collection."

Seth stood. For a moment, he looked frightened. Angry. Like a cornered animal. Seconds later, he smiled. "Hey, you still hungry for that sandwich?" he asked.

Gabe couldn't bring himself to smile back. This whole exchange had been so weird. "I should probably get going."

LATER, AFTER A QUICK SHOWER, Gabe put on his new bathing suit. He packed a towel into one of his grandmother's old L.L. Bean tote bags and asked if he could borrow her bike — the one with the big basket on the handles — to ride into town. She gave him a few stern words about being careful and looking both ways at intersections, but otherwise she seemed happy to oblige.

He found his mom, dad, and sister in the second-floor sun-room studio, where Glen was working on what appeared to be a life-sized puppet — a shaggy gray monster with large googly eyes and a mouth full of dull, marshmallow-shaped white teeth. Dolores was sewing together pieces of a large clawed hand as Miri slept in her playpen.

"Wow," said Gabe. "This guy's for the new show?"

Glen nodded. "This guy *is* the new show. Have to whip up another prototype to present to the producers in Boston." He sighed, then winked at Dolores. "Starting from scratch is painful, but I'm so happy to have an assistant."

"Can I help later?" Gabe offered. "After the pool party?"

"Oh," said Dolores, "is that today?"

"Yeah," said Gabe, trying to sound nonchalant. "Mazzy said to show up around one o'clock. It's actually at her next-door neighbor's house, Felicia something. I left the phone number on the kitchen table in case you need to call."

Dolores glanced at Glen, smiling a wide, silly smile. "Look at this. Our son is growing up."

Glen batted his eyelashes in a mawkish reply. "Oh . . . so . . .

responsible!" he said, then threw his head forward, pretending audibly to cry. His parents did this to him sometimes, like it was a game they all played whenever they thought he was being too serious, which was often. Years ago, it made him chuckle. Now that Gabe finally *did* feel responsible, he merely blushed and rolled his eyes.

"Just wanted to let you know."

"Is Seth going with you?" Glen asked, wiping at his fake tears.

"Uh, no," said Gabe, his mouth suddenly dry.

"Didn't you invite him?" Dolores asked. "He's been so nice to you this summer."

"Yeah, well, he's probably busy," said Gabe. He waved goodbye, then closed the studio door behind him, already feeling a sponge of guilt expanding in his stomach.

Gabe had met Mazzy Lerman the week before, at the Slade Middle School orientation for new students. They were the only two joining the upcoming eighth-grade class. During a tour around the school, Mazzy kept making ridiculous faces whenever the vice principal, Ms. Yorne, wasn't looking. Gabe struggled to keep himself from giggling the entire time. Afterward, Mazzy asked Gabe to walk her home a few blocks away. They chatted about their old towns, about their old schools, about their favorite movies and teams and bands.

Gabe couldn't believe a girl was actually interested in anything he had to say. At his old school, no one paid any attention to him, except to call him a loser or names like *dorkface* and *Puppet Boy*. Some kids in his class were obsessed that his father had created famous characters for that old children's television show. They'd teased Gabe about it, convinced everyone that he played with dolls. And the more he protested, the worse it became.

When Mazzy invited Gabe to Felicia's party, Gabe had mentioned inviting his new friend Seth too. But when Mazzy asked Felicia, Felicia informed Mazzy that if Gabe wanted to bring Seth Hopper, then neither Mazzy nor Gabe would be welcome anymore. It was the first time Gabe realized that Seth might just be this town's version of a *dorkface*. A *Puppet Boy*.

In Slade, Gabe had a chance to start over, something he'd long wished for. The price of its fulfillment had been everything his family had owned and nights filled with ghastly dreams. Gabe told himself that the cost would be worth what they'd lost in the fire. He would not gamble by inviting Seth to the party. Nothing would ruin Gabe's new beginning — not if he could help it.

On the bike, Gabe skidded to a halt at the curb in front of the Lermans' house — an attractive gray saltbox cottage with white trim. He flicked down the kickstand, went up the walkway to Mazzy's front door, and pressed the doorbell. Inside, a soft chime rang. As he waited, he glanced around.

The street was well kempt, the lawns manicured, the landscaping tidy and clean. The house next door was a little bit bigger. A tall white fence ran along the property line toward the backyard. Sounds of water splashing and people chatting drifted up from behind the sharp wooden pickets. Felicia's party had started.

Gabe blushed as he wondered if Mazzy had gone ahead without him. But then he heard footsteps. The doorknob turned, the door swung open, and Mazzy stood smiling at him, already dressed in a shiny black swimsuit, camouflage shorts, and orange flip-flops. Her blonde hair fell in ringlets to her shoulders. "Gabe!" she said, giving him a hug. "You made it!"

Gabe felt his limbs grow numb, but he managed to stay on his feet.

PARTY CRASH

ONCE HE STEPPED ONTO THE PATIO next door, Gabe was certain he'd made a huge mistake. About twenty kids were swimming, lounging on plastic furniture, or eating hot dogs and burgers. They chatted and laughed as if they'd known one another for centuries. Again, already, he was the outsider.

When Mazzy called out to Felicia — a petite, pretty girl with short brown hair who was sitting on the opposite edge of the pool — a hush fell over the group. All eyes were like lasers. Gabe held his breath as he followed Mazzy across the concrete, keeping his gaze at his feet so that he wouldn't trip over anything or stub his toe and embarrass himself before he actually met anyone. "Hi, Gabe," Felicia said as he approached, her voice sounding kinder than he'd expected. "Thanks for coming."

"Oh," said Gabe, as some of the feeling flickered back into his fingers and toes. He hadn't realized how worried he'd been that Felicia would kick him out as soon as she saw his skinny frame, his freckled shoulders, his grandmother's (suddenly inappropriate) flowery beach towel. "Thanks for the invitation," he managed to say.

Felicia stood. "Hey, everyone," she called out. "This is my neighbor Mazzy and her friend Gabe. They're new here. Be nice!"

A few minutes later, Gabe had plopped the tote bag and towel on the poolside pile next to everyone else's stuff. Felicia's father, a man who'd introduced himself as Mr. Nielsen, offered Gabe a hot dog, but he politely declined and followed Mazzy into the pool, where an intense game of Marco Polo was already in progress.

Since Gabe didn't know how to swim, he confined himself to the shallow end and was captured a few times in a row. But he didn't mind losing. By the end of the game, he'd already learned the names of several of his new classmates. Two seemed particularly friendly: a girl named Ingrid Jessup and a boy called Malcolm Sedgwick. Both lived nearby and were "best friends" with Felicia. Sitting at the edge of the pool, they told Gabe and Mazzy what to expect at school, which clubs to join, and which intramural sports to sign up for. When Gabe mentioned that he was staying with his grandmother in the house on the hill, their eyes grew wide.

"That place is huge!" said Malcolm. "A real mansion."

"Yeah. And Elyse Ashe is so famous," said Ingrid. She turned to Felicia, who sidled up beside them. "She did all the covers for Nathaniel Olmstead's books."

"Oh my gosh, I love those," said Mazzy. "So totally creepy."

Gabe didn't know what to say, so he shrugged and reached for his towel. How long before they started to think *he* was creepy too?

"I've always wanted to see inside that place," said Felicia.

"You guys should come over some time," said Gabe. "I'm sure my grandmother wouldn't mind." But playing the words back in his head, he couldn't believe he'd just said them. What if they happened upon his father's studio? Would someone think to start up the *Puppet Boy* nonsense again? And what about Seth? Would Dolores and Glen force him to offer an invitation?

"You hear that, Mazzy?" said Felicia. "Next party is at Gabe's house."

Mazzy wrapped her towel around her head in a tall turban. She smiled at him, as if proud that he'd fit in so easily.

❖

When the sun sank low enough to create long shadows across the patio, Mr. and Mrs. Nielsen invited the group into their large kitchen for ice-cream sundaes. Everyone helped themselves to extra-large scoops, chocolate syrup, sprinkles, and whipped cream. As Gabe was adding a maraschino cherry to the top of his own sundae masterpiece, a scream came from outside. The sound shocked him, and he nearly dropped the jar of cherries.

Outside, Felicia stood at the edge of the pool. She pointed at something large and dark hovering just below the water's surface. "Dad!" she called. "Turn on the light!"

Moments later, everyone gathered outside. Gabe found Mazzy a few feet from the deep end. "What is that thing?" she whispered. Gabe's imagination raced. It looked like a large animal. A bear. A moose.

A person.

Gabe fought off dizziness. For a moment, Seth's game flickered through his mind, and he thought of the Hunter, as if this were some trick he'd think to play, a trap to lure them all close.

Mr. Nielsen flicked a switch in the kitchen and an underwater light illuminated the bottom of the pool. Now the sunken shape became a little bit clearer. As Gabe stared, he realized that it was no animal. No person. In fact, it wasn't a single object. It was many.

"Our stuff!" said Malcolm, pointing across the patio to where everyone had earlier dropped their towels and bags. "Someone threw all of it in the pool." A collective groan rose from the group.

Felicia turned on them. The bright blue eyes that had earlier appeared to be so kind were icy with anger. "Who would do this?"

No one spoke for several seconds.

"We were all in the kitchen," said Ingrid. "Maybe someone snuck into your yard through the gate."

"But why?" Felicia asked. "What'd *I* ever do to anyone?"

At the Lermans' house next door, Gabe perched on the top step beside Mazzy, feeling like a drowned cat. Felicia's party had dispersed quickly. With nothing dry to wear, and his grandmother's tote bag still soaking wet, he'd called home to ask for a ride. The sun had set, and the brisk breeze would have made a bike ride up the hill even chillier. Thankfully, after Mazzy had changed her own clothes, she'd brought him a fresh white T-shirt to wear.

"Sorry about the end of the party," said Mazzy. "Felicia got *so* upset." She shook her head somberly for a moment. Then she cracked a smile. "I actually think what happened was kind of funny."

"Funny?"

"Yeah." Mazzy chuckled. "I mean, it's horrible and all, but it made things interesting."

"You weren't having fun?" Gabe asked.

Mazzy shrugged. "I liked meeting our new classmates. But that doesn't compare to the thought of a mad party crasher who has it out for all of us." She smiled mischievously. "There's nothing cooler than a real-life mystery."

"I guess," said Gabe. "I feel like I've had enough mystery for the summer."

Mazzy stared at him, as if trying to peer inside his head. "Did they ever figure out what started the fire?"

Me. I wished my life away. . . .

"Some sort of electrical glitch in my dad's studio."

"Studio?" Mazzy perked up. "What kind of studio?"

Shoot. A month ago, Gabe had promised himself he'd never mention his father's career to anyone here in Slade. "He's . . . an artist. Like my grandmother."

"He draws?" Mazzy pressed.

"He makes things," Gabe answered, his stomach beginning to flutter. "Sort of like a sculptor."

"I love sculpting!" said Mazzy. "In my old town, I used to dig out fresh clay from underneath this boulder in my backyard. My teacher let me use it in class. I made a clown-head cookie jar. I glazed it and fired it in the kiln and won second prize in the school art contest."

"Doesn't surprise me," said Gabe, forcing himself to smile. "You seem talented at lots of things."

"We *are* going to have a hula hoop contest one of these days, you and me. I'll prove to you that I was the official hooping champion of Cradlebrook, Virginia."

"But I already believe you!" he said, then laughed, happy that she'd changed the subject. "I mean, who would make that up?"

She smacked his arm, but chuckled anyway.

Gabe was suddenly aware of how quiet everything was out here. No cars. No birds chirping. Only Mazzy, looking right at him. He was suddenly acutely uncomfortable. Thankfully, she broke the silence. "So . . . how do we solve the mystery?"

"Mystery?" he said, purposely examining his pruned hands.

"Of the party monster," Mazzy said, lowering her voice to a grumble and turning her fingers into little talons.

"Maybe someone was angry about not being invited."

"But who?"

"Got me. I don't know anyone in this town."

Mazzy stared at him, raising an eyebrow. "That's not quite true."

A name floated into Gabe's head. Another wave of chills overcame him. These, however, had nothing to do with the evening air.

❖

After Dolores arrived, Gabe placed his grandmother's bike into the car's trunk. He thanked Mazzy and promised to get the T-shirt back to her soon.

During the drive up into the hills, Dolores mentioned that Seth had called looking for him that afternoon.

"What did you tell him?"

"I told him to find you at the pool party." Gabe clutched the car seat. "What's wrong? I thought you'd invited him."

"I kinda never got around to it."

"Why not?"

"Well . . . turns out that he and Felicia don't really get along."

Dolores sighed. "He sounded upset," she said. "Did he show up?"

"I didn't see him there." Gabe glanced at the soaking mess of his towel and clothes wrapped in a ball in the backseat.

"I'm sorry if I messed up," she said. "Just . . . be prepared to answer his questions, you know, in case you see him again soon."

Gabe breathed out slowly. "Oh, I'm sure I will."

THE SHADOW MARKET

THE TWO ROBBER PRINCES SLINKED through the hallways of Slayhool, the shadow market in a traders' village just outside of Haliath. Having chanted a charm-spell before stepping inside, they held their breath to remain mostly invisible. The hint of magic seemed to be working. So far, no one paid any attention to them. All around them, the crowds trudged along, moving through the passageways like sludge through rusted drainpipes.

Wraithen had asked Meatpie to be his lookout during a secret errand. So Meatpie followed several paces behind, glancing around at a multitude of unfamiliar and indifferent-looking faces, keeping watch for anyone who appeared to be harboring any hostility. The Robber Princes had driven several unscrupulous characters out of the borderland forest, and it was possible that those villains were now hiding in Slayhool. If they spotted the boys, there would be trouble, to say the least.

Meatpie had been to Slayhool only once before, under his parents' insistence, to familiarize himself with the shadow market — a notoriously dangerous area filled with nefarious tradesmen who were known to hold on to a grudge even tighter than they would a pouch of gold. During that first visit, a powerful warden had guided Meatpie safely through the nearly empty market, but this morning, people pushed and cursed at one another, and the warden was nowhere to be found.

Several days had passed since the incident at the Altar of the Crooked Tree, when a disembodied voice had warned Meatpie not to disturb the pile of rocks. Wraithen claimed that the warning had come from a forest spirit who was bound in service to the Hunter — a sign that they'd been on the right track.

There had been whispers throughout Haliath that a hulking silhouette had been seen lurking in alleyways late at night, watching families through windows, and growling at dogs with enough vehemence to send them running with their tails between their legs. The Hunter was toying with the boys, they knew, and it was only a matter of time before he stole another child.

Wraithen stopped outside a grimy wooden door. "Wait out here," he whispered. A sign posted on the wall was marked with a few crossed lines attached to a circle, a rudimentary symbol that resembled a tall man. "And remember the warning knock. Three, pause, then one." He opened the door and slipped inside.

Meatpie kept a lookout, trying to appear as inconspicuous as possible. He ran his fingers through his hair, then unclasped the top button of his shirt. He brushed at his pants, and made sure that his shoes were still tied. All the while, the crowds continued to pass as if he truly were invisible. He couldn't remember why he'd allowed Seth to talk him into this . . .

. . . especially on the first day of school.

Surely, the bell would be ringing soon. He had a fair idea of where his homeroom was, but he'd wanted to get there early to find a seat near the back of the class.

"Gabe!" cried a voice.

He jumped, slamming his shoulder into the bathroom door.

Mazzy stood in front of him, wearing a huge smile. "How's your first day going so far?"

"Just got here." Gabe sighed, wishing it were possible to erase the intense blush that marked his cheeks. "Hasn't really started yet."

"Duh," she said, poking his chest. "Who do you have for homeroom?"

Gabe fumbled a slip of paper from his jeans pocket. He unfolded it and read, "Mrs. Applebaum?"

"Me too! Room A3. I'm on my way there. Come on. We can walk together."

Gabe glanced back at the door he was supposed to be guarding. "I have to wait for —" The first warning bell chimed, igniting the other students into a frenzy. Lockers slammed, voices raised, and a few kids dashed down the hallway, careening into others, who called out obscenities in response.

Mazzy shrugged. "I think that means we have like a minute or something." She turned, but when Gabe didn't follow, she paused. "Oh, wait. You said you're waiting for someone?"

Gabe glanced at the door again. Quickly, he reached up and pounded the secret knock that Seth had made him memorize. One, two, three. Pause. And then one final knock that rattled the hinges. After several seconds, he turned back to Mazzy and said, "Not anymore."

LUCK OF THE
SECOND LUNCH

AFTER HOMEROOM, THE MORNING WENT QUICKLY. Gabe's mind raced as he located each classroom, met his teachers, and accumulated a pile of heavy textbooks. The distraction of Slayhool had faded. There were so many staring eyes, so many faces he didn't recognize, that he considered crawling into his locker and closing the door. He felt alone and lost, and he clutched his heavy backpack as if it were a talisman of protection. He tried to remember the kindness with which the kids at the pool party had greeted him, but so far, he hadn't seen any of them.

Halfway through the day, Gabe glanced at his schedule and realized it was time to head to the cafeteria. As he stepped through the doors into the harsh fluorescent light that filled the cavernous room, his throat grew dry and scratchy. In his old school, this had been the time of day he'd dreaded most, when the name-calling had been the worst. In fact, last year, Gabe had taken to eating lunch alone in a dark corner of the auditorium. It was the only way to avoid the constant chant of, *Puppet Boy! C'mere, Puppet Boy! Are you a* real *boy? Prove it!* At least here no one knew him.

"Gabe!"

Squinting, he noticed Felicia, Ingrid, and Malcolm waving from a booth near a window. Cautiously, he made his way to them, watching for anyone carrying a precarious lunch tray. Malcolm scooted over and patted the seat.

"Thanks," said Gabe with a sigh of relief.

Mazzy and Seth must have had another lunch period.

"So," said Felicia. She gripped the edge of the table and leaned toward him dramatically. "*Day one*. How goes it?"

Gabe was unsure if she expected him to be nonchalant or excited or disappointed or disgusted. Thinking quickly, he settled on "Fine, so far."

Felicia smiled. "Fine is good," she said. The way her voice lifted up, almost like she was singing, made Gabe laugh out loud. "If I could go through the rest of my life feeling just fine, I'd be perfectly happy."

"Liar," teased Malcolm.

Felicia waved the comment away as if it were a gnat. She seemed to have forgotten how upset she'd been two days ago.

Yesterday morning, Seth had called Gabe and asked if he wanted to get together again. If he'd been upset about the pool party, he didn't let on. Dolores ended up driving the boys to a local shopping center to pick up some last-minute school supplies. As they'd wandered a department store aisle, perusing ballpoint pens, unspoken secrets seemed to hang between them. Later that evening, when Seth had phoned about an expedition to "Slayhool" in the morning, Gabe had agreed if only to appease him.

Gabe unpacked his brown-bag lunch, and Malcolm and Ingrid warned him which teachers to watch out for and which ones to brownnose. They told him the quickest routes among the many sections of the building, as well as the best places to just sit and chill out. Throughout the period, a number of kids stopped by the booth to say hello. With every introduction, his discomfort diminished, and soon he felt like he'd won the lottery. Was he actually part of a popular crowd?

Then Felicia squinted at him and said, "So Mazzy Lerman says you're friends with Seth Hopper."

Gabe felt the blood drain from his face. "We're neighbors."

"Careful with him," said Ingrid.

"He's weird," added Malcolm.

"Seth?" Gabe played dumb. "Weird *how*?"

"He mumbles to himself all the time," said Felicia. "I've never heard him, but some people say it's like another language."

"And he can be a real jerk," said Ingrid. "If you happen to look at him at the wrong moment, he'll stare back at you like he wants to stab you or something. Totally creepy."

"Really?" Gabe asked, truly surprised. "He's been nice to me so far. . . . I guess I don't know him that well," he added quickly.

"You don't *want* to know him," said Felicia. "Trust me."

Gabe thought about how welcoming Seth had been when they'd first met. And despite Seth's intense passion for their game in the woods, Gabe couldn't deny that their adventures had become a fun distraction, an escape from every bad thought Gabe had brought with him to Slade.

"He's been through a lot lately," Gabe said. "I'm not saying it's an excuse, but his mom's been sick. And you guys heard what happened with his older brother last year, right?"

They all nodded, but their expressions remained the same. Apparently, nothing would change their opinion of Seth.

"My older sister, Becca, says his brother was just as strange as Seth is," Ingrid chimed in. "She told me he was always talking about this fantasy world he'd invented, warning the other freshmen about some sort of monster. I mean . . . Wow!" She guffawed. "Becca said he called the monster a strange name. . . . The Warrior?"

"Not the Warrior," Gabe said quietly. "The Hunter."

Ingrid pointed at him, surprised. "Yes! That was it! *The Hunter*. How did you know?"

"Seth mentioned it to me," Gabe said. "The Hunter . . . the fantasy world. He and his brother must have talked about it with each other." As the words escaped his lips, Gabe realized that Seth hadn't been making up the game as they went along. There'd been more to it than a couple of kids wasting time at the end of summer. David had played too, probably with his little brother. He'd run away, but he'd left something behind — a fantastic world in the woods, haunted by the hulking shadow of a beast, separated from the reality of life in Slade by a thin veil of imagination and memory that belonged to a boy no one really knew. His little brother. Seth. Wraithen of Haliath. The Robber Prince.

Malcolm scoffed. "So lame."

Felicia smacked his shoulder. "Have some compassion. The kid's big brother is *missing*."

Malcolm rolled his eyes. "Seriously? Do you want to invite him to sit with us at lunch tomorrow?" He glanced toward the cafeteria entrance. He emitted a harsh snort of surprise. "There he is! I'll go get him." Malcolm went to stand, but Felicia simply reached up and touched his shoulder, lowering him back to the bench as if she contained a hidden strength. She glanced around the table, silently demanding quiet. Gabe got it: No one was to invite Seth to do any such thing. But Felicia couldn't keep them from peering across the chaotic room toward the entrance.

Seth stood in the doorway, an emblem of stillness, his skinny frame rigid, his face a blank mask staring back.

Ingrid gasped, ducked, and turned away. *"He's looking at us."*

The bell chimed, and the cafeteria erupted in a clamor of voices. Trembling, Gabe shoveled the uneaten portion of his lunch into his paper bag. By the time he glimpsed the double doors again, Seth had disappeared.

RIDING HOME

LATER, AS HE CLIMBED THE STAIRS onto bus #5, Gabe smiled to himself. He'd survived the first day.

At his seat near the back, the air felt like a furnace. He reached up and fiddled with the window latch. The pane dragged open slowly, scraping an obnoxious cry that made the hair on his neck stand up. He stuck his head out the window and breathed deeply.

"Gabe!" a voice called. "Hey!"

Gabe glanced around. Mazzy galloped over to the bus.

"Hey!" he answered, calling down to her. "I couldn't find you inside."

"It's a madhouse," she said. "No worries. Felicia's having some people over this afternoon. She told me to invite you."

"Really? Me?"

Mazzy chuckled, and he realized how dumb he sounded. "Yes, really. You."

"I'd like to," he said, trying to hide his disappointment, "but my mom's expecting me home."

"You can't call her?"

"First day check-in. You know?"

"I know," said Mazzy, shrugging. "I have it easier since I can walk home from here. No fancy buses for me."

"Oh yeah," Gabe said, laughing, "this bus is *so* fancy. Green vinyl seats are the epitome of luxury."

"Anyway . . . I just thought I'd ask. Felicia's gonna be sad. I'll tell her you'll tag along some other time?"

"Definitely."

Gabe felt a pair of fingers walking up his spine. Jolting upright, he nearly knocked his skull on the windowsill. Seth stood behind him, frozen in an awkward pose, having just yanked his hand away. "Sorry," he said through his teeth. "Didn't mean to scare you."

Gabe blinked. "That's okay," he said. He glanced back out the window to find that Mazzy had already rushed away with a group of girls who were heading down the sidewalk. He watched her blonde hair swing between her shoulder blades, softly reflecting the afternoon light — a halo contained within a greasy fingerprint on the glass.

Seth sat next to him. "Who was that?"

"Mazzy? We met at the school orientation last week. She's new too."

"She's pretty," said Seth, biting the inside of his mouth.

"Yeah, I guess," said Gabe. The bus had gotten crowded. He raised his voice over the din. "She's nice too."

"You'll introduce me?" said Seth. "I mean . . . I want to meet your other friends."

Gabe didn't like the way Seth had said *other friends*. It sounded hostile. "Sure," he replied, his voice cracking. "I think she'd like you."

The driver shut the door. The bus shuddered into gear. Seth slouched down in the seat. "I doubt it," he said matter-of-factly. "In the end, nobody does."

The bus pulled away from the curb. Gabe thought of what everyone at lunch had been saying about Seth, that he was a weirdo, a freak. He knew what it felt like to be in that position. The worst thing Seth could do was agree with them. "If you keep saying stuff like that, it's possible that nobody ever will," said Gabe. Seth glared at him, and Gabe immediately regretted it. "I'm sorry," he added. "You've got to give yourself more credit though. You're really fun to hang out with, but if you go around thinking everyone has it out for you, they're going to start believing that they *actually* do."

"You don't see it yet," said Seth, wearing an almost smirk. "Those kids you were sitting with at lunch . . . They're the worst."

Gabe closed his eyes. He'd known this was coming.

"A while ago," Seth went on, "we were *all* friends. Then things started to change. Bit by bit. First, they started to make fun of my clothes. Then it was the way I talk. Then it was the way I played volleyball or tennis or football in PE. And I know they've done other stuff that I can't prove. Stolen my homework before I could turn it in. Written things on my locker. They've laughed at me in the hallways more times than I can count. And they say *I'm* the creepy one because I 'look at them funny.' No." His voice started to wobble. "I'm not the one with the problem. They are."

Gabe thought Seth might as well have replaced *they* with *you*.

"In my old school, kids did the same things to me," said Gabe, slowly.

Seth's mouth dropped open. "You? Why?"

Gabe shook his head. "People like to pick on whoever they think might be . . . weak. They think it makes them look stronger." He nudged Seth with his elbow. "You're not weak. And, after hunting the Hunter with you, I know that I'm not either." He paused. "I've never told anyone this, but . . . I'm almost glad about the fire."

Seth's look of shock was almost cartoonish — eyebrows scrunched together, head tilted, shoulders raised, eyes bugged out.

"It got me out of there," said Gabe.

Seth leaned close and grabbed Gabe's arm. "If this happened to you, how could you possibly want to hang out with Felicia and her gang of vicious little robots?"

Gabe didn't know how to answer. He understood why Felicia felt the way she did about Seth, but he also got Seth's point of view.

"Mazzy introduced me," Gabe said finally. "She lives next to Felicia." He pulled his arm away from Seth's grip. "They've all been really nice."

"But I was nice to you first," said Seth. "And *we* have our game. What do they have, besides dumb pool parties?" When Gabe turned red, Seth went on. "Yeah, your mom told me about it when I called the other day. I hope it was fun."

The bus swerved as it made its way up the hill toward their houses. It jerked to a stop, and a large group of kids got off. Gabe began to feel nauseous. "Yeah, it was," he whispered. "Lots of fun." Then, if only to change the subject, he asked, "So, what else are the Robber Princes up to today?"

{NEVER}
THE ART OF SPELLBINDING

SHORTLY THEREAFTER, THE BOYS returned to the altar.

Wraithen knelt at the base, hunched over some secret object that he'd taken from his satchel. Meatpie stood a few feet back, craning to catch a glimpse of what it was. The crooked tree reached toward the boys, its low branches swaying in the breeze like hands trying either to clutch at them or shoo them away. Meatpie had been nervous to come back here again. But Wraithen claimed he'd acquired a talisman so powerful that it would allow the boys to complete their task. The journey to the shadow market that morning had been for this purpose alone. Wraithen explained that when Meatpie had stood guard outside that mysterious door, he'd been inside brokering a deal with a covert agent to obtain the object over which he was now bent.

In moments, Wraithen professed, the hub of the Hunter's power would be destroyed.

A chill breeze rushed over the forest floor, rustling dead leaves into small swirling eddies. Meatpie shivered. He wasn't certain, but it sounded like Wraithen was mumbling something — a spell or perhaps a prayer. Several brisk snapping sounds erupted from Wraithen's cupped hands. Then he leapt up, wearing a weird expression of panic and delight.

"Run!" Wraithen grasped Meatpie's arm and pulled him down the slope toward a nearby brook. From behind them came a harsh hissing sound. It grew louder, and then a blast rocked the top of the hill. The boys fell with a wet splat into the mud near the shallow water. Rocks tumbled down the hill toward them. One stone, which was the size of a human skull, came to a stop several feet from where they lay sprawled in the muck.

Meatpie glanced up at the altar. Wraithen's spell had worked. Somewhat. A large chunk of the structure had crumbled away. The pile of rocks was not nearly as formidable as before. In seconds, the altar had become ruins.

"What the heck *was* that?" Gabe said, sitting up. The ground near the tree was smoking slightly.

"I didn't realize it was going to be such a big explosion," Seth answered quietly, dazed. His character, Wraithen, seemed to have been blown away with the blast, leaving an ordinary boy in his place.

"But you knew there'd *be* an explosion?" Gabe found himself unable to control the pitch of his voice. It rose with every word.

"Well, yeah," said Seth. "An M-80 will explode when you light it on fire." He turned over his palm, revealing a pack of matches — the cause of the snapping sound. The hiss had been the slow burn of the fuse.

Gabe shook his head in amazement. "You should have warned me! You could have, I don't know . . . killed us?"

Seth stood and raced back up the small slope to examine the damage he'd caused. Gabe followed reluctantly, wondering if the invisible thing that had chided him days ago was here now. How angry would it be to learn what they'd done? The boys paused at the edge of a slight crater. The earth was singed. It continued to smoke slightly. A dark gap had appeared at the base of the altar. The ground beneath the stones must be hollow, Gabe thought. The altar itself appeared to be held up by the intertwined roots of the nearby tree.

Gabe poked Seth's shoulder. "You've got nothing to say?" Seth faced him, but his mind was elsewhere. "Earth to Seth?"

Seth blinked, then shook his head. "I-I'm sorry. You're right. I should've said something. I just thought it would be . . . fun."

Felicia's warning about Seth came rushing back to Gabe. His mouth went dry. "Where did you get it? The M-80?"

"There's this kid one grade below ours. He trades for them. I brought him some of David's old comics this morning. You were my lookout." Seth smiled wanly. "In Slayhool. The shadow market. Remember?"

"Yes," Gabe said, frustrated. "I remember. It's just . . . I thought we were playing a game. I didn't realize this" — *reality* — "was going to be part of it."

"I won't do it again. Promise."

Gabe sighed. "Good," he said. "Thank you."

"But look," said Seth, nodding at the ruined pile of rocks. "Our mission's almost complete."

A moment later, Gabe found himself mesmerized by the dark cavity at the base of the altar. A soft sound breathed forth from inside, like a rush of water or wind. He stepped closer, his sneakers slipping into the shallow crater. Bending down, he touched the part of the crevice that opened beneath one of the larger stones, allowing his fingers to slide along the edge of earth. To his surprise, chunks of dirt broke off and fell into the gap, disappearing silently inside. How deep was this hole? he wondered.

The soft sound intensified, and Gabe realized that it wasn't water or wind, but someone speaking from the depths, too softly to be intelligible. A hand grabbed his shoulder, and he fell away from the stones.

"Whoa," said Seth. "Jumpy, are we?"

Gabe glared at him. "You did set off a tiny bomb about a minute ago, so yes, I suppose I am a little jumpy."

"It wasn't a *bomb*." Seth bent close to the altar too. "What did you find?"

Gabe sat up. "Nothing. I thought I heard —" But the sound had stopped. He closed his mouth, unsure if he'd imagined the whole thing. Maybe his ears had been ringing from the blast?

"Thought you heard what?" Seth asked.

"It sounded like someone was down there. Whispering."

Seth got down on his hands and knees, bringing his head right up to the gap. Gabe imagined a pale hand reaching up from the darkness. Wasted, skeletal fingers, dirty, clawlike nails inching out of the hole and searching for skin to clutch, to tear. He grabbed Seth's collar and pulled him away. Seth made a gagging noise. "Ow," he choked out, slapping uselessly at Gabe's hand. "What the heck was that for?"

Gabe stared at the hole. There was nothing there — obviously. "Sorry," he said. He glanced at Seth, who was looking at him like he'd lost his mind. "Can we please just get out of here?"

The boys wandered over the nearest hill and came upon one of the old horse trails. Gabe turned toward Temple House. "I should head back," he said. "Homework."

"Really? I didn't get any today."

"I want to get a start on some of the reading we're going to be doing in history." Gabe blushed at his lie. He tried to kick a rock but missed.

"How ambitious of you," said Seth, disappointed. "Well, maybe I'll do the same. Can't have you getting ahead of me. See you at the bus stop tomorrow?"

"Sure thing." Gabe took a few steps up the hill before stopping and turning around. "Hey!" he called.

Seth stopped and turned back. "Yeah?"

"If we destroy the altar, and the Hunter loses his power, is the game over?"

Seth shook his head. "Doubt it," he said, and smiled. "The Hunter always finds a way to come back."

THE MONSTER

AFTER DINNER, GABE'S FATHER INVITED him and his grandmother upstairs to his makeshift workshop. When Glen turned on the lights, Gabe was surprised to find that the puppet was finished. The creature stood against the windows, nearly seven feet tall. His googly eyes stared at the ceiling, irises slightly askew, and his mouth hung open, revealing marshmallow-shaped teeth. Short, sharp horns erupted from the top of his head. Shaggy gray fur hung like dreadlocks from his wide shoulders. Blunt black claws poked out from his fingers and toes.

"What do you think?" Glen asked.

"Oh, he's beautiful!" said Elyse.

"Yeah, Dad," said Gabe, forcing a smile. "Really cool."

Glen approached the puppet. "I'm still working on the inner framework and mechanical details, but I think I have at least enough to show the producers."

"What's his name?" Elyse asked.

"Milton Monster," Glen said with a smile.

Elyse crossed the room, took Milton's hand, and examined Glen's craftsmanship. "Jim Henson seams," she said. "Nearly invisible. Beautiful work, sweetheart." Her eyes glistened as she glanced at her son. "I'm so proud of you. Back on your feet so soon." Glen stepped forward, wrapped his arms around her slight shoulders, and squeezed.

Gabe felt like he wanted to throw up. He was happy for his father, of course, but he couldn't stop himself from thinking what these kinds of creatures had done to him in the past. He

considered what Seth had said about the Hunter always finding a way to come back. Apparently monsters were not so easily
defeated.

A few minutes later, as his father (the builder of beasts) led his
grandmother (the illustrator of gothic horrors) out of the room,
Gabe wondered why his family seemed to surround themselves
with this darkness. Was this his destiny too? He turned off the
light and followed them into the hallway.

Gabe wandered into his bedroom, closed the door, and leaned
against it. Maybe monsters could be useful? If you could learn to
control them, they might become essential allies, protectors, heroes.
He thought of Seth, of the game, of the whispering hole beneath
the pile of stones. He imagined the Hunter, standing at the edge
of the woods, a shadow surrounded by shadows, watching, waiting, amused by his puny efforts to understand.

ON SATURDAY MORNING, Dolores knocked on Gabe's bedroom door, waking him from yet another dream of smoke and fire. "You've got a phone call," she said, peeking in at him.

Gabe crawled out of bed, wiping sleep from his eyes. He glanced at the clock on his nightstand. Seven thirty? Who would be calling so early, especially on the first Saturday of the school year? Since his grandmother didn't have a cordless phone, he had to trek all the way downstairs to the kitchen. Miri was perched in her high chair beside the table, moving soggy apple slices around on the tray. She smiled at him as he came through the door. Gabe went over to her and rubbed her head, then snatched up a piece of apple and popped it into his mouth.

The receiver sat on the counter. "Hello?" His voice felt froggy.

"Hey!" Seth. Even with one short word, he sounded wide awake, raring to go. "What are you doing right now?"

"Um. I was sleeping."

"Get dressed," Seth said. "Meet me at the crooked tree. You're not going to believe this."

Twenty minutes later, dressed in a rumpled T-shirt and jeans he'd grabbed from his bedroom floor, Gabe hiked down the hill behind the house, still half-asleep.

It was another sunny day, but the air was cooler than it had been earlier in the week. The canopy of leaves high above were beginning to reveal hidden pigments — hints of the yellows, oranges, and reds that would soon paint the landscape from horizon to horizon.

From the trail, Gabe noticed Seth standing off in the woods. Seth wore a subtle smile, watching silently as Gabe made his way through the brush. He waved Gabe around the other side of the rock pile, nodding at the spot where the M-80 had gone off.

A sensation of pinpricks danced across Gabe's skin. Someone had restored the altar. "You did this?" Gabe asked.

Seth sniffed, amused. "I didn't do anything."

"Then how —"

"I don't know," said Seth, bending down to examine the repair. The stones fit together like perfect little puzzle pieces. "I had a weird feeling and came out early this morning to check. It wasn't you, was it?"

Gabe laughed, though he didn't find Seth's question amusing. "Um," Gabe said. "No. It wasn't me." Gabe remembered the voice he'd heard out here — *Don't!* — and the whispering from the crevice underneath the stones. It had to have been Seth. The other option was too bizarre to even consider considering. "But nice try," he added.

Seth flinched. "You think I'm making it up?"

"Well, yeah. That's how we play the game, isn't it? We make it up."

Seth went pale, his face grew grim. "I'm not lying. I didn't touch these rocks, I swear."

"Then who did?" Gabe asked, teasing. "The Hunter?"

"It *is* his altar," said Seth.

"No." Gabe paused. "It's just a pile of rocks that we found in the woods. The Hunter isn't real. The game isn't real."

"Don't say that," Seth said.

"You're joking, right?"

Seth turned away. When Gabe reached out and touched his

shoulder, Seth spun on him, waving his arms wildly, indicating the stones, the tree, the entire forest. "How do you explain all this?"

"Easy," Gabe answered quickly, frustrated. "You did it."

Seth clenched his fists. "I did *not*."

"Come on, Seth," said Gabe. "If you don't admit it, then I don't want to play the game anymore." The words came out of Gabe's mouth before he'd thought about what their effect would be.

"But I *didn't* do this," he said quietly. Seth's face seemed to slowly melt. He looked like Gabe had punched him in the stomach. "I called you as soon as I realized that someone else had been out here."

"The Hunter," Gabe said. As the truth finally registered, he shivered and stepped away from the altar. "You really do believe."

Seth closed his eyes, deflated. After a few seconds, he shook his head. His voice trembled when he spoke. "And I guess I'd have to be crazy to think something like that. Right?"

TATER TOTS & TACTICAL MANEUVERS

IN THE DAYS FOLLOWING THAT WEEKEND, Gabe kept himself busy. Homework. Chores. Watching Miri while the adults were occupied. When he saw Seth on the bus or in the hallways between classes, Seth chattered on about a variety of topics ranging from the promising new movies coming out that fall, to the best types of feed for elderly horses, to the precarious state of the comic book industry — everything but the confrontation in the woods.

Gabe assumed Seth was filling up with noise what would have otherwise been awkward silence. In the moment when Seth had denied rebuilding the altar, Gabe felt their friendship change. There was no going back.

He was happy to have found a lunch table filled with kids who were welcoming, who were intrigued by stories about the big creepy house where he lived, who hadn't once judged him or tried to trick him. And he found Mazzy to be more and more interesting. During gym class, she'd discovered a hula hoop in the supply closet and impressed everyone by keeping it going for the entire period. Forty whole minutes. It had been awesome. Even better, Mazzy came to the bus at the end of each school day to say goodbye. She really seemed to like him. And he felt the same. Every time he saw Mazzy smile, Gabe pinched himself to make sure he wasn't dreaming — it hurt, but it was worth it.

Then, on the third Thursday of the school year, disaster struck.

That day, Gabe decided to splurge on the school pizza, which everyone promised was too good to pass up. So after math class, instead of stopping by his locker to pick up his paper-bag lunch,

Gabe went straight to the cafeteria, arriving earlier than usual. When he came through the double doors, he found that someone had usurped his group's regular table. Seth turned toward him, smiled, and waved. Gabe didn't wave back. Looking around, he saw none of his other friends. He rushed to the table. "What are you doing here?" he asked.

"Oh, well, I realized that if I switched my quiet-study period, I could eat lunch with you guys," Seth said. He took a sip from an open carton of chocolate milk, then scooted over and pointedly brushed at the seat beside him.

"You have to go."

Seth tilted his head. He'd expected this reaction. "You don't want me to sit here?"

"*I* don't mind," said Gabe, "but the others won't be happy that someone else took the table."

"Then come with me to a different one. We can sneak off to Slayhool." He whispered in the voice of Wraithen, "My sources say that the Hunter is currently watching us."

Gabe felt an unexpected anger burning beneath his skin. Was this supposed to be a test? Of what? Loyalty? Before he could respond, he heard a familiar voice behind him. "What's going on here?" Gabe turned to find Felicia, arms crossed, looking tickled.

"We were just leaving," said Seth, rising from the bench. He grabbed the chocolate milk carton. "Come on, Gabe."

"Gabe?" said Felicia, hiding a hint of laughter. "Really?"

"Seth switched lunch periods," Gabe answered, feeling his lameness ooze from his skin.

"I can see that," she answered. Malcolm and Ingrid appeared through the crowd and approached cautiously.

"Yeah," said Seth, his voice dripping with false sweetness, "so if it's okay with you, Felicia, Gabe's gonna sit with me. We're obviously not welcome at *your* table."

"Gabe can do whatever he likes," said Felicia. "If he wants to sit here, he can, and if he wants to leave us . . . well, that's his decision." Her voice had an edge to it, which spoke silently of serious repercussions.

Gabe felt his chest begin to constrict. He struggled to catch his breath. "No," he heard himself say. He slid onto the bench. "I want to sit with you guys."

Felicia parked herself opposite him and grinned up at Seth. "I guess Gabe's made his decision."

Gabe lowered his eyes and stared at his lap. He pressed his fingers into his palms, feeling as though he were holding on to the planet for dear life. In the silence that followed, he could only imagine Seth's face, purple with rage. Ingrid and Malcolm sat down too, unable to hide their discomfort. They glanced at each other, then purposely looked in opposite directions.

"Evil witch," Seth whispered to himself, as if Felicia were a character in the game, a creature who needed to be vanquished.

Before Gabe knew what was happening, Felicia screamed. She scrambled rapidly out from the booth. The entire room went silent. Time seemed to slow. As she stood, Gabe saw an opaque brownish substance drip from her hair, down her face, and dribble onto her shirt. Chocolate milk. He turned toward Seth, unable to think, unable to speak.

Seth dropped the now empty carton. It hit the floor with a resounding hollowness. He backed away, then knocked into several students on his way toward the cafeteria doors. People grabbed at his shirt, shouting for him to stop, but he didn't appear to hear them. Either that, or he didn't care.

GAME OVER

GABE, FELICIA, MALCOLM, AND INGRID were all called into the principal's office to give their version of the events. No one was in trouble apparently, except for Seth, but he had disappeared from the school grounds shortly after the chocolate milk incident. They all had to call home and tell their parents what had happened. Gabe went from class to class worrying that his new friends would hate him now. He had brought the monster into their midst. But moments after the last bell, Gabe found the group gathered at his locker.

Mazzy was there too. "Everyone's talking about what happened," she said. "Are you okay?"

"Yeah, totally," Gabe lied. He felt his throat closing up as the group appeared to study his face. "I feel horrible for Felicia," he said quietly, barely able to look at her. Felicia had changed her clothes and rinsed her hair. She wore a Slade School Spirit T-shirt that Mrs. Closkey, the school secretary, had given her. Malcolm had lent her his Red Sox cap. Felicia had tied the shirt at the waist so it bloused out. Despite the baggy fit and boyish quality of the outfit, it still looked cute.

Felicia stared at Gabe for a moment, then laughed. "You can't say I didn't warn you."

Relief flooded Gabe's lungs. "I thought you'd hate me now."

Felicia nudged his shoulder. "Everyone makes mistakes. Especially when you're new. Now you know better," she said. "We're all about to head over to my house to hang out. You should totally come."

Gabe smiled. He could think of nothing else he'd rather do. "Sure. I just have to call my parents."

Later, after the sun had dipped below the western hills, Dolores picked Gabe up from Felicia's house. In the car, when she asked him about his day, he told her that everything was fine now. She squeezed his arm.

Dinner was waiting, as was his homework. His father and grandmother had already eaten and were together in the living room, watching a sitcom on the television Glen had recently purchased. Dolores carried Miri down the hall to join them. Gabe set himself up at the kitchen table, biting into a turkey sandwich and flipping through his textbook at the same time. He was deep into a reading about the American Revolution when the doorbell rang. He heard his grandmother get up and make her way down the hall. She called out, "Gabriel! You have a visitor!"

Gabe's skin went prickly. He knew who it was even before he came upon Seth on the front stoop. Seth was dressed in a light jacket. He'd shoved his hands awkwardly into the pockets of his jeans and shivered in the chilly air. Barefoot but for fuzzy slipper-socks, Gabe stepped outside.

"I tried calling," said Seth, "but your dad said you weren't home. I just wanted to make sure he wasn't lying."

"He wasn't *lying*," said Gabe. He reached behind himself, closing the door almost all the way. "I just got home a little while ago."

"What, I can't come in?" said Seth.

"Not a good idea," said Gabe quietly.

"Are you nervous that I'm going to throw milk at your grand-mother?" Seth laughed. Gabe didn't respond, and Seth's smile

·dropped away. "Look, I'm sorry about today. I shouldn't have
done that."

"You think?"

"I didn't mean to get you involved."

Gabe knew that was exactly what Seth had meant. "You're in
a lot of trouble. More than you know."

Seth shrugged. "Yeah, the school left a whole bunch of mes-
sages on our answering machine, but I deleted them before my
mom could listen. I'm not too worried. I've had detention before."

"And that hasn't stopped you from doing stuff like this?"

"Uh, no?" Seth bit his lip. "But it also hasn't stopped Felicia
and all them from being nasty jerks either."

"You're the one who threw milk all over her!"

"And she deserved it!" He took a deep breath. "*Gabe can make
his own decisions,*" he mimicked in a singsong voice that sounded
nothing like Felicia. "What a bunch of baloney."

"So then you're *not* sorry."

Seth sighed. "I'm only sorry that I put you in this spot. I know
you like them for some strange reason. But . . ." He cleared his
throat. "I don't want them to take you away." He quickly shook
his head. "I didn't mean . . . that came out wrong."

"They didn't *take* me away, Seth. I went on my own."

Seth's forehead crinkled. Gabe felt like he was standing on the
edge of a precipice. And if he stepped forward . . .

"I mean —" Gabe began. But the words felt like beestings. His
tongue was suddenly thick, his mouth dry. "I'm not playing the
Hunter's game anymore." Seth kept his face still, revealing nothing. Gabe thought of what the pastor had said after the fire, the
bible quote, about putting away childish things. "I think it's time
we both, like, grow up, you know?"

"That's fine," Seth said. He crossed his arms tightly, a deflec-
tor shield. "We can do something else when we hang out."

"I don't think that's a good idea."

"Not a good idea?" Seth's voice echoed out into the darkness of the yard. "What, we're not friends anymore?"

"I-I guess not." Gabe glanced at the sky so he wouldn't have to face Seth. "Not right now anyway."

"Then when? In a month?" Gabe couldn't tell if Seth was being serious, so he didn't respond. Seth dropped his arms to his sides. He seemed to examine the stone stoop. Then, with a calm smile, Seth glanced up. "You're going to be sorry about this." His voice was flat. "The Hunter will come for you." A breeze came upon the house from the nearby woods, rustling Seth's hair in front of his face.

"The Hunter will . . . come for me?" Gabe wasn't sure if he'd heard correctly.

"You and your new friends." Seth nodded, as if he'd planned this speech all along. It almost sounded silly. Like the wicked witch threatening Dorothy in that old movie.

Gabe chuckled out of nervousness. "You need help, Seth," he said.

Seth's face turned red. He stared with an intensity Gabe had never seen before. "You're the one who's going to need help. Trust me."

Gabe felt for the door behind him, in case he needed to put it between them. "Really, Seth, I think you should talk to the guidance counselor or something. You've been through a lot. Your parents. Your brother —"

"Don't talk to me about my brother! You don't know anything about him!"

"You've never told me!" Gabe shouted back. Seth bit his lip, which had begun to tremble. "I-I'm sorry. But you can't go around treating people like this."

"People can't go around treating *me* like this! It's not fair. It's the opposite of fair. Felicia gets to live in a huge house with a pool and parents who give her whatever she wants. Mazzy shows up at school with her blonde hair and little pixie-dust smile and everyone just falls in love with her. And you! You say your family lost everything in that fire, but you end up living in a mansion with your famous grandmother. You all get whatever you want. Whatever you need. I *have* to be the way I am. No one is coming to save me. No one is going to fix everything! Don't you get it?"

The thing was, Gabe *did* get it.

Seth hitched another breath, then added, "I thought we were friends."

The front door rattled open, but Gabe was so startled by Seth's outburst that he didn't turn around. He felt frozen, as if by magic — a spell he was no longer willing to believe in.

"You boys all right out here?" It was Elyse. Gabe felt her thin fingers touch his shoulders, and he glanced briefly at her.

Seth transformed. He stood up straight, wiped his eyes, then sniffed and smiled. "I-I was just leaving," he said. "Nice to see you, Mrs. Ashe. Good night." Before either of them could respond, Seth descended the front steps and sprinted off alone into the night.

PART TWO

❖

STONES

THE BABYSITTERS

SEVERAL WEEKS LATER, Gabe's parents took his grandmother into Boston for the evening, trusting him to care for his little sister. Malcolm had joined him for a horror movie marathon on his grandmother's new television.

Miri, however, had other plans. She'd started screaming as soon as the adults pulled down the driveway and were out of earshot.

"I'm so sorry," Gabe said, sitting on the couch in the living room. Miri squirmed in his lap. "She hardly ever does this." From the look on Malcolm's face, Gabe worried that his friend might take off, leaving him alone in the big, dark house to finish out the night on his own. The boys had tried everything to console Miri. Food, music, television. Nothing worked. Usually during Miri's tantrums, Gabe's father distracted her with one of his puppets. But there was no way Gabe was fetching one of the fuzzy felt creatures from upstairs, not with Malcolm there.

"Can't we tranquilize her?" Malcolm stared blankly at the television program Gabe had turned on to entertain Miri. On the screen, a cartoon train tooted its horn. *Hoo-hoo!*

"Yeah right. I wish. Maybe I should call my mom."

"What if we just put her in her bedroom and close the door?" Malcolm asked.

"She might get even more upset."

"We could wait outside in the hall until she quiets down."

Miri whined and twisted in Gabe's lap, releasing a series of melodramatic sobs.

"Okay," Gabe said, shaking his head, exasperated. "Let's at least try it." He hugged Miri tightly, then stood. "Come on, baby girl. Upstairs you go." As Gabe crossed the room, his sister went quiet. The lights in the hallway were off, but she pointed at the darkness beyond the doorway, staring as if she could see someone standing there. She gurgled something that sounded like, *Ah-bah-bah!*

"Whoa," Malcolm whispered. "What did you do to her?"

"Nothing," said Gabe, surprised.

Miri seemed entranced. She smiled, then laughed inexplicably. Gabe felt his stomach drop. "Hello?" he said softly to the darkness. But there was no answer. Of course there was no answer. Outside, the wind gusted, forcing itself into the roof overhang's hollow spaces, making a moaning sound. Malcolm hung back as Gabe stepped forward, reached around the door frame, and flicked up the light switch. Golden light filled the hall. Miri continued to coo, amused by something Gabe could not see.

"I'm just going to run her upstairs," Gabe told Malcolm. "Be right back."

"I'll come with you," said Malcolm, stepping quickly forward.

A few minutes later, Miri lay quietly in her crib, staring into the space directly above her. Gabe imagined that the screaming child he'd held only moments ago had been magically replaced with a changeling.

"Aha!" Miri cried out. She giggled at the shadows.

Closing her bedroom door, Gabe met Malcolm in the hall. He shook his head. "Kids are so weird."

"Tell me about it," said Malcolm.

Back in the living room, Gabe had just started the first movie, *Night of the Living Dead*, when the doorbell rang. Both boys jumped, then glanced at each other in confusion. It was only seven o'clock. Gabe's parents weren't due home for several more hours.

Seth Hopper popped into his head. Gabe hadn't spoken to him since the night he'd shown up on the front steps of Temple House. Seth had been suspended from riding the bus. In the hallways at school, Seth refused to acknowledge him. Gabe wanted to believe that Seth would try to change, that one day they could be friends again.

The baby monitor on the coffee table crackled with a bit of static. Thankfully, the bell hadn't woken Miri. Gabe raced to the hallway, in case whoever was out there pressed it again. Several silhouettes moved in the curtained windows on either side of the large front door.

A zombie on the television in the living room moaned.

Gabe latched the chain lock. Heart racing, he opened the door a crack. Someone on the other side pushed hard, throwing him off balance. The chain caught the door and it bounced closed again. He watched the knob rattle violently.

Seth's voice whispered in his memory: *The Hunter will come for you. . . .*

Gabe was about to call out for Malcolm, when laughter echoed just on the other side of the door. "Gabe?" spoke a female voice. "Was that you? I'm sorry!"

A warm sensation flooded his face. Standing on the stoop, Felicia and Ingrid smiled. Mazzy was beside them, watching him guiltily.

A hand fell on his shoulder, and Gabe turned to find Malcolm winking at him.

"Surprise!" they all said at once.

THE VISITORS

"WHAT ARE YOU GUYS DOING HERE?" Gabe asked, confused.

"We were feeling left out," said Felicia, stepping past him into the foyer. "So we asked Ingrid's older sister to drop us off."

"You don't mind," said Ingrid, following Felicia into the house, "do you?"

"Hi, Gabe," said Mazzy, smiling sheepishly. "They talked me into it," she added quietly so no one else could hear. Gabe sighed, then stepped aside, allowing her to pass as well. His parents would not be happy about this.

Malcolm led the group back toward the living room. "Keep your voices down," he said. "We just got his little sister to fall asleep."

"In a mansion this big," said Felicia, glancing through doorways along the way, "do we really need to worry about that? She's probably in another wing! Am I right, Gabe?"

Gabe shrugged. "She's just upstairs," he said, trying to downplay the grandiosity of the house.

Felicia paused in the living room doorway, waiting for the rest of them to catch up. "You don't seem very happy that we came."

"Oh," said Gabe. "N-no. I'm really happy. I just . . . didn't expect it. Me and Malcolm already ate all the pizza."

"We don't care about pizza," said Ingrid. "We just wanted to see your cool house."

"And *you*," said Mazzy, throwing a warning look at the other girls. "We wanted to see you too, Gabe."

Gabe couldn't help but smile.

"What about me?" Malcolm asked, looking hurt. "Didn't you want to see me?"

"Get over yourself, Malc," Felicia said, chuckling. She headed toward the sound of hungry zombies and plopped herself down on the wide leather couch. "So . . . what are we watching?"

After the movie ended, they were all giddy with fright. In the basement, the ancient boiler clicked on, and the house seemed to shudder. The group huddled closer together on the couch. Gabe and Mazzy bumped knees. He quickly fumbled to move away. Despite feeling guilty for having them here without permission, Gabe was glad that they'd come.

Felicia stood. "Okay, Gabe. Time for a tour."

"A tour of what?" Gabe asked, happy for a distraction.

"Dummy!" said Ingrid. "We want to see your house. Every nook and cranny."

"Oh," said Gabe, rising and brushing himself off. This was the second time Ingrid had brought up the house. Doubt flickered briefly through his mind. Was this the reason they'd wanted to be friends with him in the first place? To see where his famous grand-mother lived? To take a peek inside?

"Okay," he said, swallowing the lump that had risen in his throat. His father's puppets were upstairs, off-limits. "But — but be quiet. I don't wanna wake up Miri."

They started in his grandmother's library. The group was mes-merized by the strange treasures that filled the bookshelves. Malcolm pawed at Nathaniel Olmstead's books, the ones that Elyse had drawn covers for. "Oh my gosh, I love these!" he said. Felicia and Ingrid squealed at some of the more grotesque speci-mens on the shelves: luminescent beetles framed in shadow boxes, a baby doll made of cracked leather, a taxidermy snake half-coiled in mid-spring, with jaws wide open.

Mazzy, however, stood at the window that overlooked the backyard and the woods beyond. "See something?" Gabe asked, stepping beside her. Looking out at the darkness, he remembered the figure he'd seen out there a couple months earlier.

The Hunter will come for you. . . .

Mazzy shook her head. "I thought so, but no. Just the darkness playing tricks." She didn't sound convinced. Gabe felt a chill.

A few minutes later, he led them through the maze of rooms on the first floor: the dining room, the parlor, the kitchen, an office, a den. Felicia begged to see upstairs. Malcolm shushed the group as they approached Miri's door. Gabe briefly opened each of the bedroom doors, but when he came upon the closed door that led to his father's workshop, he passed it by entirely.

"Wait," Felicia said. "What's in here?" She reached for the knob. Gabe leapt between her and the door, almost knocking Felicia to the ground. She shrieked, then looked at him in shock. "Geez! Just kill me, why don't you?"

"Sorry," said Gabe, trembling, ignoring his urge to shush her. "It's nothing. A closet."

"A closet?" Felicia stared at the door, looking more intrigued now than she had been before. "Filled with what? Gold?"

"Is your grandmother hiding something?" Ingrid asked, wide-eyed.

"Just . . . towels," Gabe answered, holding the doorknob so tightly that his knuckles had gone white.

"Why can't we see them?" Malcolm asked.

"You want to see *towels*?" Mazzy asked.

"No," said Felicia. "But he's acting really weird."

Gabe felt his mouth dry up. He glanced at Mazzy, who only looked back at him apologetically.

Forget it, Gabe thought. *What does it matter anymore?* Seth Hopper had been right. They'd never wanted to be friends with him. If they'd only wished to see the famous Temple House, why not just show them and end it all?

He began to turn the knob. Then, from downstairs, there erupted an earth-shattering boom. The house shook. Outside, the wind wailed an awful howl. The group tensed like they'd done during the zombie movie. This time, however, the fright wasn't fun. Mazzy grabbed Gabe's arm and squeezed.

"What in holy heavens was that?" Felicia asked, turning slowly toward the staircase, her interest in the workshop door disappearing like a ghost.

WILL COME FOR YOU

FROM THE TOP OF THE STAIRS, they could see that the front door had blown open in the wind. It had hit the wall so hard, the doorknob had left a slight impression in the wallpaper. Gabe shook his head. His father was going to kill him.

"I must not've closed it all the way when you guys came in," said Gabe, skipping quickly down the stairs. He shoved against the door as the wind pushed back from the other side.

"Wow," said Mazzy. "We're so sorry."

"Why are you apologizing?" Felicia snapped. "It wasn't *our* fault."

"It's nobody's fault," said Gabe, thankful that they were no longer standing in the upstairs hallway. "Why don't you all go sit down in the living room. Malcolm can put on the next movie. I'll grab some snacks from the kitchen."

A few minutes later, carrying a tray of cheeses he'd scrounged from the fridge and crackers from an old box in the pantry, he turned off the hallway light, ready to set the mood for the next flick, though, in fact, the house had already done a fine job of that.

Ingrid yelped when he came through the door. Squished together on the couch, his friends looked terrified.

"Not funny, Gabe," said Malcolm.

"What's not funny?"

Mazzy leaned forward. "Please tell me you're kidding."

"About what?" Gabe placed the tray on the coffee table, baffled.

"That sound," said Felicia. "It was you, wasn't it?"

"What sound?"

But seconds later, he heard it too. A low-down, guttural growl. He turned toward the hallway. The sound came again — a deep, throaty threat. Inhuman. It was coming from the pitch-dark parlor opposite the living room.

Ingrid whined, bringing her knees to her chest. "*That* sound."

The floor tilted. Gabe grabbed at the door frame. His fingers began to tingle. *Breathe,* he told himself. Mazzy appeared beside him. Her slight touch brought blood back to his head, and the room righted. "Was that an animal?" he whispered. "Could it have gotten in when the door blew open?"

"I don't know." Mazzy stepped closer to him, their shoulders now pressing together. "Maybe."

The rest of the group joined them at the doorway.

"Call the police," Felicia demanded.

Ingrid shushed her as something crashed in the other room. They all screamed and stepped back. Except for Gabe. He planted his feet, straining to peer through the grainy darkness. After a moment, he realized he was channeling Meatpie. His courage was imaginary, but it seemed to work anyway. A vague shape shifted the shadows. His mind filled in the gaps, and the form became vaguely familiar. This was no dog. The intruder was something larger. Much larger.

That familiar thought tickled the back of his skull for the third time in as many hours. *The Hunter will come for you . . . you and your new friends.*

An enormous figure stepped toward the light of the living room, a shadow solidifying into something tangible. The group screamed. "What *is* that?" one of them shouted. The thing bumped into a side table, knocking the piece of furniture over with a crash.

Glancing over his shoulder, Gabe saw his friends cowering by the far wall. The thing in the other room could easily rush the doorway and trap them in here. There was no way out, unless one of them opened a window, and even then, with the meadow sloping steeply at the back of the house, a fall to the ground would be great. Too frightened even to speak, he stumbled backward.

From the parlor, heavy steps creaked across the old floor. A moment later, the living room's lamplight hit the intruder. A beastly silhouette filled the doorway. Shaggy hair hung from every inch of its wide body. It opened its black mouth in what appeared to be a smile filled with strangely blunt teeth. Ingrid shrieked. "Is that a . . . costume?" said Malcolm, sounding only slightly more restrained.

The world seemed to spin as Gabe reeled with both confusion and anger. "Not quite." He cleared his throat and wiped his sweaty palms on his jeans. "His name is Milton. Milton Monster."

PUPPET BOY

"I DON'T UNDERSTAND," SAID FELICIA, stepping toward Gabe and away from the group. She kept her eyes on the thing in the doorway. "What the heck is a Milton Monster?"

"A puppet." The word whisked from Gabe's lips like smoke, uncontainable now that it finally had been released.

"Whose puppet?" Malcolm asked.

"My father's," Gabe said. It was over. With his mask removed, Gabe had only moments before he turned back into the loser he'd learned to be.

"But how is it moving around?" Mazzy asked, coming up beside him again. "Is it robotic?"

Her question was like a punch. Gabe snapped his attention back to the doorway. "No," he said quietly. "It's not a robot. It's a suit." Milton Monster seemed to stare at them. "You wear it. The controls are inside. Hidden levers and hooks and strings."

"Then who . . . ?" Felicia's voice trailed off.

The puppet's chest moved slowly as someone inside breathed deeply.

"Seth?" Gabe whispered. "Is that you?" He almost expected the puppet to respond with another animal growl. But it only continued to stare and sway slightly.

"*Seth Hopper?*" Felicia asked. "No freaking way." She stomped toward the beast, stopping right in front of it. Milton towered nearly two feet over her. "What do you think you're doing?" she said, anger shaking her voice. "Freak!"

"Uh," Gabe tried to speak up, "Felicia . . ." But she wasn't listening to anything but the sound of her own voice.

The creature tilted its head, as if in amusement.

"You're going to regret this," said Felicia. "Big-time." She reached up and shoved at the puppet's chest. She pushed hard, but she only ended up sending herself into a backward stumble. Finding her footing, she looked unsurely back at Milton. "Seth?" she said, her voice a specter of what it had been seconds earlier.

Milton shook its head, long hair flipping back and forth across its broad shoulders. It opened its mouth again. A soft sound escaped this time, barely audible, but still Gabe recognized it. Whoever was inside the suit was laughing at them.

"Felicia," Mazzy whispered, waving her away from the doorway. Felicia scrambled back to the group by the wall.

"Stop it!" Gabe cried out at the intruder. This was his home. These were his friends. "Get out of here!"

Milton stepped lithely backward and disappeared around the edge of the doorway. For several seconds, the group stood together in the living room, unsure what to do. Then, from the hall, there came a sound of a heavy collapse, as if the intruder had tripped and fallen.

Gabe raced forward into the hall, and found his father's creation slumped against the wall across from the staircase. He approached slowly, waiting for it to move.

"Don't get too close," said Malcolm. "Someone's still inside that thing."

But in fact, the suit now lay completely still and silent. "I'm not so sure," Mazzy said after a few seconds. "If someone's in there, he's either unconscious or . . ."

Felicia shook her head. "Or what? Dead?"

Gabe kicked gently at Milton's foot. It flopped over, turning completely around. The group gasped. Tentatively, Gabe bent down, and for a moment, he was back in Howler's Notch or Slayhool or the Kingdom of Chicken Guts, crouching over some villainous beast that was waiting for the perfect moment to claw his leg, sever an artery, clutch him to its chest, guzzle his blood. Chilled, Gabe shook the thought away. This was no fantasy world. This was his grandmother's house. Edging closer, he poked its leg, but his hand met no resistance. The fabric flattened entirely, until Gabe found himself leaning against the floor itself.

"The suit's empty," Gabe said, glancing up at the group.

"How could he have slipped out of it so quickly?" Felicia asked. "That would be impossible."

"I guess we're looking at *impossible*," said Malcolm.

"What the heck is happening here?" Ingrid said, throwing her hands into the air. Gabe had an answer, but he knew none of them would understand.

{NEVER}
BETRAYAL AND THE BEAST

MEATPIE WANDERED THE WOODS ALONE. He'd had no official word from Wraithen in days, and he'd begun to worry that something was wrong.

That morning, however, from his royal bedroom in the stone tower of Castle Chicken Guts, Meatpie thought he'd heard their secret meeting cry: a piercing shriek, like the call of the weeway lizard — *WEE! WEE! WAAAAY!* — repeated thrice. Of course, the call could simply have come from the scaly pinkish creature itself, but Meatpie knew he must at least explore the possibility that Wraithen needed him.

Several nights prior, the Hunter had made it past the guards and into the castle — an act of aggression so egregious, there had been no protocol arranged to handle it. The beast had done no physical damage, but the psychological ramifications echoed boundlessly across the two kingdoms. No citizen felt safe. Everyone agreed that if the Hunter was not caught, and soon, something horrible, beyond all reckoning, would occur.

Strange, then, that Wraithen should choose this time to disappear.

"Ho, there." The voice came from inside the foliage just ahead. A thin shade of a body stepped out from behind a thick tree trunk.

"Hello," said Meatpie, his muscles tense. Wraithen smiled wearily. "Where have you been? I thought you might be dead."

"As you can see, I'm not."

"There is much to discuss."

"Not to worry." Wraithen stepped forward and reached into his satchel. "I've found a solution to all our problems."

"Have you really?" Meatpie said, unable to control the skepticism clinging to his words.

Wraithen pulled a small black object from his bag and held it up. A stone idol.

Carved to resemble a solemn monk, the object was familiar to Meatpie, but he couldn't remember why. "That's your great solution?" he asked, incredulous. "A little man made from obsidian?"

Wraithen studied the figurine for a moment, then glanced at Meatpie with amusement. "Have you no faith?" He reeled his hand back over his shoulder, then whipped the figurine forward. It flew past Meatpie, just missing his head, and landed with a crunch in the brush behind him.

Confused, Meatpie turned, trying to discern where the object had landed. A rock wall wound through the trees several feet away. He stepped forward and scanned the ground beyond the wall.

Something rose up rapidly before him, a shadow expanding, a tall neckless figure with broad shoulders, wearing a filthy leather vest, a quiver of ragged arrows strapped to his back and a rusted blade tied to his belt.

Meatpie was paralyzed with shock. The hulking figure reached out and caught him with massive hands, lifting him from the ground. Meatpie kicked, but only succeeded in knocking a small rock from the wall. The Hunter had pinned Meatpie's arms to his rib cage.

The thing's skin was pale blue and stretched so tightly across its enormous skull that in sections it had cracked open and bled. Its wide eyes were entirely onyx and as soulless as a shark's. The Hunter opened its mouth, revealing blackened teeth. Bloody saliva dripped down its chin. An aroma of rot, of waste, of putrefaction from the bowels of the wood's deepest cesspool swirled around them.

Seeing the creature up close for the first time, uncloaked and hideous, Meatpie tasted bile at the back of his throat. He felt faint, but he managed to cry out, "Wraithen! Help!"

From behind him came a cruel chortle. Meatpie could not turn to see his friend, but he knew something was very wrong.

"The *solution* to our problem is right here," said Wraithen.

The Hunter squeezed Meatpie, pressing breath from his lungs.

"I don't understand. . . ." he wheezed.

"What's not to understand?" Wraithen strolled up to the wall and glanced up at Meatpie. He was smiling.

"B-but why?"

Wraithen shook his head, frustrated that he had to explain himself. "*Why?*" he repeated. "Why should two castles exist side by side when one will suffice? One kingdom ruled by one king. Me." He gestured to the creature. "And here I've found my knight . . . errant as he is."

Meatpie tried to shout out with the little breath his lungs could catch. "You can't do this."

"Believe it or not, it was his idea." Wraithen smiled. "With this new agreement, he shall leave the Dark Forest of Howler's Notch and hold a position in my court. Not as dumb as he looks." The Hunter grunted as if delighting in Wraithen's praise, then shook his prey ever harder. "And the cost for his protection, he promised, will be small," Wraithen added with a cruel grin. He chuckled. "Well, human infants *are* small. And he only requires a meal two or three times a week — an offering that your people, the citizens of Chicken Guts, would be willing to give, I'm sure. Of course, if he is forced to *hunt* for his food, he works up quite an appetite."

"No!" Meatpie strained his head back, unable to move away from his captor. The Hunter opened its mouth wide. Tendons coated with rancid saliva stretched from its top to bottom jaw.

Meatpie didn't have time to scream before the monster put its sopping lips around his head. A metallic-tasting liquid filled his own mouth and spurted up his nose. He gagged. He struggled to take a breath, but only inhaled more fluid — the monster's spume. Choking, Meatpie pressed his mouth shut. His body slowly became enveloped by a steaming warmth, from his shoulders to his toes.

He forced his eyes open. They burned. He was blind. Despite his panic, Meatpie understood that where he was headed, he would no longer need to see, to breathe, to hear or feel, or, for that matter, to sense anything at all.

THE BLACK FIGURINE

GABE SAT UP IN BED, clutching his blanket to his chest. He struggled to catch his breath as the room solidified around him.

Only a dream . . . a nightmare. He was used to them, but he had never before dreamt of the Hunter.

Earlier, after he and his friends realized that the Milton suit was in fact empty, that whoever had watched them from the doorway had apparently evaporated into nothingness, they asked the expected questions. *What just happened? Have you ever seen it before? Is Temple House . . . haunted?* And after Gabe failed to answer satisfactorily, the group started with different questions — the ones that Gabe had dreaded ever since the fire had brought his family to Temple House. *Where did your father get the puppet? What does he do with it? Are there any more like it?* Defeated, Gabe told them the truth. He even brought them upstairs when he returned the puppet to his father's workshop and showed them what was really behind the door. *Surrender is freedom*, his mind had later translated for him. Giving in had been easier than he'd expected. The group explored the room, acting amazed and wearing expressions of wonder as they pored over Glen's sketches and models. But Gabe had seen those kinds of looks several years before, in his old town, after Glen had visited Gabe's school to talk about his job. First comes awe, then come the nicknames and the unending ridicule. *Want to know what's really behind that door, Felicia? Go ahead. Take a peek.* Now Gabe could do what he knew best, what he'd learned to do a long time ago. Hide. Fade away. Disappear.

The small black figurine that Wraithen had thrown into the

brush during Gabe's dream came into his head, and he remembered where he'd seen it before. It was the figurine he'd noticed sitting on a shelf in David Hopper's old bedroom, the one that Gabe had suspected was the missing piece of his grandmother's collection. For some reason, Gabe's dreaming mind had conjured it up.

He swung his legs over the edge of his bed. His feet met cold wood as he stumbled toward his bedroom door and out into the hallway.

After he and his friends had carried the heavy puppet back upstairs, Ingrid insisted on calling her sister to come pick her up. Mazzy and Felicia left with her, and when Malcolm asked if he could hitch a ride too, Gabe felt his fears solidify. Malcolm was supposed to have spent the night, but after Milton's inexplicable appearance, Malcolm had been too scared to hang out, even just until Gabe's parents came home.

Oh yes, this was most certainly the beginning of the end.

Gabe stepped onto the top stair, and it squeaked slightly. Staring into the dark hallway below, he realized that he might have a more immediate problem than the prospect of losing all his friends. Earlier that evening, someone had entered Temple House — someone who hadn't been invited.

Fuming, Gabe made his way to the library. For a brief moment, while the group was still together, he'd believed that Seth's game, the fantasy world and its oversized villain, was becoming a reality.

The Hunter will come for you.

So stupid.

He pushed open the library door and glanced around the room, making sure he was alone. This time, his grandmother's rocking chair was empty.

Gabe flicked the switch on a nearby table lamp, and the library filled with a dim glow. The light barely reached the bookshelves by the window, but his grandmother's figurines were visible, huddled together as if planning a secret attack. Gabe slowly came upon them, feeling his lungs tighten with every step. Even from several feet away, he could see that there were five figurines on display.

He blinked several times, certain that sleep had tinkered with his imagination. When he'd come into this room with his friends earlier in the evening, Gabe had seen only four little men standing on the shelf, the same number he'd noticed on the night he found Elyse sitting in the rocking chair. At some point in the past few hours, someone had replaced the missing figurine.

A soft cry came from the hallway. Gabe froze. The sound came again — not a cry, but the squeal of old hinges. Metal rubbing against metal.

With a floaty, almost dizzy sensation, Gabe moved toward the doorway and peeked out into the hall. A gust of chill air slapped his cheek. Several feet away, the door that led outside to the stairs and down to the backyard patio stood open a crack. He pulled the door open all the way and stared into the cold night, searching for movement on the grassy slope, imagining someone dashing toward the woods.

The Hunter will come for you.

Of course, Seth's threat had been empty, impossible. But was the prospect of Seth Hopper trying desperately to make him believe in the Hunter truly any better? Frightened and angry, Gabe cried out in a harsh whisper, "Seth! Are you there?" The only answer he received was the wind rustling the last of the leaves in the high branches down the hill.

MISSING MILTON

SHORTLY AFTER SUNRISE, Gabe awoke to a violent knocking on his bedroom door. He sat up, but before he answered, the door swung open.

Glen stood in the hallway, dressed in dark overalls with his arms crossed over his chest. He did not look pleased. "Morning, Gabe," he said. "Is there something you want to tell me?"

Wiping sleep from his eyes, Gabe asked, "What do you mean?"

"Were you not in my studio last night?" Glen stepped into the room.

Gabe clutched the blankets closer to his chin, as if that could protect him from his father's wrath. He hadn't thought to check the puppet for damage. What if it there was something seriously wrong with it? "I'm sorry, Dad. Malcolm wanted to look at him."

Glen sighed, relieved. "You know the rules. If you want to show your friends my work, just put the puppets back where you found them. Although I'd really prefer you didn't touch Milton at all. He's delicate, and if he breaks, I won't have time to make repairs before my presentation for the producers in Boston tomorrow."

"Oh," said Gabe, feeling his face burn. "But we *did* put him back where we found him."

Glen turned white. "He's not in my workshop."

"But that's where we left him."

Glen stared at Gabe for several seconds, searching his face for a lie. "So you're suggesting that Milton just got up and walked off by himself?" he said, clutching the doorknob.

Gabe clenched his jaw. Milton walking off by himself? It wouldn't have been the first time.

A half hour later, after revealing everything that had happened the night before, Gabe sat at the dining room table, surrounded by the rest of his family. They stared at him in disbelief. Gabe wasn't sure if their expressions were in reaction to the spontaneous house party or to the idea of Milton growling from the shadows.

"And you're positive that Seth Hopper had something to do with this?" Dolores asked. She bounced a wide-eyed Miri in her lap. Glen hung his head and paced aimlessly around the room. Elyse simply stared out the window as if lost in another world.

"Well, not really," said Gabe. "Not *positive*." He felt guilty pinning this on Seth without any actual proof. The return of the black figurine to the library certainly seemed like a clue. But why would Seth have stolen the figurine? When? Why return it now? And most importantly, why take Milton in its place?

"I'm going to have a talk with his mother," said Glen, standing. "Gabe, put on your shoes."

Gabe felt his face heat up. "What for?"

"I want you to tell her what you told us."

"B-but you might upset her."

"I don't care! If her son is a thief, maybe she deserves to be a little upset."

"Glen," Dolores whispered, holding her hands over Miri's ears. "Hush."

Gabe's father shook his head. "If we don't get that puppet back today, we can forget about selling this show at all. We'll be right back where we were three months ago, after the fire."

Elyse turned from the window. "If you must go, please don't walk through the woods."

"No, Mom. Of course we'll take the car."

Gabe stared at Elyse as she nodded, appeased, and he wondered what she knew that the rest of them did not. Now was not the time to ask.

"PLEASE DON'T MAKE ME go in there," Gabe said.

Glen pulled up along the side of the house and parked behind Mrs. Hopper's blue Honda. He didn't often show anger, but today he glared at Gabe with fire in his eyes. Glen pushed open the car door and stepped outside. Gabe knew that meant he was supposed to follow. He was frightened to find out what might happen if he disobeyed. And as he made his way up the lopsided steps toward the front porch, he worried also what might happen when Seth found him standing on the welcome mat.

Glen pounded on the storm door. The glass rattled, loose in its frame. "Dad," Gabe whispered. "Careful."

"Don't speak," Glen said.

The inner door opened a crack and a sleepy voice came from inside the darkened entry. "Can I help you?" Seth's mom opened the door a bit more and added, "Gabe? Is that you?"

"Yes, ma'am."

"Seth's not here right now," she said. "I'm not sure where he went."

"Actually, Mrs. Hopper," said Glen, "we've come to talk to you."

Sharon slipped outside into the cool morning air. She stood barefoot between Gabe and Glen. Her fuzzy pink robe was dingy at the hem. Her eyes were puffy and red. Either she had just woken, or she'd spent the past hour in tears. Her matted hair lifted from her scalp in an unintentional bouffant. She sighed and crossed her arms.

"What did he do now?"

Sitting uncomfortably on the porch, Gabe repeated his story to Sharon. Glen stood over them, grasping the wood railing at the bottom of the steps. Gabe told Seth's mom about their game, about the figurine, about Seth's strange behavior at school and their falling out, about Seth's threat, and finally about Glen's missing monster puppet. She listened, albeit glassy-eyed and slightly aloof. When he was finished, she said, "So what do you want me to do about it?"

Glen spoke up. "It would be nice if you let us check his room."

Sharon shook her head. "I can't let you inside."

"Why not?" Glen asked. His face was flushed the color of raw meat.

"It's a total mess. I'm in no shape for guests."

Gabe wondered if she'd meant to say, "*My house* is in no shape . . ."

"I mean no offense," Glen said, "but we're not your *guests*. Your son took something of mine, and it's very important that I get it back. Now."

As if waking from a dream, Sharon finally looked at him. "But we don't *know* for certain that he took it."

Glen scoffed. "Could you at least check?"

Sharon stood and tightened her robe. "Fine. Gimme a minute." She disappeared inside the white cottage, leaving Gabe alone with Glen, who trampled crabgrass as he paced in front of the porch steps.

When Sharon returned a few minutes later, she said, "I couldn't find anything out of the ordinary. You say that this puppet thing was big?" She held her arms out wide and glanced between her hands.

"Huge," said Glen, holding his arms out wider. "Larger than I am."

"There's no way my son could have hidden something that size in this house." She glanced toward the barn. "Unless . . ."

FALLING DOWN

MOMENTS LATER, after Sharon went back inside to put on her worn-out Keds, Gabe and Glen followed her across the yard.

They peeked into the stable on the way to the barn. The few stalls were empty except for spiderwebs and hay.

Sharon struggled with the barn's rusted lock for several seconds before the latch gave way and the door swung open. The barn was not large compared to others in the area, but it seemed vast as Gabe stepped inside. Shafts of sunlight broke through small holes in the high ceiling. Dust clouds glinted and swirled as Sharon walked through them.

"Seth?" she called out, and stared at the rafters as she waited for a reply. "Are you in here, kiddo?"

"Wouldn't the latch on the outside of the door have been open when we came in?" Gabe asked. Sharon tossed a confused look at him. "I mean, he couldn't have locked himself inside when the lock is on the outside."

"Good point," said Glen. "But that doesn't mean Seth didn't hide Milton in here. He could have locked the door on his way out."

"Look around, then, why don't you?" Sharon suggested. She pulled her robe tighter and shivered, obviously wishing to get back to the shelter of her cottage.

"Is it safe?" Glen asked, looking up at the ceiling. "Structurally?"

"Probably not," Sharon said.

"And you let your son play around in here?" he went on. Sharon pursed her lips, refusing to answer. "You haven't been in here before, have you, Gabe?"

"No," said Gabe, feeling the need to defend himself. "Seth suggested it, but it always seemed like it was about to fall down."

"Better hurry up, then," said Sharon. She leaned against a nearby wooden beam and crossed her arms, glaring at Glen.

Despite the size of the space, there wasn't much to explore. It was open and mostly empty, except for an old tractor that looked like it hadn't been run in twenty years. Through a dark doorway, they found a room full of stacked cages. Feathers were stuck in some of the rusted wires.

Back in the main room, a broken ladder climbed the rear wall, leading to a platform about fifteen feet above them. "What's up there?" Gabe asked.

"No clue," said Sharon. "Never had a reason to check it out." She called out as Gabe approached the ladder. "Careful. I don't think the rungs are sturdy."

Gabe paused. "So it would've been difficult for Seth to drag the Milton suit up there?"

"No clue."

Gabe grasped a rung and shook it. When he stepped up, Glen shouted out a warning, but Gabe only made it a few feet before the wood twisted in its socket and splintered. His foot crashed through several other rotten rungs below. "Sorry," he said, dropping down, brushing himself off, and glancing guiltily at Sharon and Glen.

"Well, I guess that answers that," she said. "No puppet up there."

But something creaked across the loft floor above them. The group froze, staring at the cobwebs hanging over their heads.

"Probably a squirrel," Sharon said. "Maybe a raccoon." If she were protecting Seth from Glen, her face gave away nothing. "Also, the building settles sometimes," she added. "I'm just waiting for it to collapse."

"Why wait?" Glen asked.

Sharon snorted a cold laugh. "You wouldn't believe the amount of time and money it costs to simply tear things down." She led them toward the exit, then stepped onto the grass outside.

Glen followed, but Gabe turned back to the loft. For a moment, he struggled to hear through the peculiar hush of the barn. After all the things he'd experienced lately, it wasn't difficult for him to believe that someone — or something — was up in the loft, straining to be quiet.

Monday's Dread

IN THE SEVENTH-GRADE HALLWAY the next day, Gabe noticed Seth standing at his locker, his shoulders stooped, his blond hair sticking up in the back. He flinched at every door slam, every cat-call, every footstep, as if he were expecting someone to sneak up on him and attack. When he noticed Gabe approaching, he shut his locker and darted around the nearest corner.

Surely, they'd have another chance to talk before the end of the day. Gabe dreaded the prospect, but he knew it was necessary. Neither Seth nor his mother had returned any of Glen's calls the previous afternoon. Eventually, the Hoppers' phone line went dead. It was at that point that Glen called the police. Later, when the pair of officers showed up at Temple House, they asked Gabe to tell his story again. The cops pledged to visit the Hoppers next, but they also explained that there was no guarantee they could get past Sharon without a warrant. Glen waited all night for a call that never came.

At his locker, Gabe felt the heat of staring eyes burning through the back of his head. He turned to find a few of his classmates glance quickly away. He leaned forward into the tight, dark space, swallowing down nausea.

Wow, he thought, they worked quickly here. Had it been Felicia who'd spread the word about his father's puppets? Or Malcolm? Or maybe Mazzy, whose betrayal would hurt the most. He never should have allowed any of them to come to Temple House. Now he'd have to pay the consequences.

Strong fingers clutched Gabe's shoulder and he tensed, turning to find a couple of kids from his homeroom standing behind him. "You okay?" asked a tall boy.

"Yeah," said another boy, who was shorter and had a runny nose that he wiped with a tissue. "You don't look so good."

"I-I'm fine," said Gabe.

"You heading to class?" said the tall boy, looking unsure. Gabe nodded. "Wanna walk together?"

Confused, Gabe headed down the hall with the pair.

"I heard that your grandmother is Elyse Ashe," said the short boy.

"Uh-huh," said Gabe, unsure where this was going.

The short boy's face lit up. "I told you!" He nudged his friend. "Her drawings are so cool. She did all the covers for the Olmstead books."

"Yup," said Gabe. "She did." He blushed, hoping he didn't sound obnoxious.

But the boys didn't seem to care. "Word is your dad works on television shows," said the tall boy, turning the corner. "He builds monsters?" Gabe stopped short, his sneakers skidding on the linoleum. Were they making fun of him? What was next? *I also hear that you're a big fat loser?*

The boys continued on but paused, then glanced back, concerned. "What's wrong? You forget something in your locker?"

Was it possible that they were being genuine? Were they truly impressed that his house was filled with puppets . . . that his grandmother was the creepy old lady who lived on the hill? Gabe had a strange and surprising thought: What if the things that had made him the weirdo at his old school made him interesting to the people here in Slade?

"Where'd you hear all this stuff about my family?" Gabe asked.

The boys grew sheepish. "People talk," said the short boy as the three found their way into the classroom.

People talk? That was what Gabe had been afraid of. But maybe now, for the first time, it wasn't a bad thing.

RATS IN CAGES

By LUNCH PERIOD, Gabe's anxieties had evaporated. The group at the table went on and on about what had happened at Temple House on Saturday night, rehashing all the scariest moments. No one blamed Gabe. In fact, they were amazed that he'd actually stood up to the intruder in the monster suit.

When Gabe mentioned that Milton went missing on Sunday morning, the rest of the group called Seth a criminal, a thief, a stalker. They laughed and whispered and made promises to get him back for messing up Mr. Ashe's presentation. Only after the bell rang did guilt creep into Gabe's conscience. Yes, Seth had been an absolute weirdo for the past month or so, but did he really deserve what they were saying about him?

Halfway through science class, a girl named Melanie Gilder raised her hand and asked the teacher, Mr. Hamill, what he'd done with Vincent Price, the albino rat that lived in a terrarium at the back of the room. "What do you mean?" Mr. Hamill asked. Melanie pointed to the glass case. It was empty.

Chaos erupted. Screaming. Scuffling of chairs. Several students even stood on their desks. Though Vincent Price was as tame as any pet rodent could be, Gabe lifted his feet off the floor in case the rat decided that his pants leg would make a good hiding place.

Mr. Hamill raised his hand to hush the class, then swiftly closed the classroom door. "He can't have gone far." Gabe wondered how the teacher could remain so calm. "Everyone stand up. I want this rodent found."

The class searched every inch of the room, but apparently, Vincent Price had escaped. Secretly, Gabe was happy for him.

A half hour later, as Gabe wandered into the hall someone grabbed his elbow. He knew who it was before he even turned his head. Seth glared at him, his face as red as a cherry. Gabe pulled away. "What do you want?" he asked, sounding harsher than he'd meant.

Seth stepped into an alcove doorway just outside of the school auditorium. Keeping his voice low, he said, "Since you asked, I'd really love it if you and your new friends stopped telling people that I broke into your house and stole some sort of stupid puppet from your dad." Gabe felt his own face burn. "Yeah," Seth continued. "Thanks to you, today, my nickname is *Stalker*. I wonder how long this one'll stick."

"I-I had nothing to do with that."

"Maybe not." Seth squinted. "But I'm pretty sure you had something to do with the police showing up at my house last night."

Other students streamed past the doorway where they stood, not noticing the argument. Or pretending not to notice. A tightness pressed at Gabe's chest, but he tried to stay calm. "My dad was furious. He was blaming *me*."

"So you told him *I* took it?"

"Can you honestly say I had no reason to think you might have? The last time we talked, you said some pretty nasty things."

"Like what?"

"Well . . . You said, 'The Hunter will come for you.'"

Seth's face went blank. "And so what? You think the Hunter has *come for you*?" Gabe said nothing. The words sounded silly now. "It's just a game. Remember? I was angry that night. So were you."

Just a game? Well, he was willing to play if Seth wanted to keep it up. "Listen . . . something strange is going on," Gabe said slowly, struggling to keep his voice even. He explained how someone wearing the Milton suit had growled at his group of friends inside Temple House on Saturday night. A real growl, like something you'd hear in the woods at night. He shared that the person inside the suit disappeared into thin air. How, later, someone had snuck into the house and returned the missing black figurine to his grandmother's library. Gabe thought it was most likely the same person who'd crept back upstairs and taken Milton from the workshop.

"Well, it wasn't me," said Seth. He stared at Gabe with a look that said, *You deserved this*. "I was home Saturday night watching TV. You can ask my mom."

Gabe tucked his hands into the pockets of his jeans. "Can you at least check David's room for the figurine? Maybe there was some sort of mix-up."

"A mix-up?" Seth blinked. He looked confused. "Whatever. Yeah, I'll check, but on one condition."

Gabe nodded.

"Tell your friends to stop calling me Stalker."

Right, thought Gabe. *Like that'll do any good.*

OFFENSE, DEFENSE

LATER, INGRID INVITED THE GROUP to cheer her on during the after-school intramural field hockey game. Gabe figured it would be a good distraction. So when the last bell rang, he called his mom, then headed out to the athletic fields with Mazzy, Malcolm, and Felicia. By four o'clock, Ingrid's team, the red jerseys, had trounced the yellows. Gabe had shouted so loudly after she'd scored two goals in a row that his throat felt raw. Ingrid promised everyone hot chocolate if they walked her home through the woods by the fields. The route was much shorter than taking the winding roads around the middle school.

This late in the year, the sun had begun to set almost as soon as the school day ended. Now, over an hour later, the sky had turned that familiar pale indigo that came just before the arrival of stars. The air lacked the warmth that only a month earlier would have been provided by a late afternoon glow.

In the woods, surrounded by bluish shadows, the constantly falling leaves were transporting, dreamlike. Even as Ingrid gabbed about the game, leading the group through a narrow culvert and up a small slope, for a moment, Gabe was right back in Howler's Notch.

He remembered his promise to ask them to stop calling Seth Stalker. But Gabe knew better than anyone that once a nickname was released into a group of eighth graders, it was impossible to retrieve. They'd simply laugh if he tried. Besides, who could say that Seth would uphold his end of the bargain?

Suddenly, Ingrid fell forward. It happened so fast, she didn't have time to gasp before she hit the ground. Felicia bent to help. The rest of them instinctively stepped back.

Ingrid winced, then sat up and clutched her foot, groaning. Felicia grabbed at something lying near Ingrid's sneaker. "What the . . . ?" She held it up. "Fishing wire."

The ground began to shake. From up the hill came the sound of branches snapping, of leaves being flattened. Several large rocks tumbled swiftly down the steep gully, heading right for them. "Move!" Gabe shouted.

Mazzy noticed the avalanche and dashed up the edge of the rut as the boulders crashed through the spot where she'd been standing. Felicia wrestled with Ingrid's T-shirt and managed to pull her out of the path just in time. Malcolm and Gabe leapt onto the small crest of ground beside them, watching as the boulders slowed and eventually stopped where the ground leveled out several feet away.

"What the heck?" said Malcolm, gasping for breath.

The sound of blood pounded at Gabe's eardrums with a deafening, almost tribal beat. He glanced up and down the trail where only moments earlier they had been gathered. The broken piece of fishing line glinted slightly where it now lay. "It was a trap," he said.

"A trap?" said Mazzy. "Someone planned this?"

"*Someone*," echoed Felicia. "You really have no idea who it was?"

No one spoke the answer aloud, though a name glinted clearly in each of their eyes. During lunch that day, they would have looked angry. Now, they seemed frightened.

"How could he have planned it?" Mazzy asked. "We didn't decide to come this way until after the game ended."

Ingrid struggled to stand. She placed some weight on her

injured foot and flinched. "He's a total *Stalker*," she spat out. "He probably knows I walk home this way every now and again. He could have rigged up this trip wire days ago, knowing I'd eventually come by."

"That's sick," said Malcolm. "He could have killed someone."

Gabe cleared his throat, worried that this was getting a little too heated. "I talked to him today," he admitted. The group stared at him, curious. "He said he didn't do any of it. Not the Milton masquerade. Not the theft. Also . . ." *Oh, just say it.* "He asked me to tell you all to stop calling him Stalker."

"Fat chance now!" Felicia shouted, looking around the darkening forest as if Seth might be watching. Her voice echoed through the trees.

"The point is," Gabe continued, delicately, "Seth insists that he had nothing to do with what happened over the weekend."

"Yeah," said Malcolm, nodding at the rocks sitting at the bottom of the slope. "But this is a different story."

"Ever since I moved to Slade," said Gabe, "strange things have been happening. Especially up near my house."

"Like what?" asked Mazzy.

Gabe blinked. Would they think he was nuts if he told them more? Or would they simply blame Seth again? He thought of the silhouette by the woods, the feeling that it was watching him. There *was* something weird in the woods, and none of them would understand until they'd seen it for themselves. Then Gabe remembered how, on Saturday night, Mazzy had stood by the window in Elyse's library, staring out into the darkness. She'd said something about —

"Darkness playing tricks," Gabe said. Mazzy flicked her wide eyes toward him. She understood what he meant.

"*Someone's* playing tricks," said Felicia, slinging Ingrid's arm over her own shoulder. "But I'm pretty sure it's not 'Darkness.' Come on. Let's get out of here."

As Felicia stepped back onto the path, bypassing the broken fishing line, Gabe felt a tingle up his spine. "Watch your step," he said, his voice cracking as he followed the group up the hill.

TALES OF THE HUNTER

SETH HOPPER DIDN'T SHOW UP at the bus stop the next morning, and Gabe didn't encounter him at school the entire day. When classes ended, Seth never came to his locker. Things went on this way for the rest of the week. Either Seth was out sick or he was playing hooky. His absence left Gabe feeling ill himself. Since Monday, when he and his friends had come upon the elaborate trap in the woods, Gabe had wanted to see if Seth would show a hint of remorse. At least none of them had encountered any more trip wires.

Gabe concentrated on other things. A few times, in the evening, he chatted with Mazzy about silly stuff like movies or YouTube videos. Once, over the phone, they listened to the college radio station coming out of Boston, rating each song, then comparing notes. It was almost enough to make him forget everything else.

Stories had begun to spread around the school about a tall, broad-shouldered man who was following kids on their routes home. Some had seen him watching from the shadows of the woods near the school grounds. Others claimed he'd been walking about a block behind them, ducking out of sight when they'd turn. The tales had become so common that several parents complained to the board of education, as well as to the police, that the school needed to hire more safety officers immediately.

At lunch, Gabe discussed these incidents with his friends, who, of course, wondered if Seth Hopper was behind all of it.

"What doesn't make sense is how large they say the man is," Ingrid said. "Seth isn't nearly as big."

"What about Milton?" Malcolm suggested. "Gabe's dad's puppet is still missing, right? If Seth's the one who stole him, maybe he's trying to freak everyone out by wearing it around town."

"What an idiot," said Felicia, tearing into her sandwich. She slowly chewed and swallowed. "I swear, if I ever see that kid again, I'm gonna seriously give him one."

"One what?" Ingrid asked.

Felicia chuckled. "I haven't decided. Whatever it is, he's not going to like it." That sweet girl Gabe had met at the beginning of the year was gone. He kept silent. Didn't all of this seem like too much trouble for one boy to cause on his own? he wondered. If so, did he have help? And from whom?

Later, in science class, Mr. Hamill was handing out copies of a pop quiz when someone at the back of the classroom screamed.

The students turned at once to find Melanie Gilder rise and back slowly away from her desk, which sat beside Vincent Price's old terrarium. Since the rat's escape, Mr. Hamill had cleaned it out, emptying the wood shavings that had filled the bottom, leaving the terrarium as barren as a new mausoleum. Now, however, something lay inside it.

"Melanie," said Mr. Hamill, not realizing what she'd seen, "I know these quizzes can sometimes be frightening, but I assure you, there is no reason to run."

"Uh-uh," the girl mumbled, pointing at the case. She didn't need to say anything more. Clearly visible through the glass, a pile of bones, bleached white, lay scattered on the terrarium's mirrored floor. A small skull had been boiled clean. Its empty eye sockets stared blindly at the class. Vincent Price had returned, though not of his own volition, and not in the form the class had last seen him.

Everyone burst into chatter, and once more, Mr. Hamill raised his voice. "Take your seats! Please!" This time he sounded as shaken as everyone else.

Gabe felt the room tilt and clutched at his desk to keep himself from tipping over and landing on the floor. He caught snippets of talk, mostly one-word questions — How? Who? When? Why? — and felt shame that he was the only one who had a clue. This was the Hunter's method. He stole away someone you cared about. And when he was done, he returned only what remained. Bones.

COMING CLEAN

BEFORE LONG THE ENTIRE SCHOOL was buzzing with speculation about what had really happened to the science room rat.

One faction of kids guessed that a twisted student was sick of Mr. Hamill's frequent quizzes and, in revenge, had boiled Vincent Price alive. Others surmised that Mr. Hamill himself was guilty, that he'd snapped and that one of his students would be next! A few more were convinced that the science teacher was simply teaching them a lesson about the nature of life and death, that in a couple days, he'd reveal that the bones were fake and then return the real rat to the terrarium, alive and well.

Gabe ignored the gossip. It was only a matter of time before Seth Hopper's name came up in connection with the strange episode. If he didn't find his group of friends, or Felicia at least, before the end of the day, he knew they'd demonize Seth even more. Deep down, Gabe still wished to protect Seth from all that.

Before the last period, he asked Malcolm and Mazzy to tell Felicia and Ingrid to meet him in the library as soon as possible after school. Gabe was the first one there, and he planted himself at a quiet table in the back of the room. Each of his friends arrived wearing curious expressions, but he insisted on waiting until they'd all shown up. And when Mazzy, who arrived last, sat down, he began. "This is really difficult to talk about." No one said a word, just listened. "Some things have happened over the past few months — things that have to do with Seth Hopper." His mouth was dry, and the sound of his lips smacking made him blush. "Ingrid, a while ago, you mentioned that your sister,

Becca, heard Seth's brother, David, talking about this game he'd created."

"Yeah," said Ingrid, wrinkling her brow, "the one with the Warrior?"

"The Hunter," said Gabe. "His name is the Hunter. You all know that when I moved to Slade, Seth was the first person I met. We're neighbors. Well, he invited me to play a game with him too — David's game."

Felicia flinched. "You went along with it?"

Gabe felt his face flush even hotter. "I didn't realize that Seth and David used to play it together. I thought the two of us were making everything up as we went along. Our characters. The world itself. But Seth had been leading the way. It was easy for him because his brother had already invented most of it. Including the big bad villain that Ingrid's sister mentioned."

"The Hunter," Ingrid said.

Mazzy leaned forward. "What *is* the Hunter?"

"A deformed monster," said Gabe. "He carries a blade and a bow and arrows to, well, hunt. Only the things he hunts are humans."

"Gross," said Ingrid.

"It was a weird game," said Gabe, trying to sound nonchalant. "But I didn't know anyone else in town. And Seth kept inviting me over. It took me a while to realize that he was obsessed in a way."

"With the game," Malcolm said, "or with you?"

Gabe ignored him. He breathed deeply. "What happened today in my science class, with the rat bones . . . According to David Hopper's mythology, it's a sign that the Hunter was there."

"I don't understand," said Felicia.

"In the fantasy world of the game, our characters fought to stop the Hunter from taking village children from their beds. If he succeeded, after he finished his meal, he'd return the bones to the family. To taunt them."

Each one of them sat agape as Gabe's words sunk in.

"Everything that's been going on . . ." said Mazzy.

Gabe nodded, finding it easier to speak now. "It's not just the rat. It's what happened at my house last weekend. It's the trap we discovered in the woods on Monday. It's the dark figure kids say they've seen watching them from the shadows when walking home from school."

"I'm confused," said Felicia. "Are you saying you know for sure that Seth is responsible for all of it?"

Gabe shook his head. "I can't see how he could be."

"Then what *are* you saying?"

"Well . . . there's more." This was the worst of it. Gabe felt his heart beating faster. "After Seth tossed that carton of chocolate milk at you, I told him we couldn't play the game anymore. He flipped out. He told me 'The Hunter will come for you . . . and your friends.'"

Felicia stood up, knocking her chair backward. It fell to the floor with a resounding thump. "He threatened us and you didn't think it was necessary to say anything?"

"I-I didn't want to freak anyone out," Gabe said.

"Yeah, well, good job with that." Felicia's eyes glinted with anger. "Ingrid nearly broke her ankle this week because of him."

Because of you, Gabe, he heard.

"That's the thing though," Gabe said, clutching at the bottom of his chair, forcing himself to go on. "Seth's connected to it, but I don't think he's the one who's responsible."

"Then who is?" Felicia slapped the table between them. "The Hunter?" she said, unconvinced. "Can't you see he's manipulating you? *It's what he does, Gabe.*"

Mazzy touched Felicia's shoulder. "Maybe we should just listen."

Felicia sat down in a huff and crossed her arms.

Gabe glanced at Mazzy, silently sending a message of appreciation. "Something strange is going on. Something bigger than us. Something bigger even than Seth. I can't explain it. I just have this feeling. We're targets, and we need to be careful. More careful than ever."

"Well, I have an idea," said Malcolm. "We head over to his house, knock on his door, and when he answers, we kick his butt." He paused, then added, "*Carefully.*"

"I think the best thing we can do is ignore him," Gabe answered. "Let's not spread rumors. Or call him names. We need to just leave him alone."

DEATH BY CHOCOLATE

MONDAY WAS THE START of Slade Middle School's weeklong Halloween countdown. An event had been planned for every day, concluding with a haunted house maze in the high school gymnasium on Friday afternoon, Halloween. The kickoff was a bake sale supporting the town's athletic programs.

After the last bell, people gathered in the lobby. Folding tables displayed the donated goods. There were plates filled with cookies and several different kinds of cakes and pies, as well as sweet and savory breads. An enormous bowl containing what looked like a mixture of chocolate mousse, whipped cream, and ladyfinger wafers sat upon the middle table as a centerpiece. A jumbo wooden spoon pierced the dessert's gooey heart. The aroma wafting through the halls was mesmerizing. Soon, students and parents swarmed the spread. Faculty volunteers passed money back and forth as the treats slowly disappeared into backpacks and canvas sacks and, of course, salivating mouths.

Gabe had shown up early and purchased the largest chocolate chip cookie he could find, then stood back, picked at it, and waited for his friends to show up. That weekend, he'd taken an overnight trip into Boston with his grandfather to see the aquarium and the Museum of Science while his parents visited their old property. He didn't have a chance to check in with anyone back in Slade, but they never reached out to him either. So things with Seth seemed to have finally quieted. Maybe the conversation between Gabe and his friends in the library on Friday had done the trick.

Something in Gabe's gut whined it wasn't as simple as that.

"Yo!" a voice shouted in his ear.

Gabe nearly dropped the cookie. He turned to find Malcolm standing behind him, already doubled over with silent laughter. Gabe forced a laugh too.

"Where are the girls?" Malcolm asked when he was able to breathe again.

"Haven't seen 'em."

"That's odd. Felicia said she'd be here with her mom's famous Death by Chocolate cake. She's so proud."

Gabe pointed toward the eighth-grade hallway beyond the bake sale tables. Looking frazzled, Felicia clutched a plate carrying a massive Bundt cake, thick with black frosting. Mazzy and Ingrid followed a few steps behind her, purposely keeping their distance. Felicia placed the cake on the table, smoothed her hair, and then, as if by magic, transformed her face into one that exuded joy and serenity. Better for sales, Gabe figured.

The other girls made their way to the middle of the lobby.

"Something wrong?" Malcolm asked.

Ingrid shook her head. "Oh, you know how she is. The frosting got messed up in the refrigerator in the teachers' lounge. She had to make it perfect before the debut."

"It looks delicious anyway," said Mazzy.

"Should we show some support?" Gabe asked. "Before it's all gone?"

"We'll never hear the end of it if we don't," said Malcolm, rolling his eyes.

"Oh, the things we do for our friends," said Mazzy. Gabe thought he heard a hint of sarcasm in her voice, but she simply smiled as if everything was as peachy as warm cobbler.

Felicia was busy cutting thin slices of her chocolate Death. She looked like she was in heaven now — the frosting crisis forgotten. She glanced up and saw her friends approaching. She waved them forward and mouthed, *Hurry!*

"I saw Seth in school today," Mazzy whispered into Gabe's ear.

"Really?"

"Yeah, he was near the principal's office with one of the guidance counselors. I smiled at him. He smiled back."

Gabe felt horrible. About so many things. "Well, that's good," he said in spite of himself.

Mazzy bit her lip. "There's more."

"More?"

Mazzy picked at her cuticles for a moment. When she answered, her voice was soft, barely perceptible. Gabe had to lean close to hear her. "Over the weekend," she said, "I went to see him."

His skin felt like an electric current was running through it. "At his house? Alone?" Mazzy nodded. He glanced at Malcolm and Ingrid, who were lost in their own conversation. "Why would you do that?"

"Someone had to," she said. "I would have asked you to come, but after last week, I had the sense you weren't really game." Gabe sighed, but she went on. "Everyone's been tossing around blame. I figured I'd ask him about it myself. And I'm glad I did. I feel like we made a real connection."

Gabe shuddered. "About what?"

She paused, secret thoughts playing out in her head. "Well, he explained that he'd been home from school for most of last week because his mom lost her job. He was afraid to leave her there alone."

A pang of guilt rippled in Gabe's gut. "Really?"

"I told him what's been going on here at school. With poor Vincent Price. With the trap we found in the woods after the field hockey game. He looked genuinely worried. But he denied having anything to do with it."

"Of course he would," said Gabe, trembling, showing more hurt than he'd meant to reveal. "That's what he does."

Mazzy pressed her lips tightly, then shrugged. "Maybe we can go visit him together. See if he's all right. See what's going on with his m —"

The room rocked. People screamed and fell away from the tables, knocking into others, spilling everyone backward like dominoes.

With a ringing in his ears, Gabe realized that there'd been an explosion. Mazzy was clutching his arm. He found that he was clutching hers as well. They had been far enough away and had managed to stay on their feet. Others weren't so lucky. Ahead, several people were sprawled out on the linoleum floor, apparently too stunned to get up.

From the looks of the bake sale, the target had been one of the desserts. Remnants of what looked like crust and fruit compote were splashed across the crowd. Little bits of black icing clung to the ceiling, looking strangely like blood. After a moment, Gabe realized it was what was left of Felicia's cake.

The throng slowly realized what had happened. People turned to the exits and pushed forward, trying to escape the lobby. Their energy was becoming increasingly frenzied. Malcolm and Ingrid were caught up with the crowd and soon disappeared past the double doors.

Gabe was still too befuddled to move. He planted his feet and knocked shoulders with anyone who came close. Mazzy did the same.

From the opposite side of the table, the vice principal, Ms. Yorne, raised her arms and signaled for attention a few moments too late. Frosting speckled her pale skin. "Please, everyone, stay calm. Do not panic!" As she spoke, someone pulled the fire alarm. The crowd shouted collectively, like the cheering section at a local football game, and pushed even harder to reach the doors. Some of them were getting crushed.

Gabe and Mazzy broke toward the side of the lobby and leaned against the cinderblock wall, barely escaping the wave. Mazzy nudged Gabe and pointed toward the tables. Felicia sat on the floor behind what was left of her display, her spine hunched and her legs splayed in front of her. The two squeezed past a few stunned stragglers.

Mazzy bent cautiously toward Felicia. "Hey!" she shouted over the loud buzzing of the fire alarm. "You okay?" She lifted Felicia's chin. Her blue eyes were glazed, unseeing, but when Mazzy poked her shoulder, Felicia flinched.

"What . . . what happened?" Felicia said, noticing her friends.

"We don't know," said Gabe. "Let's get you out of here." Mazzy helped Felicia to her feet. Gabe crouched and looked around. There was shattered ceramic and glass everywhere. Several singed dollar bills fluttered to the ground. The multitude of coins strewn about the floor made it look like the bottom of a wishing well. Amidst the destruction, most everything seemed to be covered in pitch-black frosting. The blast had likely originated near Felicia's dessert. If her cake hadn't been famous before, it certainly would be now.

Gabe was overcome by the need to laugh. He raised his hand to his mouth to hide an uncontrollable grin. An explosive Death by Chocolate cake? Either it was a terrible coincidence, or someone had been trying to make a very silly pun.

"Gabe!" Mazzy shouted from the other side of the table. "You coming?"

"Yeah." He stood and at that moment he noticed a different sort of object lying on the floor. This one was a thin, burnt string connected to a small twist of blackened paper, the ends of which were ash.

Gabe recognized it — he'd seen something similar only weeks ago in the woods, at the altar of the crooked tree. He'd located the remains of an M-80.

THAT EVENING, GABE SAT curled up on the couch next to his baby sister. The television murmured from across the living room. Elyse sat in her recliner and watched a game show, but he wasn't paying attention. The sound of the fire alarm at school still echoed in his head.

Miri burbled something nonsensical. The phone rang. Elyse got up and sauntered down the hall to answer it. Moments later, from the kitchen, she called for Gabe's parents to pick up.

When she came back into the living room, she stared at Gabe, looking like she was about to say something. Instead, she turned around, disappeared into the darkness of the hall. Her cold expression chilled Gabe even more than the prospect of seeing his father's puppet walking around by itself.

That afternoon, Gabe had told his family about the bake sale disaster. He left out the part about finding the M-80; that was his secret for now. His mother and father had listened, nodding with concern, but almost immediately afterward, they had gone back to discussing plans to rebuild Milton Monster. As it turned out, the producers had seen potential in the new project and given Glen another shot.

Gabe straightened, trying to hear the telephone conversation from across the house. All he caught were hushed murmurs and pieces of words. He listened to the clack of the receiver being put back into the cradle. Now his parents were whispering to each other.

Seconds later, they appeared in the doorway, both looking pale, their expressions slack, as if they'd just gotten news heavy enough to break a camel's back.

"Did someone die?" Gabe asked, sitting up straight on the couch. He'd meant it to be a joke, but no one laughed. Miri clung to his arm, her little fingernails digging into his skin. He tried to pull away, but she had too strong a grip.

"Not yet," said Dolores. Her face filled with color. Too much color. She turned red. Stepping closer, she lifted Miri away. The baby whined and reached for Gabe, but he didn't move. "That was your principal on the phone. He was not happy."

Gabe was too baffled to respond.

"He wants us to meet with him first thing tomorrow morning," said Glen. "You too, buddy." He said *buddy* in the way you say *buddy* when you mean the opposite.

"For what?" Gabe asked. Now his own face felt flush. Burning up.

"Something about what happened at the bake sale," said Dolores. "Something about it being your fault."

They arrived at the school early, before any of the buses had shown up, before most of the staff had even pulled into the parking lot. Gabe had not slept at all the night before. It had felt as though the shadows in his bedroom were watching him, and if he closed his eyes, they'd come at him with hidden claws.

He followed his parents through the main entrance. Miri was at home with his grandmother. He'd begged them all to believe him that he'd had nothing to do with the bake sale fiasco, that there must have been some sort of misunderstanding. Eventually, his parents considered what he was saying, but it had taken so much convincing, he decided not to share the rest of the story.

About the shadow, about the game, about how very frightened he was of Seth Hopper. Not yet.

The principal's office was smaller than Gabe expected.

"Please," said Mr. Drover, standing behind his desk, "have a seat." Ms. Yorne, the vice principal, was there too, leaning against a crowded bookcase, looking much more put together than the last time Gabe had seen her.

He and his parents squeezed onto the stools that the secretary, Mrs. Closkey, arranged for them. The adults all shook hands, a formality that made Gabe uncomfortable, as he was very pointedly left out of it. Mr. Drover sat down in his large leather chair and spoke. "We asked you here this morning because we believe that your son was responsible for yesterday's incident."

Glen sighed. "Gabe says he didn't do it," he said, "whatever *it* was."

Mr. Drover and Ms. Yorne nodded, as if they'd expected this reaction. They both turned toward Gabe. "You can come clean now," Mr. Drover said. "I promise you, it'll be less embarrassing for you if you do."

"But I didn't —"

"We have proof," Ms. Yorne interrupted. "We have so much proof it's not even funny."

Gabe closed his mouth and squirmed in his seat. He wasn't laughing.

"What *proof*?" asked Dolores.

Mr. Drover leaned forward, placed his elbows on the desk, and rested his chin in his hands. "An abundance of chocolate frosting," he said. "Footprints and cake crumbs leading from the lobby directly to Gabe's locker."

Glen laughed. "You've got to be kidding me. How is *that* proof?"

"Let me finish, Mr. Ashe. When we opened your son's locker,

we discovered these." Leaning back, he slid open a drawer, removed three compact gray tubular objects, and carefully set them down on the bright green desk blotter. When Gabe realized what he was looking at, his breakfast's orange juice burned the back of his throat. "These are dangerous explosives," Drover said. "M-80s, I believe they're called. Maybe you're unaware, Mr. and Mrs. Ashe, but not only are they illegal to sell in this state, but merely bringing them onto school property is a serious offense."

"Now, Gabriel," Ms. Yorne went on, "are you going to tell us where you got these? Or are you going to continue playing games?"

"But those aren't mine." Gabe's voice came out like a whisper.

"*Games* it is, then," said Yorne. "The school policy for a violation of this magnitude is no less than three days' suspension. This, however, doesn't include the county's plans, which may involve a fine or even incarceration at a juvenile detention —"

"Hold on here!" said Glen, trying for a moment to rise before realizing there wasn't enough room. "Let's not get ahead of ourselves. Gabe was adamant last night that he had nothing to do with what happened yesterday. And, I beg your pardon, Ms. Yorne, but your *proof* is hardly irrefutable." His voice shook, as if he were the one being accused. Hearing this only made Gabe more nervous. "Exactly how secure are these lockers? You were able to get inside easily enough. What about someone else? Someone who might have something against my son?"

"Entirely possible," said the principal blankly, as if he'd heard it all before. "Highly unlikely."

Dolores spoke up. "I think Gabe deserves a chance to explain himself."

"*My point exactly.*" Ms. Yorne pulled her lips into a tight smile. "Please, Gabe, I wish you would."

Gabe stared at the M-80s. Their potential origins raced through his mind, but one rose clearly above the others.

"Go ahead, honey," said Dolores. "You said you don't know where they came from."

"But I didn't say that," Gabe answered. "I said they weren't mine." His mouth was dry, his tongue like sandpaper. "I know exactly where they came from."

THE CULPRIT

GABE TOLD THEM ABOUT THE GAME in the woods, about the altar of the crooked tree, about Seth and the explosives. He explained that, according to Seth, a boy in one of the younger grades had met him in the (*shadow market*) bathroom that day, weeks ago, and sold him the M-80s. And no, Gabe didn't know who the younger boy was.

Even after everything that had happened, even knowing that Seth may very well have planted explosives in his locker, Gabe felt awful for telling on him. He had wanted to talk to him about it first, to get his story, to find out the truth, if that was even possible anymore.

Mr. Drover was disappointed. He couldn't punish Gabe without first speaking with Seth. But Seth, once again, had called in sick.

Somehow, everyone learned quickly what Mr. Drover and Ms. Yorne had found in Gabe's locker. As he wandered the halls, he could practically hear their unspoken question echoing through the school: *Did Gabriel do it?*

Between classes, he avoided his friends by ducking through halls where he knew they wouldn't be. He considered skipping lunch to bring his brown paper bag to the boys' bathroom and hide out in one of the stalls. As he paused in the cafeteria's doorway, he felt a tug at his elbow. He turned to find Mazzy standing beside him. He flinched — they hadn't spoken since right before the cake incident. He had no idea what to say to her. She looked concerned. "We need to talk," she said, and pulled him from the door.

Gabe tried to keep up as she practically galloped away from him. At the end of the hallway, she barreled through a pair of doors that led outside to a deserted patio.

The air was cold, and Gabe, wearing a short-sleeve polo shirt and jeans, wasn't dressed for it. The sky was the kind of pure blue that only belonged to the month of October. On any other day, the sight of it would have made him happy. Now, though, it looked like a lie. Everything beautiful seemed secretly poisonous.

Mazzy sat on one of the benches near a chain-link fence that cordoned off the tennis courts. She squeezed her knees together and leaned forward, sitting on her hands, staring at the ground. Gabe was too nervous to move, except to rub at the goose bumps covering his bare arms.

"I heard what happened," she said. "Your meeting with the principal."

"I didn't do it," Gabe said quietly.

Mazzy looked up at him. "I know that. I'm pretty sure *everybody* knows that. You were standing right next to me when the thing went off."

"Then Felicia doesn't blame me?"

Mazzy shook her head. "She's telling everyone that she wants to *destroy* Seth Hopper."

Gabe sighed with relief, but then thought about what Mazzy had just said. That wasn't good either. "Felicia won't do anything," he mumbled, as if to convince himself.

"When I went next door to check on her last night, she could barely speak, she was so livid."

"I would have been too."

"Even if Seth planted the M-80s," Mazzy said, "does he deserve to have Felicia show up at his house and break the windows? Or his knees?"

Gabe was confused. Why had Mazzy brought him out here? "I guess not," he answered.

"You *guess* not?" Mazzy stared at him quizzically.

"What are you suggesting we do?" Gabe asked. "Rescue him?"

"You *know* there's more to the story," she said. "I understand that you don't want to, but we have to talk to him again. At least to warn him about Felicia."

"After the bake sale, I'm not sure your talking-it-out-with-Seth thing is working."

Mazzy leaned forward, thrust her face into her hands, and groaned. She stayed that way for several seconds. Gabe sat down on the edge of the bench a couple feet from her. He reached out and touched her shoulder. "Why do you care so much about Seth?" he asked.

"Why don't *you*?" She looked up at him in surprise.

"I do!" he said. "But he blew up a freaking cake! He hurt people, and he tried to get me in trouble for it! I care, lots, but I also care about myself."

"Clearly."

"Why are you mad at me? What did I do wrong?"

"Because you know what he's going through. You might be the only one able to talk some sense into him."

"I've tried that already. It didn't work." She rolled her eyes at him. "I-I get it," he continued. "The Hunter's game is Seth's escape. I know what it feels like to need that. Last year, every day I wished for things to change. For people to just leave me alone. When my wish came true, when I *escaped*, it was because my stupid house burned down. Not a fair trade. But I learned my lesson: If there is a choice between living in a fantasy world versus living in reality, then I choose *reality*. And that is something Seth just doesn't seem to understand, no matter how much talking we do."

"You think *eighth grade* is the real world?" Mazzy said, then burst out laughing. It was a cold sound. She sounded so unlike the girl he knew, his goose bumps only spread farther. "Please," she went on. "This school, this town, is a holding pen. We're like sheep pressed up against the doors. You know what I think 'reality' is? I think it's the room on the other side. You sure you want to step to the front of the line?" After a moment, she slowly exhaled. "In a way, I'm like Seth too," she said. "I seek out the fantasy in my own world." She made her voice small and high-pitched. *"Hooping contests? Hooray."*

Gabe couldn't help but smile.

"And even though you try hard to hide it, I know you think the same way. Or else you would never have joined up with him in the first place. It's what makes the three of us different from everyone else. You, me, and Seth. We're explorers. We *know*. We've seen. We've encountered beasts. And we've escaped."

Gabe tried to see through her suddenly cloudy expression. "We have?"

Mazzy bit her lip. "How do you think I got so good at the hula hoop? Plenty of time outside, away from my parents. Away from . . . a lot of things. Practice makes perfect."

He suddenly felt sad for her. He wanted more than anything to lean forward, to wrap his arms around her. The breeze came from behind and rustled her hair. Mazzy sighed and ran her fingers through it, tucking it behind her ears. She stared off toward the athletic fields down the hill.

Gabe clasped his hands in his lap and said, "I just don't want to play games with him anymore. With anyone."

They sat quietly for a moment, then Mazzy stood and stepped toward the school's door. Looking back, she said, "That's too bad. I feel lucky that I'm still allowed."

GABE STAYED QUIETLY TO HIMSELF until the last bell rang. Then, as usual, he climbed aboard the bus home. Of everything that had happened that day, he couldn't get the argument with Mazzy out of his head. He tried to imagine what she'd gone through to call herself an *explorer*. What kind of beasts had she escaped? Gabe especially wondered if she was right about Seth, about the three of them being similar, and whether or not that made his former friend worth all this trouble.

When the bus pulled away from the curb at the base of Temple House's long driveway, Gabe stood at the roadside, unsure which direction to go. Up led home. And down wrapped around the wooded hill toward the Hoppers' house.

Mazzy was right about one thing. There was more to the story. And right now, Seth was probably the only one who knew what it was.

Gabe turned away from his grandmother's driveway just as someone ducked behind the trunk of a wide oak on the corner. Stories of the shadowy figure that had been following kids home from school leapt into his brain, but Gabe forced himself to pause. "I can see you," he called out.

A moment later, the figure, who was neither large nor shadowy, peeked out from behind the trunk. Seth. Of course. Gabe kept his distance, unsure of what Seth might do. Had Mr. Drover been in touch yet? Did Seth know that Gabe had told on him?

"Sorry," said Seth. He sounded calmer than Gabe had expected. And even though his eyes were bloodshot and his skin was pale, he did look happy to see Gabe. "I was waiting for the bus, but I didn't want you to run if you saw me. Can we talk?"

Gabe pursed his lips, unwilling to share that he'd been about to head down to Seth's house anyway.

Perched on Seth's tightly made bed, Gabe kept his muscles tense in case Seth gave him a reason to run. He wished he'd thought to tell his parents where he'd gone. Would it be weird to pull out his cell phone right now?

Seth closed the door. "I don't really have anything to offer you. My mom hasn't gone to the store in a while."

"It's fine," said Gabe. "I'm not hungry." Looking up at Seth's drawn face, he suddenly wondered when he had last eaten. "How is she?"

"Oh, you know . . ."

But Gabe didn't know. He couldn't imagine. Neither boy said a word for several seconds. Then, of course, they both spoke at once.

"Mazzy told me to come —"

"I'm sorry that —"

They paused, and in that moment, Gabe went on. "You're sorry that what?"

Seth blinked. "I'm sorry about . . . a lot of things. But mostly, I'm sorry that I ever met you." Gabe felt his face flush, but Seth held up his hands. "That came out wrong. I just mean . . . you'd have been better off. Lots of people would be."

"Don't —"

"It's true. It's like my family is cursed or something."

"You don't really believe that."

"There's a lot you don't know — so much I have to tell you."

Gabe waited, frightened that if he spoke, the walls would collapse and he'd wake up from a dream, never knowing the answers.

Seth sighed. "Principal Drover called my mom this morning. He told her what happened at the bake sale yesterday."

"You didn't already know?" The words came out before he could stop himself.

"He said that they found footprints leading to your locker," Seth went on. "That they found firecrackers."

"M-80s," Gabe corrected.

Seth nodded, his skull heavy with guilt. "He said you told him I got them from another student. That I put them in your locker. But I didn't. I would never do that."

"But you'd do *other* things?" Gabe tried cautiously.

"I wasn't at the bake sale. Or anywhere else you guys think I've been. But that didn't stop Drover from suspending me for the rest of the week."

"Wow," said Gabe, shocked that the principal had taken his own word over Seth's.

"But I *haven't done anything* to any of you. Really, Gabe. I promise. The same things are happening to me. I've seen that shadowy figure. I've tripped strange traps in my yard."

Seth stood and went to the window. He unlatched the lock and lifted the sash. Cold air rushed into the room. "I wanted to show you this."

"Show me what?" Gabe asked, standing and shivering.

"Last Friday night," Seth said, "just after I turned off my lamp and got into bed, I heard a noise outside. It sounded like something big stomping through the dead leaves near the woods. The noise scared me. Not sure why. There are animals out here all the time — deer, dogs, sometimes even coyotes. But this time, I could feel something watching me. Even through the wall. Like it was hungry." He wrapped his arms around his rib cage.

"After a while, I couldn't hear it moving around anymore. I went to the window and drew back the curtain. Almost immediately, something hit the outside wall. The glass rattled. I crouched down. Two more times, it came. Wham. Wham. Right outside." Seth glanced out into the yard. "I scrambled back to my bed. Got under the covers. My mom had taken something to help her sleep, so I knew I couldn't wake her up. I lay there most of the night, staring at the ceiling, hoping that the noise wouldn't come again. I peeked out here this morning. And I found these." Seth waved Gabe forward.

Together they leaned out the window. Moisture swirled in the cool breeze. Night was approaching quickly, but there was still enough light left to see by. Three small protuberances that looked like broken twigs stuck out of the frame inches below the sill. Gabe reached out and touched the knobby, shattered wood tips. "What are they?" he whispered.

"Arrows. Old. Whittled by hand. I tried to pull them out, but they'd been lodged in so forcefully, the best I could do was break them off. So you see . . . you guys aren't the only ones being hunted."

Gabe didn't know what to believe. He remembered what Mazzy had said earlier that day: *You might be the only one able to talk some sense into him.*

"Is there anything else I don't know?" he asked. Seth closed his eyes and nodded. "Then tell me now, Seth. Please . . . just tell me the truth."

THE WORLD ACCORDING TO SETH

"I LIED ABOUT THE BOY in the bathroom," Seth began, "the one who I said sold me those M-80s. There was no boy. I just went in there because *Slayhool* seemed like a cooler place than where I actually got them. I'm sorry." Gabe crossed his arms, waiting for a straight answer. "They belonged to my brother."

"David gave them to you?"

"Not exactly. I took them from his bedroom this past summer. He'd hidden them in his dresser. I'm not sure where *he* got them, but I guess that doesn't really matter. He used them to play the Hunter's game. In fact, the little bombs were how David introduced me to the Hunter in the first place."

One afternoon a few years earlier, when David was still around, Seth was in his bedroom reading when he heard a blast outside so loud it rattled the house. Looking out the window, Seth thought he noticed someone moving up the hill between the dense expanse of trees. Slipping his shoes on, he snuck outside.

In the woods, he heard voices. He followed them until he found his brother crouched in front of one of the old stone walls, whispering to himself as he struggled with a pack of matches.

When David turned to find Seth approaching from down the hill, he groaned. Piles of explosives lay on the ground. Seth was quite adept with a match, having had a short stint as an altar boy the year prior. He managed quickly to get a flame from the flint. David was so impressed that he forgot to tell him to throw the hissing object over the wall. As sparks slowly ate at the fuse, he knocked the M80 out of Seth's hand. It fell to the ground between them. David pushed Seth back just as the explosive erupted with a deafening crack, knocking David against the stone wall with such force that the largest rock tumbled from the top and fell to the other side. When he stood and lifted his shirt, a bruise had already started to form. He begged Seth not to say a word to their mother, and Seth, sensing opportunity, granted his brother's wish but only on the condition that David tell him what he'd been doing out here and whom he'd been talking to. Reluctantly, David agreed. It had been a game of imagination, enchantments, and monsters, set in a magical world. A world in which a boy could believe that he was strong. Powerful. Beloved. A world that was different in every way from the one where people thought of the Hoppers as a group of backwoods weirdos.

Seth insisted on joining the game. To his surprise, David agreed. Happily.

The brothers were separated in age by five years, and though they'd always been civil, they'd never been especially close. Their father's purchase of a horse years earlier had been the catalyst that had first made them *realize* each other. The horse had become the brothers' shared responsibility. A second binding had occurred when their father had walked out. The third was when their mother crumbled, and the fourth, almost an afterthought, was when she sold the mare to pay a pile of bills.

None of these events had been a particularly positive experience. But then, there was the game. A game that belonged only to them, an escape from what had come before. Older brothers were supposed to be strong, knowledgeable, just out of reach. When David had decided to let him in, Seth finally understood that his older brother lived as lonely a life as his own. Oddly, this became the strongest binding of all.

The first order of business was for Seth to invent a character, to choose a new name and a new personality. Wraithen of Haliath was born. For the rest of the summer, the brothers fought the Hunter, rescuing captured children from his clutches. In the game, they invented ways to master their abilities. David explained that being "Robber" Princes came with the responsibility to constantly "level up." The way they did this was to steal magical objects from secret places. David had created a map. Many of these talismans were hidden in an abandoned "castle" across the forest of Howler's Notch.

The first night that David led Seth up to Temple House, Seth had no idea what his brother had planned. When the two approached Mrs. Ashe's backdoor, Seth began to understand. By the time David had worked the lock open, Seth was too nervous to say anything, fearing that the reclusive owner of the house might awaken and find them. Silently, Seth followed David into the dark house. Moving through the shadows, he wondered how David had discovered the nerve to break in. Surely this was not his first time in the house.

David disappeared through a nearby doorway. Inside, Seth discovered what looked like some sort of library. A bright moon threw blue light onto the floor. It reflected up at the odd objects and books packed onto the shelves. Seth barely had time to look around before he saw David snatch something small off a nearby mantelpiece and shove it in his pocket. He nodded for Seth to take something too. Without thought, Seth grabbed the nearest knick-knack, a carved turquoise scarab, and clutched it in his palm all the way home.

By the time September rolled in, they had little time to continue playing. David was finding freshman year at Slade High School to be profoundly difficult. He frequently withdrew into his bedroom and ignored Seth's requests to venture together into the world of Howler's Notch. Seth worried that the progress they'd made over the summer would be lost. He missed playing the game, but more, he missed his brother.

Whenever they did play, David seemed distracted. By January, David flat-out refused to play with Seth at all. Seth didn't believe him when he said it was because of the cold temperature outdoors.

One night, after a month of Seth's pestering, David finally agreed to talk about what was on his mind. He explained that the game was dangerous, much more than Seth could ever understand. Seth pressed him further, wondering if it was something he'd done. "I know you won't believe me," his brother answered, his expression flat and humorless. "You might even laugh, but I don't care. We can't do this anymore." Seth waited as David paused for a long time. "The Hunter is real. And he wants us dead."

David was right. Seth laughed. He laughed until he cried.

SHOCK AND AWE

"THE HUNTER IS REAL?" Gabe asked. "What's that supposed to mean?"

"Just that," said Seth. "He believed that somehow he'd raised something up from the woods behind my house. Behind your house too."

"But that's crazy." *Right?* he wondered.

"I thought so too. My brother was definitely acting crazy. He grew more and more paranoid. He told my mom that he was sure someone was following him home from school. She thought he meant that kids were picking on him. She tried to get help from the school, from the guidance counselors, but David refused to talk to anyone about what was really bothering him. Eventually, he started asking my mom if we could move. Begging her. He said he couldn't live here anymore."

"That's . . . really scary."

"It's why, when he disappeared that summer, the police concluded that he'd run away, that he'd located my dad and went off to be with him. I think David was scared that if me or Mom knew where he was, the Hunter would find him."

Gabe sat on the edge of the mattress, unaware that his jaw was hanging open until his tongue felt gritty against the top of his mouth. "Do you think that's what happened to him?" he managed to say.

"I wanted more than anything to believe that David just left," said Seth. "And I did believe. Mostly. For a while, it seemed like the only explanation. Then you moved in up the hill."

Gabe flinched. "What do I have to do with any of this?"

"Well, when David went away, I'd stopped playing the Hunter's game. But, when you mentioned losing all your video games and comics and everything in the fire, I thought you might be interested to join in. Even after you came up with that ridiculous name for yourself. For your kingdom. Meatpie? Chicken Guts?" Seth smiled sadly. "I didn't even mind. I missed my brother, and I wanted to play again."

That last sentence was like a punch to Gabe's stomach. He couldn't imagine what it was like to lose a sibling. He thought of Miri, safe with his family just up the hill. What would his parents do if she disappeared — not merely died, which would have been a nightmare in itself, but just went poof! Gone! There was something much more horrific in not knowing when or if you'd ever be reunited. At least a death was final. No coming back from that.

"After you and I started playing the game again, strange things started happening," Seth said. "Even before school began again, I knew people blamed me for what happened at Felicia's pool party." Seth trembled. "If I'd denied it, no one would have listened." His voice shook as he went on. "I'm really sorry I showed up at your house that night and said that stuff about the Hunter coming for you. I didn't mean anything by it. I was upset. It was like, in that moment, I wished for bad things to happen. I never thought the wish would come true."

"You believe in wishes?" Gabe asked.

"I don't know what to believe. But I'm starting to wonder if David was right to run away. Maybe there *is* something out there in the woods. Something evil. Something that does want us dead."

Gabe's throat gurgled reflexively. "The Hunter?"

Seth nodded slightly, as if embarrassed to admit it.

"If something *is* hunting us," said Gabe, "how do we stop it?"

"I guess we start by warning your friends."

Gabe felt warm. He knew what Felicia's response would be. For a moment, he wondered which was scarier — the threat of the Hunter or of spending life as Puppet Boy. At this point, it seemed as though there was no escape from either.

LAUGHING IN THE DARK

LATER, GABE LAY IN BED trying desperately to turn off his brain.

Seth had seemed truly frightened about the Hunter's next attack. In all the storytelling, Gabe had forgotten to mention how angry Felicia was, and after Seth's warning to all of them, it felt like an especially selfish mistake.

A floorboard squeaked. Gabe opened his eyes and saw only darkness. But he knew he was not alone. He felt someone watching him. Gabe listened to the quiet, too frightened to move.

Wind whistled at the window. The wooden frame creaked. It sounded like the noise that had roused him. Maybe what he'd heard had been outside.

His imagination was getting the better of him. He let out a loud sigh, determined to put the fear away. He pulled his blanket up to his chin and closed his eyes again, hoping that this time, he'd get to sleep. A moment later, someone ripped the comforter away.

Gabe screamed. He didn't even have time to grab at the blanket before it slipped over the foot of his bed. Scrambling up the mattress, he pressed himself against the headboard.

The shadows were a clotted blur. Silence coated the room. Dressed only in a T-shirt and shorts, Gabe shivered at the sudden cold. Seth's tale flashed through his mind. David's alleged statement blared like a siren. *The Hunter is real. And he wants us dead.*

A guttural rumble came from somewhere near the end of the bed. Pins stabbed at Gabe's cold skin. As the sound continued, growing louder, Gabe realized it was laughter. He'd heard it before, echoing from inside the Milton suit.

The floor squeaked again. The thing at the end of his bed was coming closer. Gabe couldn't catch his breath to call out for his parents. He bit at his lip hard, hoping this was a nightmare from which he could awaken, but his mouth filled with the coppery taste of blood, and he knew this was no dream.

Panicked, he swung out at the shadows, but met only emptiness. He readied himself to leap out of bed and dash for the door. But he imagined black claws darting from hidden places, splitting both the fabric of his shirt and his thin skin underneath. He could only cover his mouth and hold his breath, hoping the monster was as blind as he was.

Then the muddled pattern of his quilt appeared, hovering beside his bed, as if held out, Gabe assumed, by the visitor. He fumbled for the nightstand lamp. Orange light blinded him momentarily. A blurred shape stood only a few feet away. It raised up the blanket. With his pupils dilated, Gabe hadn't made out details, but he'd seen enough to realize that the shape didn't seem distorted or monstrous. The shape had been Gabe's height, with a slight frame. For a moment, he felt relief. "H-hello?" Gabe sputtered.

Then the intruder growled, tossing the blankets at Gabe's head with such force, he almost fell off the opposite side of the bed. He scrambled to snatch the blanket away from his face, but the fabric was heavy. Tangled. He whined, expecting at any second to feel a chomp of razorlike teeth. But then the bedroom door opened and slammed shut with a resounding echo.

Gabe pulled off the quilt. He was alone. Footsteps came down the hall. The doorknob turned, and as the door began to open, he felt darkness seeping in from the edges of his vision.

"Gabriel?" It was his mother's voice. "What's going on in here?" By the time she'd stepped fully into his room, Gabe had fallen against the brass rail above his pillow, knocked his head hard, and, for the first time in his life, passed out.

❖

"It was a nightmare," said Glen, handing Gabe a glass of warm milk. Dolores sat beside him at the small table in the kitchen, rubbing his back. Elyse stood in the doorway, dressed in her silk robe, arms crossed over her chest, her face like stone. He'd woken everyone except Miri. "Sometimes dreams can feel real."

Gabe nodded sheepishly, but only to appear agreeable. It hadn't been a dream. How could he make his parents understand? Someone had been in his room. Someone had laughed at him. Someone who'd been no taller or broader than any of Gabe's classmates. He could tell them that he'd accidentally raised some sort of dark entity from the woods. Then a different idea crept into Gabe's mind: What if the visitor had been an ordinary boy? Seth had admitted earlier that evening that David had taught him how to pick the locks of Temple House. *No. It couldn't be. . . .*

With a burning sensation in his stomach, Gabe sipped at the soothing milk, wondering if he should tell his parents about the Hopper brothers' nighttime escapades, about the objects the two had stolen from his grandmother's library. Surely, his parents would call the police. Would they arrest Seth this time? Lock him away? And what if they didn't? If Seth was in fact still the problem, what might he try next? For half a second, Gabe actually thought, *Wait 'til Seth hears about this!* Immediately afterward, he realized he needed to talk to Mazzy as soon as possible.

Upstairs, he said good night to his parents again, assuring them that he'd be fine now, even though he felt anything but.

Passing his sister's bedroom, he heard a noise just inside. He pressed his ear against the door. The noise came again — a high, surprised squeal, followed by a ripple of Miri's contagious laughter.

Yanking open the door, Gabe found Miri standing by herself, grasping the bars of the crib, her face illuminated softly from below by a *Sesame Street* nightlight. He'd half expected to confront a large shadowy figure standing over her crib, claws raised, mouth open a crack, noxious liquid drooling out onto the mattress. The baby glanced at Gabe, but went right back to staring at the nothingness that hung over her, as if she could see something that Gabe could not. She giggled again and pointed at the space above her as if to say, *Look, Gabriel! A visitor!*

AN EPIDEMIC OF MONSTERS

BY THE TIME GABE ARRIVED at school the next day, strange stories were floating around, like a contagion.

During first period, Gabe overheard a pair of bubbly girls, Justine and Sarah, whispering behind him. They had each awoken the night before to find a shadowy figure by their beds. Sarah swore she'd heard a growl. Her parents told her that she must have been dreaming. Justine's mother had believed the story. When she called the police, the dispatcher told her they'd be delayed. Since midnight, the station had received a rash of reports of mysterious intruders from all over Slade. Dozens of people were all telling the same tale: Someone had been watching them sleep.

Gabe felt as though his brain was shutting down. Maybe he'd never woken up at all? Surely this was a dream, a purgatory version of reality. A few rows away, soft laughter echoed. Gabe didn't know if it was genuine or if he was hearing things.

Between bells, Gabe managed to gather Malcolm, Mazzy, Ingrid, and Felicia by the door of the auditorium. They all looked worried.

"You're not the only one who lives in monster land anymore, Gabe," said Felicia.

"He visited you guys too?"

"All of us," said Ingrid. Malcolm and Mazzy nodded. "And you?"

"I thought that would have been obvious."

"Someone wants to scare us," Malcolm said.

"Or send a message," Gabe suggested.

"Yeah," Felicia went on. "The message is: *I'm totally psycho.*" She raised an eyebrow. "Has anyone seen or heard from the kid?"

Gabe began to feel increasingly uncomfortable with Felicia's tone. He glanced at Mazzy, remembering her warning about getting revenge. "I heard he got suspended."

"For what he did at the bake sale?" Felicia asked. When Gabe nodded, she added, "Where'd you hear that?"

"He told me."

"You talked to him?" Felicia looked disgusted.

"Yesterday afternoon," he whispered. "He met me at the bus stop. He begged me to believe that he's innocent."

"Do you?" Mazzy asked.

An idea had been bubbling all morning, and it suddenly screamed forth like steam from a kettle. The investigators had determined that David Hopper had run away from home. But what if there was something they'd overlooked? Yes, David had disappeared. But what if he wasn't *gone*? Gabe felt a tingling sensation at the tips of his fingers. David had been a loner in school. It wasn't difficult to imagine him camping out in the woods, trying to escape from a life he'd hated. Was David trying to help out his little brother by getting back at the bullies? Or worse, what if the two of them were in it together?

"Gabe?" Mazzy touched his shoulder. "You there?"

Gabe glanced at the group. They were all staring at him. "I-I just thought of something." He sighed, annoyed with himself that he couldn't just spit it out, but he wanted to be sure before he started any more gossip. "We need answers. I have an idea how to get them, but I'm going to need help."

Hours later, right before last period, the group came back together, meeting in the same alcove by the auditorium doors. Each clutched

one of the town maps that Gabe had printed from a library com-
puter following their morning conversation.

Throughout the day, they'd each spoken to as many of their
classmates as possible, inquiring about the nighttime visitations.
Now Gabe collected their papers. They'd scrawled notes across
their maps of the town, just like he'd asked. He promised them
he'd share more once the last bell rang, after he'd organized the
data they'd collected.

Sitting at the back of his next class, he kept the project covered
by his textbook, peeking at it every now and again, jotting down
notes of his own. It took nearly all period, but he managed to com-
pile a master map. With a bright red pen, he marked the location
of every reported break-in he knew about, along with the approxi-
mate time it had occurred.

Gabe connected the dots, tracing the intruder's alleged route.
When he finished, he sat back in his chair, taking in the bizarre
drawing. What he saw on the page made no logical sense. Each of
his theories died in an instant, marred by a long scrawl of red ink.

"IT'S A SPIRAL," said Mazzy, leaning over the table in the library where the group had gathered after school, examining Gabe's master map. The room was quiet. Many of the other students had gathered in the auditorium for the presentation of the English department's Halloween story contest. Ironic, Gabe thought, since the scariest story he'd ever known was happening right here, in real life, to all of them.

"More of a bull's-eye," said Malcolm. "Don't you think?"

"And look at what's right in the center," said Gabe, pointing to the page.

Ingrid looked confused. "The woods behind your house?"

"Behind Seth's house too," Felicia added with a smug smile.

"The line actually seems to end at my grandmother's house," said Gabe, "but since we haven't spoken to Seth yet, I can't be sure whether or not he was visited too. His house might be the final spot on the map."

The group all glanced up at him in confusion. "But how would Seth visit himself?" Ingrid asked, seemingly for all of them.

Gabe shook his head. "That's just what this map proves," he said. And more, he thought to himself. There was no way David and Seth could have accomplished this together or alone. "Look at the time I noted at each location. Sure, some of them are off, but I guess that's to be expected when you interview a large group of people. Not everyone looked at the clock last night, and those who did might not have remembered correctly, but one thing is clear — no one person could have moved between these locations this quickly. This map of Slade encompasses at least three square miles."

Malcolm leaned back in his chair, "So you're saying that Seth had an accomplice?"

"I'm saying that if Seth had anything to do with this at all, he'd have to have had at least ten accomplices."

"I doubt that kid even knows ten people," said Felicia.

"It's pretty clear now that Seth isn't the one doing this," Mazzy said, placing her palms on the table and sitting up straight. "Unless he's built himself a jet pack." Felicia groaned. But Mazzy ignored her, speaking even louder. "That leaves us with . . . what?"

"Where are the *answers*, Gabe?" Ingrid asked. "Ruling someone out doesn't tell us anything. I mean, forget about being scared to walk through the woods. Now, being at *home* doesn't even feel safe."

Gabe placed his finger on the page in the middle of the table, touching the center of the red spiral, the bull's-eye on the map of Slade. "I think what this picture shows us is that these woods are at the center of everything," he said. "I have a feeling that someone is living there. Someone *unlike* us."

Ingrid's eyes grew wide. "Unlike us in what way?"

Gabe chose every word carefully, as someone would search a tree branch for the perfect apple. "Tall. Strong. Fast. Angry." He glanced at Felicia. "And mean."

Felicia rested her head in her palm, not buying it. "If you're so sure about this, why haven't we already called the police?"

"I've told my story to cops," said Gabe, "to the principal, to my parents. And every time, they either don't believe me, or they blame Seth." He blushed as he realized that only hours earlier, he'd blamed Seth as well.

Leaning forward, Felicia went on, "I'm sorry, Gabe, but are you trying to tell me that a large, angry man snuck into school and blew up my cake? Right in front of my face? And no one saw him?"

She laughed, a shrill sound echoing up into the room's vaulted ceiling. "You're kidding, right?"

Gabe blinked. "I didn't say he was a man."

"Oh, so now it's a woman?"

"Not a man. Not a woman." Gabe took a deep breath. "Actually, not a human."

SECRETS OF OLMSTEAD AND ASHE

LATER, GABE HESITATED just outside of his grandmother's library. Mornings, she worked upstairs in her studio, but in the afternoon she liked to sit down here, watching the wind move through the tree branches just down the hill. He knocked softly, not wanting to bother her, hoping she wouldn't be there. She'd been quiet lately, even for her. He'd decided that if she answered from the other side of the door, he'd come back after the sun had gone down.

The fresh laughter of his friends echoed in his head. As soon as Gabe had said the words *not a human*, he knew he'd made a mistake. After their amusement had died down, Ingrid actually said, wiping her eyes, "Good one, Gabe. You really had me going." The only one who sat still, silently, had been Mazzy.

He opened the library door a crack. "Elyse?" When silence answered him, he entered the empty room. She'd told him several times over the past months that he was welcome to borrow any book from her shelves, yet Gabe still trembled as he approached her collection. He wasn't exactly sure what he was looking for. He'd been thinking of that book he'd read near the end of the summer — *The Revenge of the Nightmarys*. Nathaniel Olmstead's descriptions of the pack of ghostly girls — demonlike creatures, veiled in rotting spider-silk damask, who had the power to make your worst fears come to life — had been so vivid, Gabe wondered fantastically if the man had in fact seen them with his own wide eyes.

According to his grandmother, some people claimed that the author had based his stories on real monsters he'd encountered in his town. She'd thought it was merely a ploy to spark publicity, an effective one at that. The point was, for whatever reason, Nathaniel Olmstead had known about weird things, the inexplicable, the unnameable. Elyse had been there during the creation of these stories, putting images on paper that had once existed only in the author's head.

The *Nightmarys* book had frightened him so completely, he might not have finished it if his mother hadn't begged him. Since then, Gabe had been too intimidated to return to these shelves, to choose another, but if Seth was right and they *had* raised something supernatural from the woods, Gabe figured these shelves were a treasure trove on the subject.

Gabe glanced at title after title. *The Rumor of the Haunted Nunnery. Curse of the Gremlin's Tongue. Whispers in the Gingerwich House. Horror of the Changeling. The Secret of the Stone Child. The Wish of the Woman in Black*. All fiction. With cover art by his grandmother.

He removed a book called *The Ghost in the Poet's Mansion*. Flipping through the pages, he wondered if the "ghost" of the title might give him a clue about the recent occurrences in Slade. But as the printed words blurred together, Gabe shook his head, understanding that he could never read through all of these — not this afternoon anyway.

If only his grandmother had an Internet connection, or if he'd thought to search the Web before he'd left the school that day for information on magical objects, monsters, forest spirits, legends of New England, stone walls . . . *anything*. Now, unless his mother agreed to drive him back to the town library, he was stuck for the night with nothing but his churning imagination.

Frustrated, Gabe kicked at the base of the bookcase. Several volumes near his feet shifted, then fell over onto empty shelf space. Looking closer, he noticed that these books were larger in size than the ones on the upper shelves. Heavier too. To his surprise,

Gabe saw Olmstead's name on another spine. He crouched to get a better look. *Olmstead's Incompleat Compendium of the Enigmatic Manuscript.*

Gabe handled it tenderly. One of his grandmother's familiar black-ink-style sketches stretched across the paper jacket — a simple, shadowy image of a leather-bound book, latched shut by a large locking mechanism, in the center of which was a pitch-black keyhole. Inside, photographic reproductions of ancient texts filled the pages. There were chapters about mysterious symbols, heretical and Gnostic scriptures, various spell books and grimoires. He came across an entry about a book with the odd name of *Malleus Maleficarum*, followed by an evil-looking and blood spattered tome called *The Necronomicon*. Though Gabe found the information to be very cool, and very creepy, nothing appeared to be especially useful for solving his immediate mystery. Disappointed, he shoved the book back with the others on the bottom shelf.

He was about to stand, when once again the name Olmstead caught his eye. His heart beat faster as he reached for this final book — the heaviest one yet. *Olmstead and Ashe's Big Book of Myths, Ghosts, and Monsters.* Opening the cover, his jaw went slack. Gabe couldn't believe his luck. It was an encyclopedic text, arranged alphabetically, each entry illustrated beautifully with a full-page drawing by his grandmother.

Gabe brought the book over to the desk and sat in Elyse's wooden swivel chair. The sky had grown darker, spilling a dusky light into the room. He switched on the desk lamp. His grandmother's name on the book cover was illuminated with a glowing swatch of yellow light, indicating — like a psychic signpost — that he was on the right track. Turning to the first page, Gabe took a deep breath. He had a lot of reading to do.

As the night encroached upon the little library, Gabe became lost in a series of new worlds. He was amazed that his grandmother had collaborated on such a book. Inside were folktales and legends from all over the globe. Stories of Anansi in Africa, Baba Yaga in Russia, the *bean sí* in Ireland, the *bunyip* of Aboriginal Australia, the dragons of China, the Scandinavian *fylgja*, the golem of Prague.

It was dark by the time Gabe found exactly what he'd sought — an article so specific, he wondered briefly if he might be seeing things. Staring up from the page was a tall man with a wide torso, standing before a crumbling stone wall in the middle of a dark forest. In fact, his body looked like a few boulders piled one on top of the other — bulky, bulbous muscle and fat. The man wore what looked like tattered and filthy leather armor, rimmed by cuffs of dingy and rotting fur. His chafed head was bald and spotted with what may have been blood. Though his face was mostly in shadow, Gabe's grandmother had filled the eye sockets with cold light. A quiver of arrows was strapped to one enormous shoulder, a long, wide sheath hung from his belt, and in his hand, he clutched a modest wood bow.

Gripped in the man's opposing hand, Elyse had drawn a soiled cloth satchel. Its top was open slightly. Inside, barely visible in the detailed pen work, a small, pale hand poked out, five fingers wiggling helplessly at the air.

A high-pitched, terrorized wail pierced his memory. He recalled the game in August, when he and Seth had discovered that dirty baby doll, hidden beneath a pile of leaves in the woods.

Gabe's eyes burned with unexpected tears. How? he wondered. How had his grandmother known? There was a ringing in his ears, so loud and sudden that the rest of the house seemed to have gone quiet. He looked up toward the window, but saw only his reflection in the glass, behind which was the darkness of night. He pushed back his chair and stood. With a few cautious steps, he approached the window, brought his face close to the pane, and strained to look beyond his reflection. No luck.

He shut off the desk lamp. After several seconds, his eyes adjusted to the darkness. He could again discern the details of the library — the walls, the shelves, the books, even the rocking chair in the far corner. The window was now transparent.

Down the hill, at the line of trees, a large shadow stood among the darker shadows, wavering in the night. It looked like the opposite of candlelight, if there were such a thing. After a frozen moment, Gabe recognized a difference in the figure that he hadn't seen before — were those two licks of blue flame where its eyes should have been?

Panic rose from his chest, into his esophagus and throat, over his tongue and escaped, like a siren, past his lips — a sound he could barely hear, and yet, so loud that his whole family came running.

A FEW MINUTES LATER, Gabe sat shivering in the high-backed chair in the living room. The cup of tea his mother had brought him was steaming on the coffee table. She'd retrieved the book from the desk in the library and held it against her chest. Elyse stood in the doorway, observing the scene, expressionless, like a scientist, detached, researching a colony of aliens from afar.

"I checked everywhere," said Glen, kneeling beside his son, rubbing at his shoulder. "Flashlight. The whole shebang. There was nothing." Gabe could feel the chill emanating from his father's sweatshirt. He'd only just come back in. "I swear, we are *alone* up here on this hill."

Gabe took a deep breath and glanced at his grandmother. She looked quickly away.

"Tell me again what it looked like," said Dolores.

Gabe pointed at the book. "Page eighty-five."

Confused, his mother opened the cover, turning pages until she came to the image he'd meant for her to find. "The Hunter?" she read, then glanced up at Gabe. "I don't understand. *This* was what you saw by the woods?"

His answer spilled forth in a thoughtless rush. "It's the monster from that game me and Seth were playing at the end of the summer. The one I told you about. The cannibal thing."

They all stared at him like he'd just had some sort of fit, but there was more that they needed to hear. The Hunter's eyes stared up from the page, daring him to confess. "Grandmother Elyse's drawing looks exactly how Seth described him. I don't know how, but I saw the . . . the Hunter watching me through the window just now." He glanced once more at his grandmother. She refused to meet his eyes. "I'm pretty sure this wasn't the first time. And I'm pretty sure I'm not the only one."

"Have you considered that Seth may have seen this book before?" Dolores asked. "That maybe he remembered your grandmother's drawing of the . . . the, what's it called?"

"The Hunter," Elyse mumbled.

"That Seth borrowed your grandmother's Hunter and used him in his story?"

"It wasn't a story. It was a game. And it's not like that. Stuff has been happening. Bad stuff. You've all seen it. Dad's puppet was stolen. The M-80s went off at the bake sale. My classmates are saying that a big, sort of shadowy figure has been following them home from school. And then last night —"

"Here we go," Glen muttered.

"Someone snatched the blanket off my bed!"

"And we already told you," said Dolores, frustrated, "it was a *dream*."

Gabe closed his eyes, speaking slowly now, trying to sound sure of himself, like an adult. "If that's true, then a whole bunch of us at school had the same dream."

"Gabriel, my son," Glen said, "when you're older, you'll understand how easy it is for ideas to spread, especially among people your age. A story can start with one person. That person tells another person. Someone else lays claim to it too. And so on. Soon, everyone wants to be in on the joke." He paused. "You know how kids are."

"It wasn't a joke," said Gabe. "And we're not *kids*. We're in eighth grade. We're . . ." He didn't know how to finish, but he knew that what his father had said just wasn't true, not in this instance anyway. "We're . . . in between."

"It's just a picture, honey." Dolores turned toward her mother-in-law. "Isn't that right, Elyse? You and Mr. Olmstead made it up. Just like the rest of the ghosts and monsters in this book." She stared at her mother-in-law with a thin-lipped smile as if to say, *Please don't make me regret offering those books to him in the first place.*

Elyse scratched at her neck with her short red fingernails. "Yes," she said, nodding slowly, "most of the entries in that particular book are stories and nothing more. Some are based on legends and myths. But the rest, we just made up." She looked right at Gabe when she said that last part. Gabe thought he read something in her expression. *There's more to it. Much more.*

"There you have it," said Glen, rising to his feet. "The Hunter is just a story."

"But that's not what she said."

"Well, that was the gist of it. Right, Mom?"

Elyse sighed. "The gist of it. Yes."

Gabe couldn't look at her anymore. What was she hiding? He reached for the tea mug and sipped too quickly, spitting out the liquid and wincing as the hot tea nearly scalded his tongue.

Dolores closed the book and took his mug, leaving them both on the coffee table. "Honestly, Gabe, I'm worried about you. I think that Seth boy is a bad influence."

Gabe grew warm, and he knew it wasn't from the tea. "I'm not even friends with him anymore."

"You've gone down to his house this week," she said. "If you're not friends, what have you been doing there?"

"We've been trying to figure out what the heck is happening in this town!"

"I think it might be best if you stay away from the Hopper house for a while. Is there something we can do to make that easier for you?"

Infuriated, Gabe glanced at each of them, realizing that he was now alone in this — impossibly stuck with a monster that had the ability, at any moment, to show up in his bedroom in the middle of the night.

"No, but thank you," he said in a pointedly polite tone. "I'll be fine alone."

A BEDTIME STORY

WHEN GABE GOT INTO BED LATER, he closed the window curtains and left the lamp glowing beside him. Every time he felt he might finally doze off, a noise from outside his bedroom door would knock him right back into consciousness. His parents were in the bathroom brushing their teeth, whispering to each other. Downstairs, he assumed, his grandmother was going through her own nighttime preparations. By the time everyone had settled down and the only sound within the house was the boiler's distant hum, Gabe felt so wide awake, he wasn't sure how he'd function at school the next day.

A floorboard squeaked. Gabe sat up and stared at his bedroom door, begging for the sound to have been in his mind. It came again, softly. Someone was walking through the house. *Squeak.* Footsteps. Coming up the stairs. He ducked his head under his blanket, remembering that the old-fashioned doors in Temple House had locks you could only turn with a key, all of which had been misplaced long ago. There was no way to keep an intruder out of his room.

The illustration of the Hunter flashed through his brain like a poorly animated movie. Frame by frame, the monster held out his satchel for Gabe to see. The child inside had stopped moving; its small arm hung limp. A red stain pooled at the bottom of the sack, dripping — *plop, plop, plop* — to the forest floor. Gabe knew it was only a drawing, an interpretation of a fantasy, like Seth's game, but he couldn't help fearing that he'd end up the same way, that tomorrow, his parents would find his bleached bones laid carefully on the front steps of Temple House — a taunting gift from the monster who now lurked just outside his bedroom door.

By the time Gabe heard the knob twisting, he realized too late that he might have saved himself by moving his grandmother's old wooden bureau in front of the door. With a slight squeal, the hinges gave way. Blind beneath the blanket, Gabe tried to still his frenzied breath, but now he was shaking. Uncontrollably.

A presence stepped briskly into his room, stopping by his bedside table. The muted light that seeped through the blanket shifted as the shape leaned toward him. And when he felt fingers clutch his shoulder, he covered his mouth to contain his fear.

"Gabriel?" came his grandmother's voice. "What the heck are you doing under there?"

A few moments later, Elyse sat at the end of Gabe's bed, wearing her usual black robe, as well as an expression of shame. She closed the bedroom door and apologized for scaring him. Gabe leaned back against the bed frame as she spoke. "Your parents have had enough on their plate, with the baby and their work, so I didn't want to say anything in front of them earlier."

He clasped his hands in his lap so hard that it felt like he was squeezing the blood out of them.

"When Nathaniel Olmstead asked me to collaborate on a big, illustrated book about all spooky things, I was beyond excited. I loved working with him, but I didn't say yes at first. I agreed on one condition: that he let me add a story of my own, a story that deserved a life it had long been denied."

"What story?" Gabe asked.

"The tale of the Hunter," she whispered, "was something I heard when I was your age, when I lived with my parents here in Temple House, in this very bedroom."

"This was *your* room?"

She nodded. "Why else do you think I offered it to you last

July? With this view, it's the most spectacular room in the house."
Gabe chuckled despite himself. "The story stuck with me through
the years. Memorable mostly because of the person who told it to
me — a boy in my class at school. A neighbor. A friend. His name
was Mason Arngrim, and he stayed just down the hill, through
the woods, on the property where your friend Seth lives now."

Gabe was speechless. It felt as though his grandmother had
just cracked open the planet and revealed a gleaming new Earth
hidden inside.

"I think the story of the Hunter has stayed with me all these
years because it's tied, fundamentally, to Mason's own story. I can't
help but recall his face whenever I've looked out over the woods
between our houses for the past fifty years. I've never shared this
with anyone, not even your grandfather, God rest his soul, but
Mason Arngrim was the reason I started drawing my little monsters, the ones that eventually led to my first illustration work just
out of high school. That boy changed my life.

"After what happened to Mason, I felt that his creation, his
Hunter, deserved to live on, even if only in the pages of a book."

Gabe shivered. He didn't like the way she'd put that. *Live on?*
"What happened to him?" he asked. "To Mason?"

Elyse smiled. "That's the thing," she said. "I'm not quite sure.
And the only person who may have known died long ago."

MEETING MASON

ELYSE TEMPLE, KNOWN TO HER CLASSMATES as Leesy, was born in the brick mansion that sat upon the highest hill in a small town south of Boston, a few miles inland from the rocky coast and cold waters of Massachusetts Bay. The mansion was famous in Slade, for at the time, it was visible from nearly all corners of the town. Built in the late nineteenth century by the famed industrial baron Mordecai Temple, its deed had passed to his children, and his children's children, and thus the building had become known throughout several local counties as Temple House. But if you lived nearby, you could probably have skipped the surname and referred to the gothic-looking manse simply as the House and no one would have questioned your meaning.

Growing up on a famous estate, as the lone great-granddaughter of the man who'd once been the wealthiest in the five closest towns, Leesy was unaware of how most people saw her. No one dared call her spoiled to her face, and even if they had, they'd have been wrong, for "spoiled" implies that the gifts one bestows upon a child changes them, makes them rotten, and Leesy was far from that. In fact, she was a shy, observant girl whose favorite activity was watching the clouds from her bedroom window, imagining faces winking at her and inventing brief stories about who and what these wispy, white creatures might be.

But her demeanor did not stop her classmates from whispering behind her back, that she was a faker, a liar, a cheat, that deep down, at her core, she must be terrible. In fact, the nicer she tried to be, the more distant they all became. By the time Leesy reached high school, despite all the privileges of the family that she'd been born into, she had no true friends.

Leesy had become so solitary that one day at school, when she found a tall gangly-looking boy staring at her from across the cafeteria, she wasn't aware that he was her next-door neighbor, or that she even *had* neighbors. If she hadn't spent so much time looking up at the sky from her bedroom, she might have perceived the cottage swaddled in greenery across the slope of her backyard, in the distant cradle of the hill.

On the day Leesy had caught him staring at her in the cafeteria, the boy had just eaten for the first time in two days and only because the woman in the serving line took pity on him when he'd turned out his empty pockets and had scooped a small helping of beef Stroganoff onto his plate. In fact, he explained to her later, he hadn't so much been looking at Leesy as he'd been looking *through* her, toward a hungry chasm inside his mind, filling it with bits and pieces of memory from his previous life, the one that had existed before his parents' accident, before he'd come to Slade.

"Can I help you?"

Sitting in the small booth in the corner of the busy cafeteria, the boy blinked, suddenly aware that a thin girl with dark hair and pale skin had materialized before him, as if by magic. "I-I'm sorry?" he asked. "Help me with what?"

Leesy's face filled with color. "Oh," she said, "I thought you needed something. You've been staring at me for the past few minutes."

She held back that he'd actually begun to frighten her, and that she'd decided the only way she'd be able to go on with the rest of her day was to confront him face-to-face. But now she saw that she'd been wrong; this boy hadn't actually noticed her at all.

"I didn't realize," the boy answered, standing up to greet her.

"I just . . ." He glanced down at the empty lunch tray, licked practically clean, that sat on the table between them.

Sensing his discomfort, Leesy held out her hand. "I'm Elyse Temple. But you can call me Leesy."

"I know who you are," he said. Leesy's eyes grew wide. He blushed but took her hand in his own and squeezed. "I'm Mason. Mason Arngrim."

A PORTRAIT OF
THE WITCH QUEEN

THEIR FRIENDSHIP WAS NOT IMMEDIATE — that kind of thing did not come naturally to either of them. But the next day at lunch, Leesy felt compelled to offer him the seat beside her.

At first, they barely spoke, spending the period comforted by each other's quiet presence. As days passed, they chatted. Eventually, Mason told her how he'd come to be at the Hoppers' cottage.

When Mason's parents were killed in a freak train derailment in Chicago, his aunt and uncle — Verna and Freddy Hopper, whose two sons had both been sent to the conflict in Vietnam — took him in. It was a deed, Verna insisted to anyone who asked, that "any good, God-fearing woman would have done." Of course, at church services she neglected to share with her fellow congregants that by "taking him in," she meant she allowed him to sleep in the hayloft in her barn and would only provide him with food after he'd finished his chores.

Those chores were extensive, ranging from milking the cows to chopping firewood to pulling up large stones from the yard. Coming to Slade from a city, Mason was unfamiliar with most of these tasks. Each job took him time to learn and so, when a particularly difficult chore brought him into the kitchen past sundown, Verna often refused him the meal she'd promised, comparing him to her own sons, telling Mason that the quicker they'd finished one job, the quicker they'd been able to start another, so next time, he should take a hint from his cousins and plan better.

In the evenings, after Uncle Freddy arrived home from the mill, he'd disappear into his basement workshop with a drink in hand, not noticing or caring how strict his wife was being with his dead sister's boy. Once, Mason asked his uncle why he spent so much time down there, and Freddy gave him such a shattered look, Mason later returned to the hayloft pondering the darkness that so clearly lived inside his aunt. After that, Mason decided not to mention to Verna that he had homework, or school even, especially if these "activities," as she called them, interfered with him being fed.

Following this revelation, though he never asked and often tried to refuse, Leesy always offered half her sandwich.

After school, they sometimes walked home together, up the winding road toward the steep density of trees that separated their two houses. Once, on their journey, Leesy removed her notepad from her satchel and showed him some of her cloud-face sketches. Mason was impressed with her skill at capturing tiny, telling details that revealed peculiar personalities. "But I didn't invent them," she'd explained. "The clouds did!"

Afterward, he decided to share his stories with her. Back in Chicago, his mother had taken him to the local library every other week, where he'd borrow stacks of science-fiction and fantasy novels, gobbling up the stories as quickly as he could. But in Slade, Mason had no time to walk to the public library.

With a deficit of available fantasy, Mason had begun to imagine his own stories, to create his own worlds and populate them with characters of his own design. In his head there lived monsters and heroes; thieves and scoundrels; and kings, queens, and princes. Lying upon his lumpy mattress every night, shivering inside the sleeping bag he'd once used only for camping vacations with his parents on Lake Michigan, he thought of these new worlds as if they were parts of a game, a challenge, and he wondered, if he were somehow able to exist within them, what role might he play?

Leesy listened, thunderstruck that another person saw their world swarming with as much mystery as she did. She begged him to write down the stories for her, but Mason explained that he had never thought himself capable — certainly not in the same manner as a Lovecraft or Lewis, never mind the power of Edgar Allan Poe or Mary Shelley or the great Robert Browning in Mason's new favorite poem, the nightmarish "Childe Roland to the Dark Tower Came," which his English teacher had discussed with his class earlier that month. Leesy laughed and told him that everyone had to start somewhere. He promised her he'd write the stories, but only if she agreed to illustrate them. Leesy was delighted to be asked.

Over the course of several weeks, the two accumulated pages of journal entries and doodles: Mason's tales of monsters and mayhem accompanied by Leesy's increasingly disturbing and gory depictions of the poor victims. At first, Leesy shocked herself by being so macabre, but soon, she considered that to make pictures in which Mason's monsters received a comeuppance gave her relief that she hadn't known she'd needed. For surely, monsters worse than these existed — all one had to do was open a newspaper or turn on a radio for proof.

By the time winter slammed its icy hand down on the coast of Massachusetts, Leesy's drawing skills had improved so greatly, she believed her collaboration with Mason had the potential to turn into something real, complete, true. Whenever she finished another illustration, she'd sign it and hand it over to him for safekeeping out of fear that if her parents ever found her *grotesques*, they'd disapprove.

As the cold weather continued its reign into the next year, she believed that her project with Mason just might be the only thing keeping him going. He had asked Leesy to keep it a secret that his room was in the barn's drafty loft, and that despite his diligence, his aunt continued to withhold the occasional meal.

Leesy couldn't understand why he didn't wish to alert someone to his situation, even after he explained that the alternative would be for him to leave Slade. She could never have borne such cruelty, especially from someone who was supposed to care unconditionally.

At night, safe in her own bed, Leesy imagined him shivering inside his sleeping bag, on his thin mattress, tucked into the upper hollows of the barn's roof. At school, she began to sneak some of Temple House's blankets to him. Some days, she would even wear one of her father's extra-bulky sweaters and hand it over during lunch.

No one in her family ever questioned the slow dwindling of items from the house's deep closets. Unfortunately for Mason, someone in his family did end up wondering where he'd acquired such new and fancy décor. From her kitchen window, Aunt Verna had seen Mason lugging quite a few of Leesy's gifts into the barn.

One day, after he'd left for school, his aunt explored the loft. When Mason came home, he found her waiting up there for him, her face twisted in anger. It wasn't the blankets from Temple House or the clothes that had belonged to Leesy's father that had brought about her fury. Instead, she'd laid out on his bed the pages of handwritten stories and sheaves of illustrations, using her finger to draw an invisible line of accusation between Mason and his beloved project. She demanded to know what sort of evil he'd been playing with. "What is Howler's Notch?" she'd asked quietly.

He later told Leesy that her question hadn't been about his stories. How could she be concerned about evil when she was the one who forced him to live like this? No, her dilemma was about his relationship with the "Princess on the Hill." Leesy's signature was all over the drawings. One sketch in particular shocked Mason's aunt so thoroughly that, for a moment, she'd lost the

ability to speak and instead croaked out her disgust. It was an illustration of a haggard old woman whose face bore a striking
resemblance to Verna's own. Leesy had labeled it "The Witch
Queen."

Mason knew that an explanation would never suffice, so he
refused to answer. Red-faced, Aunt Verna had instructed him to
gather up the pages from the bed and bring them into the cottage.
Inside, a warm fire was already burning in the living room fireplace. She opened the small door in the iron furnace and heat
rustled Mason's hair. He understood what his aunt was asking of
him, and judging from her expression, he thought it best to obey.

As he fed each leaf of paper into the furnace, Mason had tried
uselessly to control his tears. He'd saved Leesy's drawings for last,
as if some interruption might prevent him from finishing the worst
of his aunt's *chores*.

The next day, when Leesy found him sitting at their usual
lunch table, Mason's anger had already dried up any other emotion. In fact, his calm demeanor was more shocking to her than
hearing what Mrs. Hopper had made him do. He was cold,
detached, as if he'd encountered one of the beasts from his tales,
and in order to survive, had fed it a piece of his soul.

"We'll start over," she told him. "We'll be better than before."

"Sometimes, I wish that my monsters were real," he answered.

Not knowing what to do, she nodded with tentative sympathy.
If she were to reveal Mason's story to her parents, would she need
to confess the dark subjects of her artwork? If she somehow were
able to get her point across, what power would they have to change
his situation? Would they even care? What else might Mason's
aunt force him to set aflame? The blankets? The sweaters?
Himself? With the frigid temperatures of the approaching
February, she worried for his safety. Someone needed to talk some
sense into his guardians.

That was how Leesy ended up at the Hoppers' cottage later that evening, rapping on their front door, waiting patiently for Verna to open up and let her in. She stood on the porch, bundled tightly, a scarf wrapped around her neck and most of her face, a thick wool hat pulled over her ears. A harsh wind howled through the branches, sounding like a high-pitched cry. But as the sound grew louder, more frenzied, Leesy realized it was a *human* wail. Lifting her hat away from reddened ears, she understood quickly that it was coming from the barn.

THE BIRTH OF A MONSTER

LEESY FOUGHT AGAINST THE COLD and her fear, descended the stairs of the cottage, and traversed the path toward the dark building beyond the driveway. Every step brought her closer to what sounded like a disturbed and violent confrontation. Standing outside the barn's side door, Leesy heard the argument clearly.

"What did you do?" This came from a woman. Mason's aunt Verna? She sounded frantic, frightened, angry. "*What did you do?*"

"I didn't do anything," said a low voice. Mason. He sounded different, as if his throat had been ravaged somehow, choked raw. Had Verna put her hands on him? Hurt him? What was his aunt blaming him for? Surely something bad.

"It was the Hunter," he added.

Leesy flinched. Had she heard correctly? They both knew that the Hunter was only a character in a story.

A moment later, there came a great smashing, clattering crunch, as if metal had met wood or wood had met metal. She reached for the latch.

"Stay away from me!" Mason cried out. "Leave me alone!"

Leesy stepped back, hugging her rib cage, as if she too needed protection. One of her mother's rules was *People will not mind if you mind your own business.* But Leesy wondered whose business it would be if someone was seriously hurt. Mason and his aunt seemed to be battling, like mortal enemies in Howler's Notch.

She called out, "Mason!" as if announcing her presence here might be enough to stop them from killing each other. Another raucous scream erupted from just inside the door. What if, when she opened it, Verna attacked her too?

Leesy glanced back toward the cottage and saw Mason's uncle standing on the porch, watching and listening, just as she was doing from outside the barn. The man noticed her noticing him. He stiffened then turned, slipping quickly back inside. Leesy wanted to run over to the house, to pound on the door, to demand his help.

The barn door burst open with a crack that sounded like a shotgun. Lantern light spilled out onto the grass. A tall, thin figure dashed from the doorway and raced toward the woods. "Mason!" Leesy screamed again. The figure paused to look over his shoulder. She was certain he saw her, but he continued to run, disappearing into the mass of trees, swallowed by the shadows of the in-between. She moved to follow him, but stopped herself. Mason was faster than she and clearly did not wish to be tracked.

Seconds passed. The night grew quiet, almost silent, but for the ambient sounds of nature settling into slumber. Specks of snow floated in the cold air. Leesy stared at the forest, seeing in her mind the fantasy world that Mason had created; within, her friend was a soldier regrouping from an assault by the witch queen herself.

She remembered his aunt's desperate question: *What did you do?* It struck her, *had* Mason done something? What could be so horrible that it would cause his aunt to erupt like Vesuvius? *It was the Hunter.* Earlier, Mason had told her he wished that the monsters of his imagination were real.

A soft weeping hovered in the air between the tenuously falling snowflakes. Leesy cautiously approached the rectangle of light flickering at the wall of the barn. Mason's aunt was at the far wall. She didn't notice Leesy step through the doorway. A kerosene lamp hung from a hook on one of the posts that held up the hayloft.

Leesy glanced around the room. Shattered glass lay on the ground. One of the hayloft ladders was smashed to pieces. Animal feed was scattered haphazardly across the floor.

One of Leesy's mud-crusted shoes met a weak plank; a squeal rang out. When Verna turned, Leesy screamed.

The woman's floral dress was covered in blood. Red specks had splattered onto her face, but tears had cleared away two clean trails to her chin. She stepped toward Leesy, clutching a dripping red mess. Leesy thought of the Hunter's bag and what Mason told her the beast carried in it. Bits of ash swirled around them. Holding up her palm, she caught a piece. It was actually a black feather.

Quite a few were pasted to Verna, her clothes, her blood-slick arms. "He killed it," said Mason's aunt, her voice wobbling like the cry of an injured animal. Leesy's own throat began to swell, making it hard for her to find breath. The room spun. The kerosene lamp's flickering light was dizzying, and she fell back against the wall.

A pool of blood covered the floor in the far corner where Verna stood, holding the small bloody thing, as if in offering to her. A dark doorway stood open behind Verna. From inside came a rustling followed by the sound of flapping wings. The chicken coop. An axe lay several feet in front of the door. Not far from the blade, illuminated by the uneven light, lay a small, glistening lump of feathers. A head.

"Abraham," said Verna, her bottom lip trembling. "My rooster." Her eyes darkened as she seemed finally to understand who was standing with her in the barn — the reviled Princess on the Hill. "That boy is evil," she spat out. "The basest kind of evil. The vengeful sort. There is no reasoning with a creature like that. I should have known better than to let it in."

It. She'd called Mason *it.*

Leesy felt a white heat rise up the back of her throat. How dare this woman accuse him? It took every ounce of strength to keep her mouth shut even as she began to wonder if Mason was capable of such an atrocity.

"If you see him," said Aunt Verna, reverently placing what was left of the rooster onto the floor a few feet from its severed head, "you tell him he is no longer welcome in my home." Verna sighed. Her eyes seemed to glaze over, as if she'd gone away to some secret place. "Now, if you'll excuse me," she said, "I have a real mess to clean up."

The storm continued to gather strength, a mix of snow and sleet. By the time she'd climbed the slick road back to Temple House, Leesy was soaked. Feeling numb, she raced to her bedroom.

Kicking off her shoes, stripping away her overcoat, Leesy slipped beneath the blankets on her bed. Once she'd caught her breath, she turned her head to the window. A thin layer of ice had begun to stick to the glass, obscuring her view of the churning clouds. The wind picked up, seemed to cry out at her in a language she could not comprehend.

Was Mason still out there? she wondered. Maybe this wailing at the window was not the wind. Maybe it was him, crying for help, pleading for shelter from the storm. Every time Leesy blinked, she saw blood, glistening darkly by the light of that lantern. Deep down, she knew that Mason had done it, and though she understood why, she couldn't bring herself to condone it. The idea that her best friend had been filled with such hatred frightened her beyond all expectation.

Leesy shoved her face into her pillow and cried until the cotton case was soaked nearly through. She was sure if she thought on it all night long, in the morning, she'd still have no clue what to do or say when they met.

But what Leesy didn't know — couldn't have fathomed — was that she'd never have a chance to find out. After that night, Leesy never saw Mason again.

In a Different Light

GABE WAITED FOR HIS GRANDMOTHER to continue. She licked at her lips and brushed at her robe but said nothing more. Not immediately. Clutching the blanket closer to his chin, Gabe finally blurted out, "But what *happened* to him?"

Elyse stared at the floor. "I told you, no one knows. Not now that Verna Hopper is dead. A car accident, many years later."

"You think Verna did something to him?"

The tilt of her head told him she wasn't sure. "The next morning, after my guilt caught up with me, I told my parents what I'd seen in the barn. Of course, they called the sheriff's office. When the officer arrived at the Hoppers', Verna showed him what had become of her rooster and shared who she thought was the culprit. She claimed that hours earlier, Mason had snuck back to the barn, gathered what was left of his stuff, and taken off. She said she didn't know or care where he'd gone.

"Later in the week, Verna called my parents and told them what she'd found in her hayloft — my drawings of Mason's monsters. Turned out, she'd kept one to show them."

"The Witch Queen?" Gabe asked, appalled.

Elyse nodded. "It was the first time I saw how spiteful a person could be. Needless to say, they weren't happy.

"My parents sent me away to the Nettleburn Academy for Girls, a boarding school in New York State. I left Slade in a smoke cloud of shame.

"More than anything, I wished to see Mason again. To ask

him what *really* happened that night or, at the very least, to say good-bye. I did try to find him. Unsuccessfully of course.

"I returned to Temple House on holidays. But it no longer felt like my home, just another stopping place where I was lucky enough to have a bed and a roof over my head. I spent many of those holiday breaks doodling in my notebooks, trying to re-create the sketches that Verna had forced him to feed to her furnace.

"The Hoppers' two sons returned and took over the house. The oldest boy married soon after that and his wife gave birth to a boy, who grew up, I believe, to become your friend Seth's father.

"A lifetime later, after my father's funeral, I never would have imagined that, when I stepped through Temple House's front doorway, I would be overcome with a sensation that I mustn't leave, that it was imperative I make this house my home once more. It was not a bad feeling, merely a voice insisting it was time for a change.

"I packed up my apartment in New York City — every prize I had acquired over the years — and came home." She smiled, looking inward, seeing the picture of her story. "Only recently have I understood what truly called me back here." Elyse paused. "Do you know what it was?"

"I-I have no idea." Gabe grew tense.

"It was *you*," she said.

"Me?"

"You and your sister and your parents. If I hadn't returned to Temple House, I most certainly would have sold it to one local nincompoop or another. Do you realize what would have happened then?"

He shook his head, confused.

"After the fire, you would have had no place to go. No place to start over. The apartment where your father grew up wasn't nearly large enough for all of us. Oh, I'm sure he'd have found *something* for you. But here, you have space, an okay school, friends. You have every advantage I had when I was your age." For the first time since she'd come into his bedroom, his grandmother took Gabe's hand and held it firmly. "But as you know, I didn't visit your room tonight to give you a pep talk." He tried to control the sudden trembling that was creeping down his arm. "I came because you found that drawing in the book I did with Nathaniel all those years ago. The one of the Hunter."

Gabe wasn't sure if he was ready to hear the rest. "Wh-what about it?" he forced himself to ask.

Elyse squinted at him, as if into a clouded mirror. "You say you've been playing this *game* with that boy Seth. Somehow, your game is all mixed up with my memories of Mason's stories — Howler's Notch and whatnot."

Gabe nodded cautiously.

"Now, your mother was correct in thinking that Seth or his brother could have read the old book of ghost tales and mythologies. The local library has a copy of it, I'm sure. It is entirely within the realm of possibility that those boys based their game on my drawing and my memories." Elyse squeezed his fingers. "But I have a feeling that's not quite it."

Gabe couldn't control himself any longer. "You've seen it, haven't you?" he blurted out. Her lips opened with a crisp smacking sound. "The shadow by the woods," he continued. "The thing that hides just inside the line of trees." To his surprise, she remained silent. Not a denial. "That's what you meant when I found you in the library that night — you said you like to watch the night because sometimes the night watches you back. But it's not the *night* that watches. It never was the night, was it?"

As she sighed, her thin rib cage expanded visibly beneath her silk robe. "No. It wasn't."

THE BLACK BOOKS

GABE LEANED FORWARD. "You never believed Verna that Mason just up and left Slade."

"No. I didn't," Elyse answered.

"So, then, what happened to him?"

Her eyes flicked back and forth, as if she were searching for an answer written on the ceiling.

"Did he *stay* in those woods?" Gabe went on. "Did he grow up there, hiding out?" These questions were bizarre, he knew. But not impossible. "What if *Mason* is the one who's been watching from the shadows." What if there was no monster, no magic, no conjuration from the burned journal of an adolescent boy, but merely Leesy Temple's old friend. In the flesh. Out there in the woods. A man who'd lived in the forest for years and years, teaching himself how to survive, learning the land better than anyone in Slade.

In Elyse's eyes, Gabe saw the girl she'd once been, that quiet girl in the cafeteria who'd taught herself to stare at clouds and see things in them that others could not. He was suddenly certain she believed, somehow, that he may be right. So when she shook her head no, it felt to Gabe like a sharp poke in the chest.

Elyse reached into the deep pocket of her robe and removed several small black notebooks. With a slight tremor, she laid them on the bed, opening their covers so Gabe could see inside. Dark pencil drawings filled every page. She'd written dates for each of them, going back several years. He looked closer and recognized the images she captured. Every page, every drawing, the shadow within shadows, the shape that had watched him from the darkness of the woods. The similarities between these sketches and the drawing she'd done for the Olmstead book were unmistakable. This was Mason Arngrim's Hunter.

"I started these books almost as soon as I came back to Slade," she said. "At first, I didn't know why, or where the ideas were coming from. But then I realized. Every time I looked out over the forest toward that old barn at the bottom of the hill, I remembered him."

What his grandmother had collected on these pages was not simply her newest project, but a strange compulsion, a record of a lingering hurt. She'd told him the story of her past in order to make him see how it was affecting his present. Mason. His tales. Her drawings. Dots that, when connected, made a bigger picture. And now the picture was becoming clear.

"If you never believed that Mason left Slade," Gabe whispered, "then what happened to him?"

"In my heart of hearts, Gabriel, I never thought Mason survived that storm."

"And these," he said, his hand hovering over the notebooks, "what do *they* say to your heart?"

Elyse stood. "I suppose they say that I'm right. That *we're* right. We've both seen something out there. Who knows what it is or how long it's been around?" She shook her head, as if astonished at herself for thinking it. "I wonder if Mason had seen the 'something' himself. And if so, had this *thing* inspired Mason to write in the same way it inspired me to fill these pages?" She nodded at the books.

"I've wondered for ages what happened to Mason that night. I'd heard him tell Verna that the Hunter had killed her bird. Of course she'd scoffed. But what if he'd told the truth? And worse . . . what if Mason encountered his monster when he ran off into the woods?"

Gabe suddenly felt very small. "Y-you believe the Hunter is real too?"

"Funny. When I was a younger woman, I might have seen a priest or a doctor for even considering something like that. But after I started working with Nathaniel Olmstead, I saw things differently. When I was hired to illustrate his first book cover, people whispered to me that he was crazy, that he believed the monsters in his books were real. I figured *he'd* constructed the rumors to market himself, but the closer we became, I realized that he really did believe."

"Mr. Olmstead told you that monsters lived in his town?" Gabe asked.

"Oh yes," said Elyse. "And he was scared of them too. He never actively tried to convince *me*, but once, I discovered a note shoved between a few loose manuscript pages he'd sent me. It was a list of seemingly unrelated items, and at first, I thought he'd accidentally tucked in his grocery list. I reread the note several times before I understood its meaning. The items were all from his books. They were what his characters had used to defeat his monsters. Chicken bones, wind chimes, marbles. Little talismans like that."

Gabe thought of the library downstairs, packed with strange objects. He wondered if she'd begun the collection before or after reading the note.

"What gave me chills, though, was the postscript I discovered scrawled on the back of the page. It read something like, *Keep these at home. For emergencies only.* When I asked him about it, he only smiled mysteriously and questioned me about whether I'd collected the items."

"And did you?" Gabe asked. "Collect them?"

"I did," Elyse answered.

"Did you ever need them? For an emergency?"

Elyse smiled. "Thankfully, no," she said, "not yet." Glancing at the small clock sitting on the nightstand, she looked surprised. "Oh my. I think it's about time we get some shut-eye. You've got school tomorrow."

Gabe flinched. "After everything you just told me, I don't know if I'll be able to sleep."

"If that's true, please don't tell your parents on me." She gathered up her notebooks and shoved them into her pocket.

Before she opened his bedroom door, Gabe sat up and swung his legs over the edge of the bed. He almost asked her to stay with him. "What do I do now?" he asked.

She turned the knob and pushed carefully, familiar with the room's squeaks and squeals. "For starters, you can stay out of those woods."

"And for finishers?"

Elyse blinked, her eyes filled with concern. "I'll have to give that some thought," she said. "You do the same. I'm sure we can figure this out."

Gabe wished he could agree.

PART THREE

❖

BONES

SECRET MEETING

GABE ARRIVED AT SCHOOL in a daze, his grandmother's story stuck in his mind. He'd never imagined that her past had contained such horror. At his locker, he stretched and groaned. His backpack was heavier than usual. Bending down, he unzipped the top pocket and removed the Olmstead and Ashe book. He shoved it quickly into his locker. Next he found Mazzy, who was at the water fountain near the gymnasium. He asked if she could meet with him after school. When she asked him if there was something wrong, he shook his head and promised to tell her everything later. "This'll be between us," he said, and after a pause added, "plus one other person."

Gabe tried to focus on his classes, but throughout the day, the shadowy sketches from his grandmother's black notebooks appeared in Gabe's mind. These were followed immediately by visions of the figure by the woods — the dark man with eyes of icy flame.

He skipped lunch in the cafeteria with Felicia, Malcolm, and Ingrid, opting instead to hide out in the library. Since they'd laughed at his suggestion that they were all being haunted or hunted by something not human, he knew they'd never understand the story of Mason and Leesy, or where the Hunter's game had truly begun.

Minutes after the last bell, he met Mazzy outside the wood shop classroom door. From there, they slipped out the side door and bolted for the driveway. Mazzy assured Gabe that she'd seen Felicia and the others heading to the auditorium for the PTA's showing of *Frankenweenie*, but as he ran, his bag heavy again with

Elyse's book, Gabe glanced over his shoulder to make sure no one followed.

"I heard people say they saw it again last night," Mazzy said, when they crossed the street from the school. "The figure. I didn't. Did you?"

"Sort of," he said. The shadow hadn't come into his room, but he'd certainly seen something out by the woods again. "I'll explain when we get to your place."

At the Lermans' house, they found Seth sitting on the top step. He stood as they approached. After an awkward hello, Mazzy opened the door. Her mom was busy in her office at the back of the house. The trio crept upstairs. "She doesn't like me having friends over during the week," Mazzy whispered. "Homework policy." Once inside her bedroom, the boys plopped down on the floor, while Mazzy sat cross-legged on her mattress. Reaching over to her radio-alarm clock, she turned on some music. "Keep quiet, okay? Don't want to get you guys kicked out before I even know why you came."

Everything in Mazzy's room was yellow and bright, and in the late afternoon light, it all seemed to glow with a warmth that didn't exist at Temple House. Gabe smiled at the large rainbow-sparkle hula hoop hanging on the wall over her bed, wondering if that was the one she'd used to win that championship she was so proud of.

"Is anyone gonna tell me why we're here?" Seth asked.

Gabe pulled his bag close and unzipped the largest pocket. He removed the book he'd brought from home and laid it on the floor between them.

Mazzy leaned forward to see over the edge of the bed. "*Olmstead and Ashe's Big Book of* . . . what does that say?"

Seth answered, "*Myths, Ghosts, and Monsters.*"

"I found this last night in my grandmother's library. It's filled with lots of useful information." Gabe flipped open the cover and turned to page eighty-five. "And pictures."

NO SUCH THING

WHEN MAZZY AND SETH SAW Gabe's grandmother's illustration, they both gasped. After a moment, Seth read aloud the description of the Hunter. With every sentence, he became paler and paler, until by the end, he lay on the floor and stared at the ceiling.

"How is this possible?" Mazzy asked. "I thought you guys made that character up."

Seth shook his head slightly. "I thought my *brother* made it up."

"It doesn't belong to Olmstead or my grandmother either," said Gabe.

"Then where did it come from?" Seth glanced at him. "Is it some kind of obscure myth?"

"It's not a myth," said Gabe. "A boy named Mason came up with it. He was my grandmother's friend when they were kids. She's always remembered the story. And when Mr. Olmstead asked her to illustrate this book, she asked him to include this entry in memory of her friend."

"In *memory*?" Mazzy said. "Is he dead?"

"See," Gabe answered, "that's the thing . . ."

They hung on Gabe's words like climbers dangling from a cliff — as if a simple blink would plunge them into an abyss where they'd never learn the truth.

When Gabe finished, Mazzy and Seth stared again at Elyse's illustration of the Hunter, digesting the details. "So strange," said Seth, after a few seconds. "He looks exactly how we imagined him."

"My grandmother had the idea that maybe David had seen this book somewhere," said Gabe. "The town library maybe. She thought he'd lifted his version of the legend directly from this page and used it to create a game. The game that he shared with you. The game that you shared with me."

"Sounds like a virus," Seth said, and shuddered.

Mazzy plucked nervously at her bedspread. "Gabe also said his grandmother wondered if maybe something out in those woods had planted a seed in Mason's head. And the seed sprouted into the stories that Mason wrote down." The group paused, trying collectively to nullify years of being told that such things were impossible. "Let's throw reality out the window for a few minutes," Mazzy went on. "Just *suppose* that fifty years ago, some sort of mysterious entity gave Mason the idea for the Hunter legend." The boys scoffed, and Mazzy raised a hand. "Hear me out. When Mason transcribed the stories, something happened to allow the entity to materialize. To live. On the night his aunt found the muti-lated rooster, the entity . . . took Mason away."

"And a couple years ago," Gabe added, "David might have found a copy of this book in the library. When he started playing his game, that same entity returned . . ." His curious expression fell away as a hard realization took its place.

". . . to take David away too," Mazzy finished. She glanced at Seth, who seemed fascinated by the floor.

"We played the game, just like David did." Gabe felt the blood rush from his face. "And now things have been happen-ing to us."

Seth tore the pillow out from beneath him and threw it against the wall, where it hit with a pathetic whoomp. "No!" he said. "I won't believe it. David ran away. All the rest of it's not . . . It's just not . . ." He closed his eyes, letting out a long breath.

"We're only talking," Mazzy said, sliding off her bed next to him. She squeezed his shoulder. "There's got to be a logical explanation."

"Oh yeah?" Seth asked, raising his voice. "Stories that travel like viruses? Monsters that set traps to catch children for supper? Beasts that creep into our bedrooms at night? You mean logical explanations like those?"

"There has to be an explanation, even if it isn't logical," Gabe answered. "I brought this book here today to show you what I learned. To tell you what my grandmother told me. Something is not right in Slade. It's not just a story." Gabe reached into his backpack and removed the bull's-eye map of Slade. "No one but us wants to see the truth. If there is something supernatural occurring in this town and in our woods, *we* might be the only ones insane enough to end it."

Seth and Mazzy flinched. "Insane?" Mazzy asked.

"I only mean, we have the *imagination* to look for answers where anyone else would stop." Gabe nodded at the book on the floor. "Just like Nathaniel Olmstead." *And Leesy Temple,* he thought. He turned the pages, revealing more and more monsters, folktales, and fantasies. "My grandmother said that Nathaniel was a little bit crazy himself. He believed his monsters were real, that he'd fought against them with talismans. He'd discovered the monsters' weaknesses: the same sorts of everyday objects his characters used to survive."

"Okay," said Mazzy. "So then our first task is to figure out *our* talisman." She flicked on the lamp next to her bed. Until then, none of them had noticed how dark the room had become.

"No," said Seth. "What we need to do first is figure out what we're dealing with." He ran his finger along the spine of the big book on the floor, as if his touch might extract the answer.

"Why don't we start with Seth's family?" Mazzy suggested. "Your cousin Mason lived in your barn. His awful aunt and uncle were your great-grandparents." Seth stiffened. This connection had not yet occurred to him. "Verna was there when Mason disappeared," she went on. "And she might have been the only one who had a clue where he'd gone. Or *if* he'd gone."

"But she died years ago," said Gabe.

"I'll check at home anyway," said Seth. "See if there's anything about my family lying around."

Gabe picked up his grandmother's book and held it in his lap. "We also have pages of possible answers right here too. I can glance through it again tonight. How about I bring the book to school tomorrow? We'll settle down somewhere and catch up."

"But I'm still suspended for the chocolate cake thing," said Seth. "Unfairly, I might add. I can't set foot inside school for another few days."

Gabe sighed. "After school it is, then."

"We're going to need some time to go through everything," said Mazzy. "Where will we be able to do that?"

"My house isn't good," said Gabe, remembering his mother's warning to stay away from Seth.

"What about Seth's house?" said Mazzy.

But Seth shook his head. "My mom's definitely not going to want us traipsing through her beloved hellhole."

"What about back here?" Gabe asked. "It worked well today."

As if in response, there was a knock on the door. "Mazzy? Who are you talking to?"

Wide-eyed, Mazzy scrambled to stand up. She tucked her long hair behind her ears. Gesturing for the boys to remain silent, she tiptoed to the door and opened it a crack. "It's just the radio, Mom."

But Mrs. Lerman pushed at the door and Mazzy skidded on

the carpet. The door swung open. "I cannot believe you," said Mrs. Lerman. She stood in the hall, hands on her hips. "Lying to my face?" She pointed at the boys sitting on the floor, then flicked her thumb toward the stairs. "You two are welcome to come back when my daughter learns to ask permission."

THE HAUNTED GYMNASIUM

THE NEXT MORNING, Slade Middle School was abuzz with excitement. The final event of the week had been arranged to occur later that evening, on Halloween night.

The high school sat upon a hill adjacent to the middle school. Working together, the student governments of the upper and lower schools had organized a "haunted house" in the high school gymnasium. Students and faculty had constructed a labyrinth of corridors and chambers, each room populated with various horrors. Black-lit ghosts hovered on fishing line. Plastic snakes and bugs fell from above. Volunteers dressed in ghoulish costumes jumped out from hidden partitions.

The haunting was a town tradition and the school's biggest moneymaker of the year. People came from all over the eastern part of the state to experience the frights of Slade High's ghostly gym. And according to the senior-class president, who'd been interviewed in the local newspaper that day, this year's spook show might just be their best yet.

Lacking other options, Gabe figured the event was the perfect spot to meet.

Gabe passed through the rest of the day with a knot in his stomach. After his grandmother had picked him up from the Lermans' the night before, he'd told her about their discussion. Elyse agreed that he might find some answers in the mythology book. She promised that she was still thinking about what to do.

He ate lunch in the cafeteria with Felicia and Ingrid and Malcolm, if only to keep up the appearance that everything was okay. Felicia was her usual outspoken self, talking up her costume for that evening. She was going as Maleficent from Disney's *Sleeping Beauty*.

Malcolm and Ingrid oohed and aahed like good little worker bees, but Gabe simply smiled, half listening. He kept thinking about the Olmstead and Ashe book. During his research, one entry in particular had stuck out, and he couldn't wait to discuss it with his friends.

After the last bell, Gabe called Temple House to remind his family about the fright fest at the high school. After listening to his grandmother's stern warning to "be careful," he trekked up the path to the other campus with Mazzy.

The light was low in the sky, the air crisp. The scent of burning leaves drifted on the breeze. Young children dressed in colorful costumes were accompanied by tired-looking parents through the front door of the high school, carrying bags and satchels and jack-o'-lantern-shaped buckets they hoped to later fill up with candy.

Gabe and Mazzy had been sitting on the low wall outside the entrance for several minutes when an odd figure approached them. His thin frame was bulked up by a suit of plastic armor under which he wore a dark sweatshirt and a pair of dirty jeans. A red cape hung from his shoulders and a centurion's helmet hid his face, a Mohawk of synthetic hair rising from the top of it like a horse's mane. In his belt was tucked a long wooden sword, painted silver. "I figured if we're gonna be fighting monsters," Seth's slightly muffled voice came from the helmet, "at least one of us should gear up."

"We're not fighting monsters," said Gabe. "We're just talking about what to do."

"Same thing at this point," Seth answered. From inside the helmet, he flashed some teeth. It was the first time Gabe had seen Seth smile in at least a month.

"Okay," said Mazzy, "but just to be sure, this isn't part of your game, right?"

Seth glanced at his costume. "This? No way. A Robber Prince would never wear something so obvious." He knocked the sword against his helmet. "I'm just being cautious in case one of the faculty recognizes me. Don't want to risk getting sent home, right?"

"I guess that makes sense," said Gabe, holding back a smile. "Come on. Let's head inside."

LEAVING THE LABYRINTH

"You have the book?" Seth asked, trailing Gabe and Mazzy into the lobby.

"In my bag," said Gabe. They stood at the end of a long line. "Should we try to find a place inside the gym? It'll probably be dark. Maybe private. Quiet even?"

Mazzy nodded. "We can sneak off if we need to."

The hallways off the lobby grew dark as the sun went down. Accordion gates stretched across their wide entrances, blocking access to the rest of the school. Classes here must have ended early in preparation for this haunting, Gabe thought.

"Can't we just talk out here?" Seth asked. The line was packed closely. Despite the white noise that filled the lobby, someone could listen in, so Gabe shook his head. He recognized several teachers from the middle school. It was a good thing Seth had come in costume, or he'd have been noticed immediately.

Creepy music and sound effects were being piped out of the intercom speakers overhead. Volunteers dressed as zombies greeted everyone, alternately scaring and delighting the youngest visitors. More and more people crowded into the lobby, until finally, the last of them were forced outside onto the patio.

When the gymnasium doors finally opened, the crowd raised a cheer. Easing forward, Gabe glanced over his shoulder to see if they were being watched, but there were so many people, it was impossible to tell.

❖

Minutes later, they were inside. Moans and groans filled the darkness and every few seconds screams erupted and echoed up into the cavernous ceiling. It turned out that the gym wasn't such a good place to chat after all.

They'd traversed several twists and turns of the dark makeshift maze, before Mazzy located a gap in some plastic sheeting and motioned for the boys to follow her through. On the other side, they pressed up against the gymnasium wall. A light from a nearby exit sign guided them forward down a narrow path. At the door, when Mazzy pushed the handle, Gabe expected an alarm to sound, but it swung open without even a squeak. On the other side, at the end of a dark hallway, another red exit sign glowed.

"Where are we going?" Seth whispered.

"Away from all the people," Mazzy answered.

"Keep moving," said Gabe. "I'm sure we'll find a good spot."

Mazzy pushed open another door, and a blast of cool air escaped another darkened space. The group flinched at the aroma of stale milk. She whispered hello, and received a tinny echo in response. Reaching around the doorway, she felt for a light switch.

Fluorescent light strobed and rung out a barely audible hum. Metal surfaces gleamed all around. Countertops, cutting boards, a griddle, food trays were tucked cleanly inside the glass casings of the serving line. On a wall above a large sink, a steel rack held several utensils — spoons, spatulas, skewers, knives — of all shapes and sizes. In a far corner, the baritone drone of refrigerator motors added discordant harmony to the tone emitting from the lights.

"Nice," said Gabe, following Mazzy inside.

"I think this is as private as we're gonna get," said Seth, accidentally bumping his wooden sword against the stainless steel countertop. It rang out with a *Brrrng!*

Mazzy rushed back to the door and closed it quietly, hoping to trap the noise inside. "Yeah," she said, "but we still have to be quiet."

"If anyone asks, we'll just say we got lost," said Seth, pulling off his centurion helmet.

They sat on the floor between two food prep stations. Gabe unzipped his backpack and removed his grandmother's book. He laid it on the floor, then opened to the page he'd marked with a white note card the night before.

THE GHOSTS OF SLADE

HE WAITED FOR HIS PARTNERS to notice the passage. When they glanced up at him, they looked as confused as he'd expected. *"Ghosts?"* said Mazzy and Seth at the same time.

"A revenant, specifically," said Gabe, nodding at the page open between them. "A vengeful, angry spirit. The walking dead. Humans, or even animals, who have risen from the grave." He waited for them to take a peek. "Vampires are a type of revenant. Zombies too. But most people who believe in this stuff say that they're ghosts. They can take different forms. They have the ability to move objects. They can talk or cry or wail — basically scare the stuffing out of people. Some even say they can kill."

"Kill?" Mazzy echoed.

Wide-eyed, Seth asked, "How does that relate to . . . us?"

"Maybe it doesn't," said Gabe. "But yesterday, after reading late into the night, I couldn't get this entry on ghosts off of my mind." He pointed at his grandmother's illustration: a young girl standing in the doorway of a ruined building. The girl was dressed in what looked like a white hospital uniform. A strange light seemed to swirl around her thin, transparent body, coiling up from her toes to the top of her head. Her face was all shadow, but her eyes managed to reach out from within the page, clutch your throat, squeeze. It was classic Elyse Ashe.

"I know it's hard to believe that any of these myths and legends are real," said Gabe. "According to this book, they come from our primal fears. Parents pass them to children." Like a virus, he thought, remembering Seth's earlier words. "And that's how the ideas survived. Ghost stories are everywhere. Every town has at least one legend. An abandoned house. A sprawling hospital. An ancient graveyard. For some reason, people are much more willing to accept the existence of spirits than of monsters."

Mazzy nodded. "In my church, I've heard the priest talk about Lazarus rising from the grave, and because it's in the Bible, nobody even blinks. I'm sure they'd never call him a ghost, but still . . . Same species, right?"

"All of the strange occurrences fit," said Gabe. "The voices, the stolen objects, the mysterious traps, the growlings, the night-time visitations, the shadows and figures that we've all seen following us home from school. A small group of people would be challenged to pull it all off" — Gabe stared down at the glowing girl on the page — "but if we were dealing with a spirit . . . a very angry spirit . . ."

"A revenant," Mazzy corrected.

Gabe nodded. "Well then, that's a different story."

"But whose spirit is it?" asked Mazzy.

Seth whispered a name so quietly, the others barely heard him. He looked up and repeated himself, louder this time. "Mason Arngrim. My cousin."

THE NEW GAME

SETH PEERED UP FROM THE BOOK, licked his lips, and glanced back and forth between Gabe and Mazzy, nodding with certainty. "It's him. Mason. After everything Gabe said last night, I know he's been here." He clutched his middle. "I can feel it."

"So Seth's cousin is haunting the entire town of Slade?" Mazzy asked, skeptically. "He's masquerading as a character from his stories?" She raised an eyebrow. "Mason is the one who stole Mr. Ashe's puppet?"

Gabe remembered the night Milton disappeared, recalling how close he'd come to reaching up and trying to pull the puppet's head off. What would he have found inside?

"And Mason set up the trap in the woods behind the school," Mazzy went on, "and shot arrows at Seth's bedroom window. If all this is true, wouldn't he need a reason? Unless Mason was just a psycho. In life and now in death."

"From what my grandmother said about him, he didn't sound like a 'psycho.' Disturbed, yes. But insane?" Gabe bit his lip. "He'd been through a lot. Maybe he reached a breaking point on the night his aunt accused him of killing that rooster, but I don't think Mason was beyond reason."

"True," said Mazzy. "But as far as we know, he simply ran off that night, took a bus right out of town."

"My grandmother believed he never left Slade."

"This isn't about Mason being crazy," Seth interrupted. "It's about him being lonely."

"I don't think we're dealing with a friendly ghost situation here, Seth." Mazzy patted his knee, not unkindly.

"He's trying to hurt people," Gabe added.

"But for us, it started as a game," Seth said. "And games are meant to be played." They were quiet for a moment, considering. "David introduced me to Howler's Notch. And I invited Gabe. But where did David find out about it? From this book?" He reached out and flipped to the page where the Hunter glared up at them with his flaming eyes. "Or did he learn the story from somewhere else? Some*thing* else? The afternoon David told me about the Hunter, I heard him talking to someone in the woods. Remember? What if it was Mason? Like, what if Mason's ghost was pretending to be the Hunter?"

Silence. The refrigerator's motor hummed.

"We were playing the game with a ghost," Gabe said finally. He felt numb. "The whole time. With a ghost. A *revenant*."

"I told you those woods were weird," said Seth.

"But didn't you guys hang out there all summer without any . . . incidents?" Mazzy asked. "The scary things only started later."

"Yeah," said Gabe. "They started after Seth told me the Hunter would come for me." Seth blushed. He opened his mouth to object, but Gabe went on. "All in the past now," he said. Not exactly true, he thought, but it'd be better to stick together at this point.

Mazzy scrunched up her forehead. "Could Mason, as the Hunter, have taken a cue from Seth that night? After you guys had the fight, he *really* came for Gabe?"

Gabe shook his head, as an idea came to him. "We stopped playing the game that night. I know I did. Seth too. Right?" Seth nodded. "And David wasn't around to keep up his part. If Mason had been playing with us as the Hunter, who was left to participate?"

"No one," said Seth.

"That's it, then, isn't it?" said Mazzy. "Mason never stopped playing the game. The Hunter is still hunting. Only his target is no longer just the two Robber Princes. He's been searching all of Slade for another participant."

Gabe closed his eyes, trying to process these possibilities. "It's like he's been trying to lure us back. Everything he's done recently has been bigger, scarier, more dangerous. It's like he's setting a trap."

"So, do we play?" Seth asked. "To keep him happy?"

"And what if we don't?" Mazzy asked. "What if we leave it alone? Ignore what's going on? If it's only the spirit of Mason Arngrim, what could he do next?"

"He's already done a lot," said Gabe. "We shouldn't underestimate him."

"There's really no question. Is there?" Seth stood, grabbing his wooden sword from his belt, and shouted out, "I, Wraithen of Haliath, do challenge Mason Arngrim, the Hunter of Howler's Notch, to battle here in Slade High School! Reveal yourself finally to be the villain we know you are!"

Mazzy stood too, her mouth open in shock. Seth slipped away, racing down the aisle toward the kitchen sink. He swung his wooden sword around wildly. His centurion helmet lay on the floor at Gabe's feet.

"Seth, come on." Gabe climbed wearily to his feet, unsure how he'd subdue him if it came to that. "I really don't feel like being arrested."

A squeal echoed through the room. Hinges turned. The trio froze. Gabe turned to find someone standing in the doorway, a shadow surrounded by shadow.

A DIFFERENT KIND OF BEAST

THE SHADOW SPOKE IN THE VOICE of Felicia Nielsen. "What the *heck* are you guys talking about in here?"

The girl stepped into the light, wearing a warped smile that, unfortunately, was not part of her Maleficent costume — a long, dark purple dress, a shawl wrapped tightly around her scalp, two twisted black horns rising from her skull. She was the picture of evil — exactly what she'd been going for. She glanced between Gabe and Mazzy. "I trusted you guys. And you were all in it together?"

"In *what* together?" Mazzy asked.

"Right. Play dumb. The firecracker? The cake? I could have lost a freaking finger!"

Gabe took a deep breath. "You've got it wrong, Felicia. We're only trying to figure out what's happening here. We want to stop whoever it was that hurt you."

"*Whoever?*" Felicia stepped forward, laughing. "You're kidding, right?" She nodded at Seth, who was now by the sink across the room. "Just a theory, but do you think it could possibly have been the kid with the wooden sword?"

Seth dropped his arm to his side. "It's a costume," he said quietly. "It's Halloween."

"Every day is Halloween for you," Felicia answered. "I would have thought you'd have learned by now not to mess with me, Seth." She nodded at Mazzy and Gabe. "I tried to help you guys understand what you were dealing with here, but you didn't listen.

Gabe, I saw you and Seth leaving Mazzy's house last night. I didn't bring it up at lunch today because I wanted to be sure." He opened his mouth to answer, but she cut him off. "Whatever you've got planned is not happening. You're not gonna freak out any more of my friends." She stepped toward the open door behind her. "In fact, when I'm done with you, I doubt you'll set foot in Slade Middle School again."

"Would you shut up a second and listen to us?" Mazzy shouted. Felicia flinched, surprised at the outburst.

Something slammed out in the hallway — a locker, a classroom door — reverberating so loudly, Gabe wondered briefly if a piece of the ceiling had collapsed.

Felicia turned toward the darkness beyond the door. "Who's that?" she cried out, breathless. She must have seen something then, because she staggered against the door frame, her shoulders slack, as if someone had punched her hard in the stomach. She turned around and faced the group. "H-how are you guys doing this?"

"We're not doing anything," said Seth, calmly. "We're standing right here. With you."

"What do you see?" Mazzy asked Felicia.

Felicia turned reluctantly back toward the hallway. "There's someone down there," she said. "Watching."

Gabe held out his hand and waved her forward into the kitchen. "Get away," he whispered. A beastly roar erupted from the passage and Felicia fell into the room. She screamed and scrambled across the linoleum on her hands and knees. Gabe's muscles had turned to cement.

A slithering, sliding sound echoed forth from the darkness. Claws scraping against tile. It was coming closer.

Felicia stood, then slipped and knocked Gabe into action. Glancing around the room, he noticed another door, half-hidden beside the refrigerator. Taking Gabe's silent cue, Seth turned toward the exit. He threw himself into the door, sending it swinging wide open. Gabe waved frantically for Mazzy and Felicia to follow. Scrabbling sounds resounded into the kitchen. Mazzy bent down and picked up the book, then Gabe and Felicia followed her, stumbling into the darkness beyond the new doorway.

PREY

THE HALLWAY WAS A TUNNEL of shadow. As the group careened toward what looked like the emptiness of outer space, Gabe remembered his dream in which the Hunter had eaten him alive. He felt that same weightlessness, as if he were falling, floating, waiting for one final crunch.

Ahead, he heard a whump followed by a shout of pain. "Wall!" Seth cried out sharply, then added, "This way. Quick."

A cacophony exploded from the kitchen behind them. Something large must have passed through the workstation aisle, knocking over utensils, plates, glasses.

Gabe knew his sneakers slapping against the floor was like a trail of crumbs for the Hunter to follow. His only thought was to find light, a place with people around. The high school lobby. Even the gymnasium would do. He wasn't sure if anything could protect them now, but at least they wouldn't be sprinting through darkness.

The sound of claws scrabbling on tile erupted from the kitchen door. Something hit the wall of lockers back there, releasing a clang that echoed in all directions. It was coming closer. Fast.

Suspended in the pitch just ahead, another red exit sign glowed. Seth led the way forward, his sword raised, as if he were still pretending to be the hero of the story. He pushed open a pair of double doors, revealing a pinpoint of light at the end of a long hallway — the lobby. The group dashed ahead and didn't glance back, not even when the doors slammed shut behind them.

Focused on their goal of the lobby in the distance, none of them noticed that the hall was blocked by one of the accordion gates until Mazzy smashed into it at full sprint. Felicia, trying to avoid the same fate, swiveled to the side. But she slipped on the hem of her polyester costume, and her leg extended into Gabe's path. He flew face-first into Seth. Together, they bounced off the blockade and fell to the floor.

For a moment, the hall was quiet, then they groaned together and rolled away from one another. Everyone managed to climb to his or her feet, hearts and minds still racing.

"Is he gone?" Mazzy asked, peering back down the dark hallway. The double doors were fifty yards behind them.

"I can't see," said Gabe.

"He's hiding," said Seth. "We need to keep going."

Felicia shook the bars of the accordion gate. The contraption rattled but didn't give.

"Wanna try and keep it down?" Seth whispered.

"We're locked in," Felicia said, not acknowledging him. Her voice wavered at a high pitch, panicked and very un-Maleficent-like.

"Can we climb it?" Mazzy asked.

"There's only a few inches at the top," said Gabe. "There's got to be another way around."

"Wh-what's going on here?" Felicia asked, her brain finally catching up to reality. "Who's chasing us?"

"Long story," said Seth. The sneer in his voice was unmistakable. "We'll be sure to tell you at lunch on Monday, you know, if there's room at your table."

The double doors slammed open down the hall, smashing against the walls with such force it sounded as though they'd been ripped from their hinges.

CAN'T RUN

GABE BURNED WITH FEAR AND ANGER. He spun toward the gate, trying to see beyond the inky blackness and the fuzzy spots that danced in his vision. This was Seth's fault. He'd taunted the Hunter, dared him to show up. To battle. To play the game. And now the beast, or Mason, or whatever, was coming.

The light of the lobby was unreachable by about the same length as what they'd just run. Surely the crowd there would hear them.

Felicia grappled the bars again. "Help!" she screamed. "Someone! Please!" The rest joined in, shouting until their voices were raw. But no response came. "Can't they hear us?"

Mazzy glanced over her shoulder and whispered, "The sounds of the haunted house must be blocking us out."

A new growling stirred from the darkness behind them. Gabe turned quietly with the others toward the thing in the shadows. An obscure mass in the center of the hall was slightly distinguishable from the rest of the darkness, moving forward, shifting like the silhouette Gabe had seen at the edge of the woods by Temple House. Here, it was only a blur, a blob, but its rumbling voice gave it a new shape.

"Mason!" Gabe called out. "Stop! We're not playing anymore."

The mass grew as it slunk closer. The group pressed against the gate, keeping their eyes focused on the thing. The growl rumbled louder and a foul aroma drifted toward them — mold and mildew and freshly exhumed earth.

"On the count of three," Gabe whispered, "everyone push as hard as you can." The others tensed. He counted aloud and then, together, the group slammed their backs against the cage.

It held fast.

"Again!" Gabe said.

The thing was running now, its claws slipping and sliding on the tile, trying to catch a crack, a groove, anything to push itself forward faster.

"One. Two. Three!"

An earsplitting squeal and a jolt rocked the group as a piece of metal gave way.

"Here!" Seth shouted.

Gabe turned to find Seth already pushing Felicia through a small gap between the gate and the wall. "Go!" Seth ushered Mazzy through next, then grabbed Gabe's shoulder and shoved him forward.

When Gabe turned around, an enormous darkness rose up behind Seth. Two arms extended from the shadow, reaching for Seth as he raised his foot to step into the opening. Gabe took hold of Seth's hand and pulled as something swiped through the space where he'd stood. Seth's sword clattered to the floor.

A large, dark shape slammed against the cage, but it bounced away before Gabe was able to get a good look. The gap they'd created was clearly too small for the thing to fit through.

"Come on," said Mazzy, waving them farther down the hall, toward the light of the lobby.

"There's another gate," said Felicia.

The growling continued from the other side of the cage.

"We smashed through this one," said Gabe. "We'll do it again."

"But what if this was just good luck? What if we get stuck?"

"What other choice do we have?" Mazzy asked.

"There's gotta be another way through," said Seth. He pointed to the hall that branched off to their left, then stepped quickly into its shadows.

"Are you sure?" Gabe asked, following hesitantly. The thing rattled the gate and released a howl of frustration. He realized then that he didn't care if Seth was sure or not.

CAN'T HIDE

AFTER A BRIEF SPRINT, Seth stopped short. He clutched at a doorknob on his left. When he pulled the door open, the smell of chlorine nearly overpowered them. The four stumbled down a small corridor and into a yawning space.

Allowing their eyes to adjust yet again, they found themselves standing by the deep end of an indoor pool. Tall windows allowed light from streetlamps outside to filter in. The water was only steps away.

"Careful," said Mazzy. "Floor's slippery." She and Seth crept toward the shallow end on the other side of the room. But Felicia seized up, clutching at Gabe's elbow.

"I'm sorry I didn't believe you," she said.

"We can apologize later." He pulled his arm from Felicia's grip. "When we're safe. Okay?"

The door in the corridor behind them crashed open, and a large figure darted out. Gabe froze as the figure plowed into Felicia. She screamed and plunged into the water.

Even after she slipped below the surface, her voice continued to echo around the room.

"Felicia!" Mazzy shouted, racing several steps back to the deep end of the pool and kneeling at the edge. The boys crouched beside her, trying to peer through the pitch-black below.

"I can't see anything," said Seth.

Mazzy took a deep breath, then leaned forward into the water. With a splash, she too disappeared.

Gabe instinctively scooted away from the pool. He peered at Seth. "I can't swim."

Seth stood and quickly released the Velcro that was holding his centurion armor in place. The plastic pieces rattled to the tiled floor. "Look for a light switch," he said. Then he jumped, pencil-diving feetfirst into the deep end of the pool.

Gabe stood and tried to catch his breath. He glanced around the room, looking for anything that resembled a switch. But the shadows erased all detail. He turned back toward the corridor where they'd come in and slid his hand along the walls on either side of the doorway. His palm scraped across a metallic knob, and a moment later the water came alive with illumination. He skidded back to the side of the pool to find a dark mass twisting and turning at the bottom. It reminded him of Felicia's party.

The shape began to rise, finding form as the diffuse light from the pool wall struck it, pale legs and arms moving frantically, struggling against the bulk of the water. Three heads burst through the surface a few feet from the wall. Gabe dropped to his knees and held out his hand. "Here!" he called.

Mazzy and Seth climbed out, dragging Felicia behind them, but another dark shape remained at the bottom of the pool — the thing that had chased them. Was this what a revenant looked like? Gabe stared for several seconds, until he was sure it was still. Dead. Then cold laughter rang out from the other side of the room, near the shallow end of the pool.

Glancing up, Gabe saw a thin silhouette standing at the edge of the water, a person made of shadow. The other night, he'd heard the same harsh chuckle ring out from the darkness beside his bed, right before someone had torn away his blanket. "Mason?" he whispered. "Is that you?" The thin silhouette seemed to feed upon the surrounding shadows, gathering up the darkness and swelling into a new, bigger shape. For a moment, it resembled a broad-shouldered man: tall, thick, impenetrable. Then, in a blink, the shape faded away, blending into the far wall, taking the laughter with it.

Gabe turned to find the others sprawled out on the ground beside him. Felicia was sobbing. Mazzy stared, wide-eyed, at the ceiling. Seth sat up and scooted toward him. "It was Mason?" he whispered. Gabe nodded. "Is he still here?"

"I-I'm not sure. I don't think so." He glanced at the blackish blot that was now drifting around the bottom of the pool on a slowly whirling current. "What's *that* thing?"

"I don't know. It was wrapped around Felicia. It felt like skin. Or fur. Mazzy and I had to untangle her."

"Fur?" Gabe shook his head. Pins and needles pressed painfully into his legs where he knelt. "What kind of fur?"

Mazzy groaned as she too struggled to sit. She rested her hand on Felicia's forehead. Felicia flinched but finally stopped crying. She leaned toward Mazzy, wrapping her arms around her waist. "I'm pretty sure it was your dad's puppet," Mazzy said after a moment, stroking Felicia's sopping hair. "Milton." Gabe hadn't imagined he could feel worse, but this news had done the trick. "By the time we reached the suit, it was as empty and lifeless as the night we found it lying in the hallway at your house."

SOON AFTER THE FOUR STUMBLED into the lobby, wet and panicked and in obvious distress, the school's administrators turned on the gymnasium lights, effectively shutting down the haunted house for the night. Several teachers stationed at the event took care of Felicia, who needed the most attention, until the paramedics arrived.

Later, Gabe, Seth, and Mazzy answered questions from a long stream of adults. Of course, after the group shared their story, the officers and others merely gifted them with skeptical stares before turning and whispering to one another.

Gabe purposely neglected to mention the silhouette of the boy at the shallow end to the police. But now he mentioned it again to his friends. "Did you guys see him?" Gabe asked. "The boy by the side of the pool."

"I saw *something*," Seth answered. "Couldn't tell what it was though."

"A boy?" Mazzy asked. "What boy? Who?"

A couple cops walked through the lobby carrying the soaking rag that was Milton Monster. By the front doors, they zipped the suit into a large plastic evidence bag and delivered it to a squad car waiting just outside.

Gabe felt a knot in his stomach. "When you guys were all safe on deck, when Milton was at the bottom of the pool, I saw someone else in the room with us." He described what he'd seen, the way the silhouette had changed shape, expanding before fading away, the harsh laughter that had echoed across the rippling water.

"I heard that too," Mazzy said. "It was Mason?"

Gabe nodded emphatically. He had no doubt.

"I asked him to come and play," said Seth, looking mortified. He covered his face with his hands and mumbled through his fingers, "So he did."

"He'd have shown up anyway," said Gabe. "If not tonight, then soon. We haven't set foot in Howler's Notch for weeks now, but that hasn't stopped him from visiting us."

"How do we keep him from coming back again?" Mazzy asked. She'd collected the Olmstead and Ashe book from the pool deck. Now she handed it over to Gabe. "Is there something in here that tells you how to destroy an angry spirit?"

"*Revenant*," Seth corrected.

Gabe clutched the book to his chest. The cover was damp and for a moment he felt bad that it would probably be crinkled when it dried. "Olmstead does mention that you can quiet a restless spirit by burying its remains in, what was it called . . . consecrated ground?"

"Like a cemetery," said Mazzy.

"Yeah. Or if the spirit's body is already buried in a cemetery, people believe that if you dig up the grave and destroy the bones, you send the spirit away."

"Great," said Seth. "Then all we've got to do is locate Mason's grave and burn whatever's left of him. Easy!"

"Easy?" Mazzy answered. "You're suggesting that grave robbing is *easy*? Please don't tell me you have any experience with that sort of thing."

"Doesn't matter whether grave robbing is easy or not," said Gabe. "Mason *disappeared* over fifty years ago. Remember? My grandmother said she was sure that Mason never left town. If she's right, and he's still here in Slade, Mason's resting place must be unmarked." He shook his head. "It's going to be impossible to find."

"Not impossible," said Mazzy. "Just . . . tricky. It'll take some time is all."

"That's exactly what we don't have," said Gabe. "We don't know what else Mason has in mind. I mean, it's Halloween. According to Nathaniel Olmstead, tonight is the one night of the year that the restless dead are at their strongest. I wouldn't be surprised if our little revenant showed up again, next time with more success."

"*Success?*" Mazzy asked.

"David said the Hunter wanted us dead," said Seth.

"Oh," she whispered.

"But why?" Gabe asked. "What would Mason gain from . . ." The end of the thought stuck in his throat. "From *killing* us?"

"Simple," said Seth, his voice hollow. "If we die, he wins the game."

THE MAIN INGREDIENT IN HUNTER'S STEW

WHEN THE AMBULANCE ARRIVED, Mazzy rode with Felicia's parents to the hospital. She promised that she'd check in with the boys later, to let them know about Felicia's condition.

As the ambulance left, a voice called from near the school's entrance. "Gabriel!" Gabe turned to find his grandmother walking briskly toward him. "Oh, thank goodness," she said. The look on her face made him feel like he might faint, and when she grabbed him and hugged him close, he nearly did. "I was looking all over for you."

"But I told you I'd be here. And I have my cell. . . ." Gabe caught a glimpse out the lobby windows. Night had fallen over Slade, the sunset long past. He hadn't realized how long he and his friends had been here. He yanked his phone from his pocket to check the time and saw that the battery had died.

Elyse glanced around, noticed the solemnity of the crowd, the gathering of cops and medics who were filling out paperwork. The front doors swung open and flashing red and white lights streaked into the lobby. "What's going on?" she asked.

Gabe flinched. He'd imagined that somehow his grandmother had learned about what had happened to him and his friends, and that was why she'd hugged him so hard. But now he realized that she must have come looking for him for a different reason. "Felicia almost drowned," Gabe answered. He quickly added, "They say she'll be okay, but they took her away in an ambulance."

His grandmother covered her mouth in shock. She closed her eyes. Sighed. "Awful night," she said. Then she added with a whisper, to herself, "A curse to suffer nights like these." Then, as if struck by a jolt of electricity, she opened her eyes and looked at Gabe with such pity, it frightened him.

"If you didn't know what happened here, why did you come?" Gabe asked, trying to control his rising panic. He felt Seth move in close beside him as if to protect him from whatever news his grandmother might deliver. Elyse stared at him, holding inside what seemed like a hurricane of emotion, then she clasped his shoulders with her long fingers. Her grip felt like Death itself had taken hold of him, was toying with him, as the Hunter had been doing for the past few months. "Please tell me what's wrong."

"It's your baby sister," said Elyse. "Miri is missing."

Gabe was suddenly glad that she was clutching his shoulders, otherwise, he might have collapsed.

Elyse offered Seth a ride home. On the way, Gabe and Seth sat in silence while Elyse explained what had happened.

Earlier in the evening, Dolores had left Miri in her high chair to answer the doorbell. Groups of trick-or-treaters had been arriving sporadically all afternoon. But when she got there, she found the stoop empty except for a few scattered leaves. Returning to the kitchen, Dolores discovered the high chair vacant as well. Miri had only just started crawling; there was no way she could have gotten down on her own. Glen was coming home late from a meeting in Boston, so Dolores and Elyse searched Temple House on their own. Almost ten minutes had gone by before Dolores was worried enough to call the police. Now, hours later, according to Elyse, Dolores was inconsolable.

As his grandmother turned a sharp curve, heading up into the hills west of the schools, Gabe was seized by a thought more terrible than any other. He blinked, remembering what had happened to Vincent Price, his science teacher's rat. If Mason was imitating the habits of the monster he'd invented, then Miri was in bigger trouble than anyone knew.

BEASTS OF SHADOW,
BEASTS OF LIGHT

SEVERAL MINUTES LATER, the Cadillac turned onto the Hoppers' long gravel driveway. Gabe felt helpless as the car slowed to a halt, stopping between the cottage and the old barn across the way. He knew that once Seth had gone, he'd be left alone with the reality of his missing sister.

"Thank you for the ride, Mrs. Ashe." Seth opened the car door. He paused, as if searching for just the right thing to say. "Gabe, will you call me if anything changes?"

If he replied, Gabe knew he'd burst into tears. Instead, he merely nodded.

Elyse craned her neck over the steering wheel, peering out into the meadow. "Something's burning." She was right. As soon as Seth had cracked the door, an unmistakable aroma had drifted into the car. It brought Gabe back to his old neighborhood, standing on the sidewalk, watching flames devour his house across the street.

He clutched the door handle and squeezed, trying to force himself back to reality. The nightmares that had terrorized his sleep over the summer nipped at the edges of his vision. The fire demon. Arms made of flickering light and melting plastic reached out for him. He pressed himself backward, into the seat.

"My mom's probably started a fire in the fireplace," said Seth, stepping outside, "Weird." He flinched. "It's been a while since she's done that. I didn't even think we had any firewood. . . ." He trailed off, staring into the distance.

Smoke was seeping from the roof of the barn. Seth darted across the driveway, then skidded to a halt. He clutched at his hair, then turned back to the car. Gabe opened the front door. "I've gotta call the cops," Seth said. "The fire department. Someone . . . I don't know. Will you guys wait here?"

Elyse calmly leaned forward across Gabe's seat. "Of course we will," she said.

She yanked the gear into reverse before Gabe could close his door, then spun out onto the Hoppers' lawn, moving a safe distance from the smoldering building. Once parked, they got out and made their way to the driveway ahead. Seth had already disappeared inside to call the authorities.

They stared up at the barn's roof. Ribbons of gray curled into the sky, dancing gracefully between pinpoints of starlight. Elyse reached for Gabe's hand. He imagined her thin fingers clutching a pen, dipping the nib into a well of ink, scratching across a white page, creating the monster that Gabe was certain had caused all this trouble. Was his grandmother to blame? And could she do something about it now? Backlit by the porch light, she looked otherworldly. When Gabe blinked, he could almost picture her as a girl, standing in this very spot, listening to the cries of Mason's aunt Verna weeping for the slaughtered rooster.

"You know what this is," he whispered. His grandmother turned to him. The evidence that Gabe was right was written on her face. "You know who's responsible. Why else would you have told me that story?"

Trembling, she glanced at the cottage, pretending not to hear.

"Grandmother Elyse." Gabe tugged at her coat, trying to capture her attention. "Talk to him. Ask him what we can do to make him stop."

She shook her head, refusing to listen. "That noise," she whispered. "Do you hear?"

The smoke was growing thicker at the roof; the barn was fighting against a beast that was trying to devour it. From inside,

there came a kind of cry, as if moisture within the wood was heat-
ing, turning to steam, escaping from tiny sealed pockets in the
same way it would spew from the mouth of a boiling kettle. It was
a harsh wail, and it pierced the night.

Elyse's face went slack. "Oh my goodness." She stumbled
toward the barn, her limbs hanging limp. "That's the baby crying,"
she said. Then she screamed. "Miri's in there!"

HOUSES OF FIRE

THE PREVIOUS SUMMER, at the end of a July day, when his house went up in flames, Gabe watched carefully from the sidewalk across the street.

It had happened fast, but he remembered every detail as if it were a movie he could pause and rewind and replay. First came the smoke, light gray and wispy, like the kind that you see going up a chimney from a controlled blaze in the fireplace. Then, at the front windows, the first licks of flame appeared. Soon, the orange bursts turned hefty and thick, like lava, but hovering, pulsating in the air over his front yard. The firefighters scrambled around like swarming insects, pulling the hoses from the trucks, spraying massive streams of water onto and into the rapidly faltering structure. Pieces of siding appeared to melt and fall away from the house's frame, and other crisp, unrecognizable objects simply floated away on the hot breeze.

The strangest part was the birds chirping in trees nearby, like they would on any other summer afternoon. Listening to them sing almost made the fire seem like a hallucination, a dream, an illusion. It was the birdsong that made Gabe remember the wish that he'd made — the one about making the *Puppet Boy* nickname disappear. And after the fire had been extinguished and Gabe sat on the Parkers' front stoop, watching his parents rushing around, making calls, talking with neighbors, it was the birdsong that echoed in his head.

Now the disturbing cries of the birds in Gabe's memory became the wail of a child. Standing beside his grandmother in the Hoppers' yard, Gabe made no wishes. Dashing forward, he was determined to tilt back the scale he'd upset months ago. His grandmother called out to him as he ran toward the barn, but his heartbeat pounding in his eardrums drowned her out.

The small wood door appeared before him. He grabbed the warm handle and pulled. Stepping inside, he remembered searching for Milton with his father and Sharon in this spot a month before. The door slammed shut behind him, and Gabe shouted in surprise. He turned around and kicked at it, then tried the inner latch but it wouldn't budge. For a moment, he thought he heard the hushed laughter that had been haunting him for weeks. "Mason!" he shouted. Gabe realized that the sound wasn't laughter. A hissing was coming from the old tractor that sat in the center of the barn. The engine hood was engulfed in smoke and flame. Some sort of fluid was dripping to the floor from under the tractor's carriage, carrying with it small drops of fire. A pool was forming, spreading outward. A few feet away, several large bales of hay were stacked against the wall.

Miri's screaming echoed around the vast room. Gabe listened, trying to pinpoint where it was coming from. He glanced up. The hayloft. Looking around, he noticed the wood skeleton of the only remaining ladder clinging haphazardly to the barn's support columns. The last time he'd been here, he'd broken the rungs at the bottom. Sharp remnants stuck out from their former pegs. The rungs near the top looked weathered.

Gabe leaped toward the lowest solid rung, several feet above his head. His fingers barely grazed it; the dowel turned slightly at his touch. He needed to get closer to grab hold.

"I'm coming, Miri," he called, hoping his voice might calm her. Glancing over his shoulder at the tractor, through the opaque air, Gabe saw that the pool of liquid fire had crept outward a couple more inches. A moment later, Miri began coughing. Gabe needed to get up there. *Now.*

Several plastic crates sat next to a darkened doorway on the opposite side of the room. Gabe rushed over and grabbed them. He peeked briefly through the door. Seeing only empty cages, he made a mental note that the coop was just another dead end.

He returned to the ruined ladder and placed the two plastic crates below it. Stepping up, he easily grasped the lowest rung. Gabe pulled himself upward using what felt like his last bit of strength, silently begging the wood to hold. He pressed his sneakers atop the remains of the splintered rungs to lessen the burden on the ones above. He grasped the next rung and the next. At the top, he reached for the platform of the hayloft and pushed off from the ladder, launching himself upward. But the lower rung twisted. His foot slipped and his chest crashed against the ledge. He howled through the pain, his palms slipping frantically over the boards, searching for something to clutch. He shoved his index finger into a large knothole, then quickly located a crack between two other planks and found a grip.

Trying to ease his breathing, he shimmied forward until he felt solid flooring beneath his body, then he collapsed. Dead weight. He felt a darkness pressing at the edges of his vision. He pushed himself up onto his hands and knees and shouted out an unintelligible grunt, forcing himself to stay awake, aware.

Though the firelight from below was growing steadily brighter through the cracks in the flooring, it was still difficult to make out details of the space. The air was murky, the heat like an oven, but what Gabe could see gave him chills.

He knelt on raw wood planks, several feet from a rug blackened with mildew. On top of the rug, near the sloping of ceiling, a dresser sat, its water-damaged sides bulging out. Beside the dresser stood a twin-sized brass bed frame. A thin mattress lay on top, its springs poking through the worn fabric like bones through skin. This was Mason's old bedroom.

To Gabe's relief and horror, Miri sat in the center of this old bed, reaching out for him, her mouth open in a silent scream, her face grimy with soot and damp with tears.

From downstairs, Gabe heard a pounding. Someone outside was trying to get through the stuck door. "Gabe!" It was Seth. "Let me in!"

Gabe didn't respond. He needed to save his breath. He crawled across the filthy rug to his sister, then, rising to his feet, he snatched her up and hugged her tightly. She whined into his ear, but it was a comforting sound. They were together at least. When her small fingernails scratched his neck, his own eyes stung with tears.

In the distance, sirens shrieked. The fire trucks were coming, but they still sounded so far away. Gabe stumbled back toward the ladder. Looking over the edge, a wave of dizziness overtook him and he sunk to his knees. If he tried to carry his sister down, they'd end up crumpled atop the plastic crates below. Miri choked again, her whole body heaving. Gabe coughed too — a long, painful rumble. The air was getting hotter by the second. Sweat poured from his skin, his clothes clung like plastic wrap. Gabe glanced around, searching for another solution. The one that he kept coming back to was the one where they ended up on the floor below, their bones shattered.

Light-headed, almost giddy, Gabe imagined himself as Meatpie. The Robber Prince of Kingdom Chicken Guts would no sooner leap to his demise than he would lie down and die. No. A Robber Prince would never surrender.

Struggling up, Gabe carried Miri to the other edge of the loft, where the smoke was now coming like a solid wall. He peered over the rail. Stacks of hay bales stood about fifteen feet down. The pool of ooze from the tractor had reached the dry grass at the opposite end of the long row. Flames climbed the bales, munching greedily at the straw. Several untouched feet of tightly rolled hay still leaned against the wall of the barn; in a moment the entire pile would be engulfed.

Gabe held Miri close to his chest. Feeling that this was a dream, a memory, a fantasy, he swung himself over the loft railing and, without thinking, stepped into the void.

STRAW & STICKS & STONES

THERE WAS AN EXPLOSION OF SPARKS. They swooped and swirled all around.

Gabe lay on his back, his sister perched precariously upon his chest. The sharp ends of the hay poked through his coat, and a wave of heat slapped at Gabe's cheek. When he turned his head, which throbbed with a warmth all its own, he saw that the flames had crept along the tops of the bales, inches away from where he and Miri lay.

The baby was screaming, her tears and snot spraying his face. Gabe wobbled on the bale, searching for a slope that would indicate which direction was down, twisting his body around and holding Miri to his chest. Gabe slid down the bale, feetfirst.

When his sneakers touched the dirt floor of the barn, he crouched, sweeping one arm in front of him, trying to sense where he was. The smoke irritated his eyes and noises assaulted his ears. Knocking sounds, hissing sounds, sounds of heavy things collapsing. And the sirens screamed from just outside.

But Miri wasn't making any sounds.

Gabe jostled her. When she didn't respond, not even a kick, he brought his head down low. Her warm breath tickled his cheek and he sighed in relief. "They're almost here," he said, as if Miri could hear or even understand his words. "Don't worry." This time, he wasn't speaking to her.

Gabe stood tall, and the room spun. Smoke was everywhere. He groped and stumbled his way to the door. He kicked it again, but, as before, the door did not budge.

"Seth!" he cried out, the air scraping at his throat. Seth must have run to meet the firefighters. There was no way he'd just leave them in there. Was there? "Grandmother Elyse!" he tried instead.

No voice answered from the other side.

The sirens wailed louder than ever. Gabe thought he could see flashes of light seeping through the gaps in the wood, but it might have been the flames against the far wall, reaching almost to the roof.

Something shifted behind him. Gabe spun. He'd thought that a chunk of the roof had fallen close by, then, through a thick veil of smoke, he saw a dark silhouette step toward him. Someone else was in here with him. "Seth?" He clutched Miri closer, bouncing her up on his hip. She moaned, exhausted. "Is that you?"

He thought he heard a reply.

No.

It could have been the fire, crackling and hushed, or maybe he'd hit his head harder than he thought.

The silhouette became solid. The person was carrying something. Large, round, flat. It hung low. Heavy. Arms raised the object, as if to toss it at Gabe, to crush him.

"Stop," Gabe murmured. "Please, Mason. Leave us alone."

I'm not Mason.

This time the voice was unmistakable. And even in the heat, he still felt goose bumps.

Behind this person who was *not-Mason*, a larger shadow rose, haloed by the wicked fire. This new silhouette stood like a tall stack of rocks. Gabe could feel Mason's presence now. Big and bad and angry as heck. The larger shadow grabbed the smaller shadow, and the two darknesses melted into one.

The heavy object that the first silhouette had carried landed at Gabe's feet. He rocked backward, away from the object, and fell against the barn door, rattling the outside latch. Gabe nudged the object with his toe. It was a large stone.

The Hunter roared. Or maybe it was the sound of fire escaping into the night sky. The massive shadow seemed to expand. Or maybe it was simply smoke, blackening the air.

Gabe placed Miri on the floor next to the door. With eyes bloodshot and open wide, she shoved her thumb securely in her mouth. The rock was bulky, but he managed to lift it. Turning away from the fire, away from the shadows and smoke, he raised it over his head, then, stepping forward, he swung his arms and released the load, launching it as if from a catapult. The stone smashed into the wood frame. The door burst open, and a furious wind rushed in.

Ducking low, Gabe grabbed Miri. The fire inside the barn howled, licking at the air just over his head. With one arm, he cradled his sister to his underbelly, then, like a wounded animal, he crawled to the surprisingly cold ground just outside the door.

WHEN THEY'D MADE IT PARTWAY across the field, Miri began crying again. Her wailing was a relief. It meant they were both alive. Firefighters ran toward them in slow motion, gas masks and oxygen tanks giving them the appearance of interstellar explorers.

Gabe didn't remember much of what happened next.

Later, he sat in the back of an ambulance that was parked safely away from the barn and the blaze and the trucks and the water gushing from hoses. Paramedics took his and Miri's blood pressure and temperature, slipped oxygen masks over their noses and mouths, asked questions, kept them both conscious. Gabe was grateful for their help and attention, but he knew that as soon as this was over, as soon as these people went away, Mason would be waiting. Every time he glanced at his sister's little form lying on the cot beside him, an electrical sensation surged through him. It was a feeling beyond anger — rage, maybe? Gabe could not imagine how someone would do such a thing to a child, even if that someone was no longer living.

Seth was with his mother off by the light of the porch. Elyse stood closer, her tearstained face illuminated by the fluorescent radiance spilling from the ambulance, hovering as close as she could while giving the rescue workers the space they needed to do their job.

Another pair of headlights appeared down the driveway. Sitting up, Gabe recognized the vehicle as it came closer. Skidding to a stop, it tore up some of the Hoppers' lawn. The doors burst open, and Glen and Dolores dashed from the car, making a beeline to their children.

Gabe was surprised by the ferocity with which his parents hugged him. They scolded him for running into the burning building. A moment later they called him a hero for saving his sister. He was confused and dizzy and his whole body ached, but he'd never felt so close to any of them.

Minutes later, Gabe listened as the adults spoke at each other, loudly. His parents demanded to know what had happened. How had Miri gotten into the hayloft? Who had allowed Gabe into the barn? What had happened in there? Elyse tried to explain, but Gabe was the only one who knew the whole truth. And the one person he was desperate to tell wasn't close enough to listen.

He glanced toward the cottage. Seth stared back. The boys understood. If they were going to stop the Hunter from returning, the clock was ticking.

"I'm fine," Gabe insisted, pulling off the oxygen mask. "Mom, please. I wanna talk to Seth. Just for a second. I'll be back. Promise." Dolores gave him a look that was both frustrated and compassionate. Glen's attention was with Miri, so Dolores looked to the EMT worker, as if for permission to let Gabe go. The worker hung the oxygen tubing on the top of the tall green tank and nodded slightly.

Dolores rolled her eyes, but kissed Gabe's forehead. "Okay," she said. "But if you feel anything, any aches or pains, I want you right back here." He barely heard this last part. He was already halfway to the Hoppers' porch.

Seth was sitting on the bottom step, staring at the firefighters who continued to battle the blaze. When he noticed Gabe approach, he leapt to his feet and threw his arms around him. Neither boy said anything; they just stayed like that for a while. Eventually, they sat down, stewing in awkward silence. The fire had consumed most of the barn's far wall, the one that had been lined with hay bales. The building's scorched framework rose in blackened shadow against the light, resembling used-up matchsticks.

Finally, Gabe worked up the nerve to tell Seth what had happened in there, or what he remembered at least. Seth listened and when Gabe finished, he released a slow, trembling sigh. "I don't think we're done yet," he said. Gabe nodded. "It's Halloween, the night when the dead come back, when the curtain that separates the worlds of the living and the dead is the weakest. And if that's true, tonight must be the night when Mason is the strongest. He still has a few hours left . . . to hunt."

"I really just want to go home," said Gabe. Every muscle ached. His throat felt like it had been scraped out with an electric mixer. His skin felt crispy.

"But what if he won't stop?" Seth asked. "What if, when we try to get to sleep later tonight, he does something else? Something worse?"

"Worse than burning me and my baby sister alive?"

"Yes," Seth answered. His certainty was chilling. Gabe covered his face, but Seth rested his hand on his shoulder. "We've got to find Mason's bones," he insisted. "Destroy them. Or bury them. And we have to do it tonight."

Gabe glanced up. The lights from the trucks splashed sporadic color out into the forest. Firefighters continued to blast water at the barn, soaking the remaining wood and the surrounding grass to keep the dwindling flames from spreading. Glen and Dolores were still huddled at the back of the ambulance, flanked by Elyse, leaning over Miri. No one seemed to notice that he and Seth were sitting on the porch steps. If they were going to disappear, they needed to do it now. "Where do we start?" Gabe asked, standing, clutching his side. "Mason's body could be anywhere."

Seth climbed to his feet too. "That map you made of Slade. The red spiral ended in one particular spot." He nodded at the darkness behind the house, toward the slope that led to Temple House at the top of the hill.

"The woods?" Gabe said. "But that still leaves us with a few dozen acres to search."

Seth rose onto his toes, peering toward the barn.

"What is it?" Gabe asked. "You see something?"

"I have an idea." Seth stepped forward onto the driveway. He waved for Gabe to follow him.

Gabe's body ached in places he hadn't realized he'd been hurt. His lungs felt as though they'd shrunk by fifty percent. As he rushed to keep up, Gabe glanced back toward the ambulance. His family would never understand what he'd told Seth; even Elyse seemed too frightened now to fight. Shadows pulsed across the lawn, similar to the shifting shape that had been chasing him all night. He quickly decided that it would be a bigger mistake to stick around here. "What are we looking for?" Gabe asked, struggling to catch his breath.

"You said you saw a boy in the barn."

"Yeah, but I also smacked my head pretty hard when I jumped down from the hayloft."

"What if there *was* someone else with you?" Seth asked. They wandered around the corner of the barn, cut off from view of the fire trucks. As they approached the broken door where Gabe had escaped the fire, he slowed his pace. "Someone besides you and Miri. And Mason. He was approaching you, but then the Hunter emerged from the smoke and attacked him?"

"I think so, but —"

Seth stopped walking and held up his hands. "After every-thing you've seen tonight," he said, "after everything that's happened, you still don't believe?"

Gabe blinked. On any other evening, this would have been a laughably dramatic gesture. Here, now, mere steps away from the burning barn, Seth appeared almost regal. A Robber Prince. A hot wind rushed from the building. Gabe felt suddenly faint. He shook his head. "Of course I believe," he whispered.

"I don't think that other boy was trying to hurt you," Seth went on. "He gave you the tool to get out of there: the stone you used to smash the door. He saved your life."

Splinters of wood were scattered across the dirt. The stone lay among them. It was pale and flat. Something about it was strangely familiar. Gabe crossed his arms, nervous to step closer.

"This is it," said Seth. The breeze blew his hair back from his forehead. He crouched down, rubbed his fingers over its surface. "Am I right?" He glanced up at Gabe.

Gabe bit his lip. Nodded.

"What if the boy wasn't *only* trying to save your life?" Seth smiled wanly. "What if, at the same time, he was trying to give you a clue?"

"A clue to what?"

"Where have we seen stones like this before?"

Despite the heat, Gabe felt a chill. He understood. Seth glanced toward the dark woods in the distance, to the place they'd once called Howler's Notch. Inside the notch, an altar stood. Someone had piled up stones like the one in the dirt beside the barn, an altar that Wraithen had believed contained the Hunter's power. Beneath the stones, there'd been a hollow spot. When Meatpie nearly uncovered it over a month ago, a voice had told him to stop before he'd been able to dig, had called out *Don't* with a voice similar to the one that had spoken to Gabe in the barn earlier that night.

"*I'm not Mason*," Gabe whispered, remembering, stepping closer to Seth. "So who was it? Who helped me?"

Seth's eyes darted back and forth as he thought. "I have no idea," he said after a few seconds. Gabe shivered. He turned to the woods, too frightened to ask Seth why he looked like he'd just told a lie.

{NEVER & BEFORE & NOW}
HOLLOW GROUND

AWAY FROM THE FIRE, the night air was biting. Already coated in sweat, Gabe's body sprouted goose bumps from the chill. Every few seconds, a red or blue flash from the trucks lit up his warm exhalations, which hung momentarily in the air before fading away.

The boys had already walked far up the horse trail, stumbling over rocks and tripping into ruts, before they thought of flashlights; too late. They continued on, careful of the pitfalls, until they turned off the path and into the forest. Seth led the way, moving through the brush swiftly, trampling dead leaves and pushing past prickly foliage. Gabe followed, sure that even to blink was to let his guard down. Every shadow, every sound, every breeze was the Hunter chasing them. He kept imagining a great, dark silhouette creeping into the kitchen, lifting Miri from her high chair, carrying her down the hill and into the barn. He and Seth were not dealing with "a bump in the night," "go back to bed," "you're hearing things, silly." This was not the wind, not the furnace, not an injured bird, not a nervous dog. The Hunter was as real as David Hopper had insisted, and the stakes of the game were unimaginably high.

They splashed through a shallow brook. A few steps more, and they were there. Above the shrunken reach of the deformed tree, the forest canopy opened, creating a dome of cold starlight. A million silver pinpoints glistened there. Last year, the sight may have taken Gabe's breath away. Now, however, he simply struggled to breathe.

The boys stood together by the pile of stones. Without a word, Seth grabbed a flat, round rock from the top of the so-called altar and tossed it to the ground. It slid to a halt a few feet down the slope. Gabe tried to do the same, but his hands were shaking so much, he managed only to loosen the structure. Stones rolled noisily to the base of the cairn. Gabe looked up, wide-eyed, but Seth shrugged. "Might as well get on with it," he whispered, pushing at the stack as Gabe had accidentally done, the catalyst for another miniature avalanche. "Faster this way," Seth added.

It took about ten minutes to spread the pile out onto the hillock. When the boys had nearly uncovered the altar's base, Gabe slowed, remembering the last time he'd been here. He had a better idea now of what was below. Together, the boys knelt down and cleared away the last few stones. Underneath, they discovered a couple rotting planks of wood. The boys glanced at each other in surprise. Seth reached out for one plank, Gabe for the other.

At Gabe's touch, numerous insects scattered across the board — some raced onto his hand. Pressing his lips together to contain his disgust, he threw the piece of wood as hard as he could. It rustled through low leaves in the distance. Gabe shook himself off, brushed at his jacket, imagining hundreds of tiny claws clutching at the insides of his clothes. Seth was doing the same. Gabe almost laughed at how ridiculous they both looked, but he managed to hold that inside too.

In the dim starlight, the boys saw what lay beneath the boards. The roots of the crooked tree had formed a type of netting, which had held up the planks and the stones. Below these roots was a deep indentation, beyond which lay pitch blackness. A musty smell rose up from the hole. It was raw earth. Decay. Moisture and rot. Gabe felt himself start to gag, but then he began to breathe through his mouth instead of his nose, which helped.

"What is this place?" Seth asked.

"The grave?" said Gabe.

"But it goes deep." He picked up a pebble from the rubble of the altar. "Listen." Seth dropped it into the depression. The pebble tumbled between the roots, then disappeared into the darkness. Seconds later, a *pip* echoed up at them. The stone had found the bottom. "I think this hole might be a well."

"A well?" Gabe leaned back. "Like, for water?"

"It's possible, though it's probably dried up now," said Seth. "My dad told me that a hundred years ago, before the trees took over, this was all farmland. That's what all those stone walls are for — they divided up the properties."

"Isn't that dangerous?" Gabe asked. An echo rose up from the chasm, and he suddenly felt like a fool. *Dangerous?* said his voice. *Dangerous? Dangerous?* "Leaving a well like this out in the middle of nowhere?"

"My thought exactly." Seth stared into the emptiness. "If this hole *is* what we were looking for, then you-know-who is all the way at the bottom."

"You think he fell in? That night with the rooster?"

"If so, we need to figure out a way to get him out."

"No way," said Gabe, shaking his head. "This isn't just a *grave*." A knot had formed in his chest. "We've got to get help."

Seth stood up. "You're right," he said slowly, his voice teasing. "Why don't you go ask the fire brigade to stop what they're doing and come out here to recover a fifty-year-old skeleton at the bottom of an abandoned pit?"

"We're completely unprepared! I wouldn't know how to do this even in broad daylight."

"I say we start by clearing away these roots."

"Why didn't we bring shovels?"

"They were in the barn," said Seth. He sighed and added, more seriously, "Mason almost killed you tonight. And Miri too.

If we leave here right now, he's free to try again. We don't have time to argue. Or to find help. And if we go back for shovels, anyone might stop us, keep us from coming back here. Don't you get it?"

"I'm sorry," said Gabe. "I'm just . . . scared."

"I am too. I really am. But tonight, I think we've both proven that we're more than *just scared*. Tonight, we've learned how to be brave." Here was Wraithen again. Spine straight. Chin tilted toward the sky. His words were cheesy, but the sentiment was comforting. "And not just brave in a game. Brave where it really counts. In here."

Gabe wasn't sure where *in here* was, exactly. But he understood that the Robber Princes' bravery now belonged to Seth, and if that gave him the strength to survive, then who cared how crazy he sounded? *Heck, I'll be Meatpie now if it gets me home,* Gabe thought. He shook his head in disbelief, knelt forward, and peered into the crevice.

Though the tangled system was fairly solid, the boys were able to pluck away some of the roots from one side of the hole, revealing enough space for a body to fit through. Even better, a few of the thickest roots looked like they might go deep enough to act as a ladder of sorts. "So?" Seth perched on the opposite side of the opening. He glanced down. "Who's the lucky one? You or me?" When Gabe's silence stretched on, Seth added. "One of us has to stay up here. Keep a lookout. Right?" But Gabe could not, in fact, speak.

In the space behind Seth, where the dim silhouette of tree trunks and branches should have been, there was only a wall of darkness rushing closer, solidifying into the shape of a tall, wide body. A pair of blue eyes wavered in the air like flame. Gabe stumbled backward as Seth glanced up to see what was the matter. The darkness seemed to swoop forward. And that's when Seth slipped.

Or was pushed. With a brief and strangely quiet yelp, he disappeared through the broken net of roots and into the rift, but Gabe was the one who screamed. Over the echo of his own voice, he thought he heard a familiar laughter. With a crushing panic, Gabe realized that they'd both fallen for another of the Hunter's traps.

DARKNESS BELOW

"SETH!" GABE CRIED OUT, then glanced around the clearing. It was now still, but the quiet was no comfort. A whimpering sound rose up from the hole. Gabe lay flat on his stomach and scrambled farther forward, peeking over the edge of the well.

Several feet down, Seth clung to a stringy root. The thin strand was slowly pulling out from the dirt. Struggling to stay near the rim, Seth placed one hand in front of the other, gripping another root. His feet scrabbled against the dirt for a foothold. Stones and clumps of earth fell from the wall and rattled into the maw.

"Seth," Gabe said as evenly as he could. "Calm down and listen to me. We're going to get you out of there, but you need to relax. Okay?"

"Okay," Seth muttered, his teeth chattering. He shook his head and said it again, this time, louder, as if to himself. "Okay."

"Now give me your hand." Gabe extended his arm. Seth let go of the first root, and the second loosened from the dirt. He slid farther into the hole.

"I-I can't," Seth said, once he'd stopped swinging. "Maybe . . . Maybe I should just go on down."

"No," said Gabe, speaking quickly. "He's here. Going down there is what he wanted. He pushed you."

"I fell," Seth insisted.

"Something snuck up behind you," Gabe went on. It wasn't reassuring, but Seth needed to understand. "The stone in the barn wasn't a clue, it was a lure. We're right where he wants us. If we go down there, he'll bury us with him."

"Wh-why would he do that?" Seth said, panting.

"So he has someone to keep playing the game with him!" An instant later, the words rang back at him, each time sounding more and more like the answer the boys had been trying to uncover all along. "There's no time to argue. We've gotta get you out. *Give me your hand!*"

Seth yowled as he pulled himself back toward the mouth of the well. He kept his eyes on Gabe's, as if Gabe could send him strength. Inch by inch he climbed, wincing and groaning, but making enough progress so that eventually, their fingers made contact. Then their palms. Finally, Gabe wrapped his hand around Seth's wrist. Starlight illuminated Seth's face, as he peered into the space up beyond Gabe. Reflected in his friend's eyes, Gabe saw movement. "Watch out!" Seth shouted. "Behind you!"

Too late. Gabe felt himself sliding forward. His chest scraped against the rough rocks. In his struggle to halt his descent, his jacket tore. His skin became slick with sweat or blood. He lost his grip, and Seth fell, swallowed by the dark. A new howl battered his eardrums. Only after a few seconds did Gabe realize the sound was coming from his own mouth.

Someone stood above him, but he couldn't see who or what it was. Something sharp pressed into his back — talons, claws, fingernails — and squeezed. Gabe tried to shout again, this time for help, but he couldn't catch his breath.

He twisted, fighting to turn over, to face the thing that had decided that his life was a prize to be won. The thing had other plans. It pushed Gabe toward the mouth of the well. The hole seemed to expand. The roots brushed at his face. Swinging his arms out, Gabe reached for something to hold on to. There was only weightlessness — a rushing black, which was followed by the certainty that, in a moment, the game would be over. He'd lost.

BENEATH THE CROOKED TREE

GABE OPENED HIS EYES. Walls of darkness surrounded him. He rolled over. Sat up and flinched. His head rung with a dull pain. It felt as though every bone hurt. Tasting blood, he knew he'd bitten the tip of his tongue.

Leaning forward, he stirred up a foul smell of rot from a thick layer of dead leaves. Water trickled nearby. Pieces of dirt and stone rained down from above, spattering his face as he looked up, trying to see how far down he'd fallen, but above, he found only a ceiling of shadow.

"Seth," Gabe whispered. No answer. He listened for movement. His lungs clenched. His skin went numb. The ground seemed to tilt. He clutched at his scalp, trying to steady himself. They'd both fallen into the hole under the altar. No. They'd been pushed. So where the heck was Seth?

Gabe knelt, feeling for wall. The space down here seemed larger than it should have been. But maybe the earth had crumbled away, like in a sinkhole. "Hey!" he cried out. "Anyone up there?" His voice bounced, its clarity like a shock. Gabe stumbled forward and finally made contact with the edge of the cavern — a wall of stone and dirt covered with spongy mosses and fleshy fungi. Or at least that's what Gabe hoped it was.

A slithering sound came from several feet away.

Gabe froze. "Seth?"

"Shh," said a voice.

"Wh-who are you?" Gabe spoke louder this time, trying to sound brave.

"Shh," the voice repeated. "He'll hear you." The voice sounded familiar, and very close.

"Seth, is that you?" Gabe went on. "I don't —" Icy fingers covered his mouth. Gabe yelped, but pressed his lips shut. The other person pushed him to the wall, positioned Gabe's back against it, then pressed into the space beside him. The hand's clammy skin emitted a scented mixture of sweat and, strangely, dried fruit, which reminded Gabe of the inside of Seth's house. He reached up, trying to tug the hand away from his face, but the fingers only clenched more tightly around his jaw.

Heavy feet squished into the mud and muck somewhere just ahead of them. Something was being dragged across the ground. The sound of brittle sticks clattered like toneless wind chimes. Bones? Then a growl tumbled through the darkness. Gabe held his breath, grateful for the stranger's warning. He listened as the footsteps retreated, echoing as if down a tunnel. Just how big was this hole in the ground?

The hand let go, but Gabe did not move. When the sounds were finally gone, the dark rushed in from all sides. He stepped away from the wall, but felt blind, exposed on all sides, so he came back again, too stunned to speak.

"You hit your head pretty hard," said the voice. Male. Maybe around Gabe's age. "It took a while to get through to you."

"I'm sorry," said Gabe as politely as he could, "but I don't —"

The boy's nervous chuckling interrupted him. "I'm the one who should be apologizing. I must have freaked the stuffing out of you." The boy paused, became serious. "But you're not safe here. He's looking for you, and he'll be back soon. We don't have a lot of time."

"Who's looking for me?"

"Mason," said the boy. "Well . . . *the Hunter*. But I refuse to call him that anymore, even though it makes him mad. Really mad."

Gabe trembled. He glanced around, beginning to discern small impressions in the dark. "Where am I?"

"The dungeon of Castle Chicken Guts." He spoke so matter-of-factly that Gabe nodded, as if the boy'd said, *The parking lot of the Dunkin' Donuts out by the highway*. "It was the best I could do under the circumstances. Of course, the towers at Haliath Keep would have been a better bet, but Seth is too far gone. I couldn't reach his thoughts as easily as I reached yours."

The words finally seeped in. "I-I don't understand," said Gabe.

"The Kingdom of Chicken Guts exists in your head," the boy answered plainly. "So I guess you could say that's where we are right now."

"In my head?" Gabe shook his skull. A dull ache blossomed behind his eyes. He pressed his fingers against his temples and winced. "But this feels so real."

"That's the strange thing," said the boy. "It *is* real. I don't have a clue how it works. I've never done this before. Not sure I'd even be able to if it weren't Halloween. Rumor has it that tonight, we're at our strongest. Through the thinnest veil, we can almost fully appear in the world of the living. But it goes both ways. Tonight, you guys can see into our side too."

"*Your* side?"

"The Realm of the Dead sounds so dramatic." The boy sniffed. "Right now, we're standing somewhere in the middle — a kind of borderland in your unconscious."

I'm dreaming, Gabe thought. *I'm at the bottom of the well. I have to wake up. I have to help Seth.* He imagined that somewhere, in the world of the awake, he and Seth were side by side, their bodies twisted, their bones broken.

"Dreaming. Awake. Living. Dead," the boy went on. "It doesn't matter what you call it right now, Gabe. Really, it makes no difference. Mason has had a long time to teach himself to navigate between these states. At this point, it's as easy for him as opening a door. As you've seen, he knows some other pretty awesome tricks. I mean, he was strong enough tonight to snatch your little sister out of your home. And that's not the worst he can do. Or *will* do. I, on the other hand, am still learning the ropes."

Gabe struggled to focus through the darkness. "You're the boy I saw in the barn," he said. "You brought me that stone. You helped me get away from the fire."

"Yes. I did."

"Why?"

"Because I want this to be over as much as you do."

"Can you show me what you look like?" Gabe asked, though he was fairly sure he already knew.

"I'll try," said the boy. "Gotta be quick about it though. Mason's out there, looking for a way in." Gabe wondered where *out there* was. "Your dungeon will only keep him at bay for so long."

A blue glow appeared in the space between them. The boy had extended his hand, and a flicker of what looked like an iridescent flame floated a few inches over his palm. Slowly, the boy brought the light closer to his face.

Gabe gasped. He was staring at someone who looked remarkably like Seth. He was a little bit older, perhaps, but they had the same sharp jawline, the same light hair, the same pointed nose. The boy smiled. "I know he's mentioned me a few times." He reached out for Gabe's hand. But Gabe was too frightened, too shocked to move. "I'm David," said the boy. "Seth's older brother." He clutched Gabe's wrist. The bluish flame joined them together, raced up their arms, across their shoulders, shrouding their bodies with a blinding light until, in a flash of pure white, the room disappeared entirely.

MASON'S TRAP

GABE WAS HIGH ABOVE THE FOREST that separated his grandmother's property from the Hoppers'. Not floating or flying; he simply existed there. Like a low cloud on a windless day. He had a view of the houses and the town and, if he squinted, he could also see the water of the bay off in the distance. The sun was shining. The trees were green. This was another time. Another season. The past or future, Gabe was not sure.

The screen door at the Hoppers' porch slammed shut. A boy raced down the front steps onto the driveway, then turned toward the woods. It was David. He looked furious and terrified. With barely any effort, Gabe swooped down, following David as he crossed into the woods, barreling like a wild animal up the old horse trail, unaware of Gabe's presence. After a few minutes, the boy stopped, hunched over, his hands resting on his knees, struggling to catch his breath.

"You have to leave him alone!" he shouted, as if to the trees. "Take me if you want, but don't touch him. If I'd known what you'd planned, I'd never have —" A rustling sound moved steadily through the woods. David spun, his chest heaving still. His eyes flicked back and forth, trying to pinpoint where the sound was coming from. Someone out there was laughing, that familiar harsh chuckle, the same one that Gabe had heard in the darkness at the edge of his bed.

Grunting, David catapulted himself into the brush, crashing through whips of foliage and lashes of tree limbs. Moments later, he came upon the small hillock. The trunk of a tree rose from the earth and twisted, leaning precariously toward the forest floor, as if it were about to topple over. There was no altar here now. The only stones nearby were the ones that made up the wall beyond the mound.

David froze. A figure stood before him, holding on to the lowest branch of the pathetic tree. A tall, lanky boy, with big hands and long fingers, was dressed in dusty overalls speckled with the brown, dried blood from a long-dead rooster. The boy smiled. His eyes were vacant, amused, curious, like a child who'd just plucked the leg off a grasshopper and was waiting to see what it would do next.

Gabe tried to speak, to warn David to stay away. But he had no voice.

"Mason," David said, direct and calm. The panic he'd displayed minutes earlier was tamped down. Hidden. "See? You *can* be yourself. You don't have to be the monster all the time."

"But if I'm not the monster," said the boy by the tree, his voice plaintive and low, "you won't play the game with me. And I'll be alone again."

"No, you won't. I'm not going anywhere."

"Not true," said the boy. "I heard you tell your brother that you wanted him to stop playing. You think I want you both dead."

"I only said that because . . . you've been a little . . . intense. The Hunter's a fun adversary, but only in the game. It's not so fun for me and Seth if the Hunter is real."

"I'm *real*," said the boy, his voice dropping further to a frightening register.

"Yes, of course," David answered quickly. "And that's why I'm not going anywhere."

The boy was quiet for a moment. Then he shook his head. "You'll grow up. You'll get old. You'll forget."

"I won't forget. I promise."

"People believe they'll be one way, but then they transform. They don't even mean to. I've seen it happen. To everyone. And when you're the one who's forgotten, who's left behind, it hurts." He paused. Shook his head. "You have no idea how much it hurts."

Gabe thought of his grandmother's story — her ruined friendship with him. Of course Mason would have felt abandoned, not only by Leesy, but by his parents, by his horrible aunt and uncle. Being discarded was pretty much all he'd ever known. What had he been willing to do to change that?

"I'll leave your brother alone if you do one thing for me," said Mason.

"What is it?" David asked.

"Come here." When David stayed put, Mason waved him forward blithely. "I want to show you something." David shuddered, then made his way up the shallow slope, crunching dead leaves and fallen sticks, until he stood beside the tree trunk.

Gabe stayed close. He peered at Mason, whose pinkish face was flecked with dirt. A mole marked his cheek just below his left eye. His hair was greasy and unwashed. He blinked and scratched at his arm and bit at a loose piece of skin on his lip. Except for the old blood that had dried onto his clothes, he looked like he could have been one of Gabe's own classmates. As human as anyone.

This boy was no *revenant*, was he?

"What did you want to show me?" David asked, his voice now shrunken.

"I never told you about what happened to me," Mason said. "Aren't you curious about how I got this way?"

This way? Did he mean dead?

David paused. "You'll leave Seth alone if I say yes." It wasn't a question.

Mason pursed his lips and raised an eyebrow. With a smirk, he nodded.

"Okay, then," David answered. "Yes."

They were standing several feet from the base of the tree. Mason simply pointed at the ground. David looked down, confused. But Gabe knew what he was meant to see. There was no dirt beneath David's boots, only a couple of wooden planks. David glanced back up at Mason, but Mason was no longer there.

In his place stood the monster. The creature from Grandmother Elyse's drawing. A mass of muscle and bone, of pale, cracked, and bleeding hide. The thing smiled hideously. It lifted one immense foot and brought it down hard. The planks shattered. David fell. He twisted his body as he realized what was happening, reaching for the low tree trunk, but he wasn't fast enough. He screamed as he fell.

In a blink, Mason — the Hunter — disappeared too.

Gabe could only watch. A sickening thump belched forth from the hole. Seconds later came a shriek that went on and on. He tried to cover his ears, to block out the sound, but he had no body, no ears to cover. Then he remembered he could follow David down into the earth. He hesitated before descending the shaft; this time, he was aware of the nightmare he would encounter below.

David lay on the wet ground. He struggled to stand, but he couldn't move his legs. Gabe could feel David's broken bones as if they were his own. His pain was immense, worse than anything he'd ever imagined. David breathed deeply, then glanced around. There was just enough light in the cramped space to see he'd landed on something, canvas or denim that had nearly rotten through. He clutched at what felt like a metal rivet — the kind of clasp you'd find on a pair of jeans. Or overalls. And inside the clothing were long, sticklike objects. Running his fingers blindly over the jumble of decayed things, he understood what Mason had wanted to show him. Bones. David had landed atop the boy's skeleton. "Help!" he cried out, through the agony in his chest. "Mom! Seth!"

"Shh," said a voice in the darkness. David froze. A sticky mix of tears and blood and mucus leaked down his face. His arm hurt too much to lift from his side and wipe it clean.

"Why did you do this to me?" David asked. "I promised I wouldn't leave."

Chuckling. "Now I know it's a promise you'll keep." A scuttling sound rushed up the well, and David knew he was alone again.

Someone would come, he promised himself. His thoughts began to race. A rescue team would find him. There'd be a television crew. There always was. Tomorrow at this time, he'd be lying in bed with a story to tell. Everyone would know his name. People would pay him just to show up places. He'd write a book about how he survived. Maybe he'd get rich. This fall could end up being a very good thing, he told himself.

"Hello down there." A face appeared at the mouth of the hole, barely distinguishable through the network of tree roots. Still, David knew it was Mason. His heart turned to stone, his blood to ice. His bones may as well have been glass. Mason sounded cold, purposeful, resigned. "I'm up here."

"I know that," David whispered.

"Good. Because *this* is what I wanted to show you." Mason, dressed in his phantom overalls, stared down at him for a few seconds. David saw that he was holding an object out over the opening, but he couldn't tell what it was. "On the night that I was unlucky enough to find this pit," he said, sounding almost robotic, "I'd done something really bad. But I'd done it to hurt a nasty person, so I felt kind of good. I don't know if God punished me for taking pleasure in my sin, but I ended up where you are now. I too called for help. I screamed and shouted over the rain and thunder, hoping that someone would hear me. There was this girl who lived up the hill. A friend. At the time, I wished that she'd been . . ." He paused, sounding for a moment like he could actually feel something other than anger. "But she wasn't . . . And she didn't . . .

"Someone else heard me instead. My aunt Verna came out here with a flashlight. She looked down at me just like I'm looking down at you. Then she snatched up a rock from one of the stone walls nearby, like the one I'm holding in my hands now. And she raised it over the mouth of this hole. And she stared at me for several seconds, full of spit and hate and spoiled blood. And I stared back, feeling the same thing. Then she let go of the rock. And it fell, just like I'd fallen several minutes earlier. Just like you've fallen today. My aunt's rock came at me quickly, just like this rock will do when I let go of it." The boy paused. "In a moment." Then he smiled sadly and, with a wistful look, he tilted his head. "Are you ready?"

David shouted, struggling to raise his arms over his head. "No, Mason. Please! Don't."

"But *this* is what I wanted to show you," the boy whispered, his voice somehow echoing in David's ear. "And you said yes."

"I changed my mind. I don't want to see."

"Don't worry. Now, we'll have all the time in the world for our game. You'll be the good guy. I'll be bad."

And with that, Mason let go.

INSTRUCTIONS

GABE CLOSED HIS EYES. He couldn't watch. He waited for the horrific crunching sound to burst his eardrums, for a warmth to splash at his ankles. Neither came.

He opened his eyes as David released his hand. The blue flame that hovered in the poor boy's palm diminished to the size of a small coin. They were back in the dungeon of Castle Chicken Guts. Wherever that was.

"I'm sorry," Gabe whispered. "I don't know what to say. You didn't deserve to die like that." He thought of Mason too, of his aunt discovering him at the bottom of the well on that stormy night and killing him simply because he'd slaughtered her rooster. Well, that and the fact that she was probably insane. "No one does."

David nodded. "When I had gone away from my body, I watched Mason cover the hole with new boards." He spoke quickly now, rushed. "Then he stacked stones on top. Organized properly, the old tree's roots supported the weight. Mason needed to hide what was left of me from the search parties that scoured the woods over the next few days. If they located me, he knew they'd take me away from him. Bury me properly. Put me 'to rest.' His ploy worked. When they came through, the people thought the stones were just part of another ruined wall. Mason laughed at me when I tried to call out to them. I didn't yet know how to be heard."

"Why didn't *you* take the stones away? Let the people find you?"

"At first, I didn't know how to do that either. When I refused to play Mason's game, he refused to teach me what he knew about being, you know, dead. And by the time I figured out how to direct enough energy to move objects like these stones, Mason had gotten to Seth. Manipulated him into rediscovering the old game. And Seth had talked you into joining him."

"My grandmother's figurine," Gabe muttered, remembering. "The black stone that you and Seth stole. It was you who returned it to the library, wasn't it?"

"I never should have taken it in the first place." David sighed. "I brought it back there, thinking it might give you a clue about what had happened to me. I wish I could have done more to communicate, but I was still weak. I mean, the day you guys tried to dismantle the 'altar,' it took all my strength to whisper at you to stop. I was scared that if you uncovered the old well, you'd end up where I did." He scoffed. "I was right. Tonight, when I realized that Mason had taken your sister, I would have done anything to save her myself. But he stood guard in the barn. Waiting for you. There was no way I could get by him, so I came up with a different plan."

"The rock," Gabe said. "The one you dropped at my feet in the barn. The one I used to smash open the door."

"A clue." David nodded. "To lead you to the well."

"But why, if you wanted us to stay away?"

"Because Mason's changed into something he can't control. He believes he *is* the Hunter. Being down there, alone for all those years, well, conditions were perfect for his anger to boil, become molten. I don't think he even meant to do it, but somehow, he turned himself into that monster."

"A revenant," Gabe whispered.

"After you've been hurt over and over, maybe it's easier to become the villain."

"Make people fear you," Gabe said, thinking of Seth, of lunch periods, of Puppet Boys, "so you can control them."

"I thought that tonight might be my only chance to warn you. The old well needed to be found, our bones buried. It's the only way." A soft rumbling shook the ground. David closed his hand, extinguishing the flame. "He's here," he whispered.

David clasped Gabe's shoulder and leaned close. "Mason is going to ask you to join him. He knows that to keep you, he needs your consent, otherwise he's stuck again with someone who will not be his toy. Like me. You must refuse, no matter what he promises. You know what happens if you say yes to him. Right?" Something knocked against the wall. Dirt tumbled to the floor from all around them. "*Do you understand?*"

Gabe felt himself trembling. "Yeah. I understand."

"But most important," David whispered, his voice barely audible, "you have to get out of the hole. I'm sorry I led you here, but you and Seth were the only ones who could see the truth. If you don't escape, Mason will find someone else to play with. Someone else to haunt. To hunt. He's already visited a bunch of other kids here in Slade. He's got his eyes set on your friend Mazzy especially." David paused, took a deep breath, then added, "Tell my brother and my mom that I love them . . . and that I'm sor —"

The earth shattered. Clods of dirt exploded into the room. Gabe screamed, fell back, landed on his side. A wide gap had opened in the wall. Hazy light filtered through a cloud of dust, revealing a massive silhouette standing in the shadows. Two flecks of familiar blue flame glowed where the head appeared to be, staring into the room with fierce glee. David was a mere outline now, a foggy figure fallen beside the beast. "Run!" he cried. With a twist of his forearm, the Hunter knocked him away.

David was gone. Shoved out of Gabe's mind somehow. He was alone with the Hunter now, in the dungeon he'd invented, in a peculiar darkness that only he knew.

"Wake up," Gabe said to himself. He slapped his own cheek. Hard. It stung the same way it would have if he'd been conscious and aware. Panicked, Gabe worried that if his body felt pain here, maybe it could die here too.

The Hunter stepped toward him. In the slight glow of its eyes, Gabe noticed its lips part. A grin. "I found you," a voice rumbled so deeply, the sound was like a quake, like continents shifting. Gabe collapsed, every inch of himself aching. He struggled to lift his head and stare into the eyes of the massive thing that had once been a boy named Mason Arngrim. "Let's play."

"N-no," Gabe said, forcing his sore jaw to move. "I want you to leave us alone."

The creature's mouth spread wider. The Hunter chuckled, then reached across its broad torso for the bow and arrows strapped at its shoulder, placed the arrow's notch against the string, pulled the bow taut until it squealed, then directed it at Gabe's forehead.

"*WAKE! UP!*" Gabe screamed.

THE SHADOWS WAVERED. The room went all staticlike. The world shifted, flickered, changed channels.

Gabe lay on his side at the bottom of the well, his eyes open, conscious. Away from the Hunter. Away from Mason and the question that David had assured him was coming: yes or no?

He gasped, then choked and ended up coughing for several seconds. His body no longer throbbed in agony like it had in the dungeon. Now he could pinpoint the pain. His elbow. His shoulder. He touched his forehead. His fingers located a tender lump above his right eye. He imagined he looked like a corpse. But he was alive. He would heal.

A tunnel of stone and dirt rose up in a cylindrical shape. A hint of pale light passed through the thick web of roots near the opening at the top. Dawn had arrived. He'd spent the night down here.

Gabe thought of his family. They must be sick with worry. But that was a good thing. It meant they were looking for him. Any moment now, they'd peer down at him. Call his out his name. Tell him they love him and assure him that in no time he'd be safe and sound. And once he was in their arms, the scolding would begin. He would welcome it. He couldn't wait for his mother and father to yell at him.

He sat up. Felt around. The ground was damp. He imagined the skeletons layered beneath him, but the thought of dead bodies was only slightly terrifying. Right now, he needed to be sure that there was another living boy in this pit. His friend. Seth Hopper.

Gabe touched damp cloth only inches away. He clutched a pair of soaked jeans. Inside, Seth's leg felt warm. Rising awkwardly to his knees, Gabe leaned forward. In the faint light, Seth's face appeared to be scraped up, covered in mud and filth. His eyes were closed. Gabe placed a hand on his chest. A heartbeat! He yelped with relief. "Hey! Seth! Wake up." He rubbed at Seth's sternum, trying to rouse him. "Seth," he said again louder. "Can you hear me?" Seth's lips parted, and he released a soft moan. "We're okay. We had an accident. We fell. Someone's coming to help."

Seth's eyelids fluttered open. He looked directly at Gabe. "Gabe?" he mumbled. Then his eyes grew wide. "Where is he?" he whispered a bit more clearly. "Did we find the body?"

Then Gabe remembered. Seth didn't yet know that his brother was dead. Should he tell him now or wait until they were aboveground? What if he was wrong? What if none of the vision had been real? "Yes," he answered. "He's here." It was just vague enough to be true.

"Good," Seth said. "Then we won."

Gabe felt his throat closing. If he looked at Seth any longer, he'd start crying. And this was no time to cry. He struggled to stand in the narrow space, trying not to step on anything *fragile*. "We haven't won anything 'til we're outta here," Gabe said, glancing upward.

"I don't know if I can get up," said Seth.

"Then just stay where you are." Gabe called out for help, his voice resounding for several seconds afterward. "Someone *must* have heard that," he said. He tried again. And again. Seth lay at his feet and merely listened. After several minutes, Gabe grew tired. He slumped against the wall. A sharp edge of rock poked into his back, and he flinched.

The light continued to grow from above. The stone walls were black and slick with slime and moss. Some parts were cracked and crumbling. The base of the well was littered with fallen rocks and leaves and a few other obscured things Gabe didn't care to think about. The space was tight, but not tight enough for Gabe to reach out and touch both sides.

Scaling the wall would be difficult but maybe not impossible. He'd been pretty good at the rope climb in gym class last year. If he could find stones that stuck out from the wall like the one he'd just leaned against, he might be able to reach the root system above. From there, he was almost certain he could drag himself to freedom.

He felt for the sharp rock by his shoulder, then carefully, he pushed on it, adding more and more weight, testing its bearing. The stone shifted, slipped out, and crashed onto the floor, just missing Seth's hand.

Seth flinched, turning his body away, but he had barely moved before crying out in agony.

"Sorry!" Gabe said. "I thought I might —" Some of the other rocks slid out too, hitting the ground. *Thud, thud, thud.* "There goes that idea."

"I hear something," said Seth.

"It was me," said Gabe, indicating the rocky mess at his feet.

"No. Something else. Someone's coming."

Gabe listened. Sure enough, footsteps crunched through the forest above. He nearly called out again, but Seth grabbed his ankle. When he looked down, Seth shook his head. And when the voice shouted out to them, Gabe felt numb. "Hello down there," Mason said with a chuckle.

FROM BELOW

"G-GET OUT OF HERE," Seth stammered, staring up at the well's mouth. Gabe crouched low and shushed him.

A wind rustled impossibly into the shaft, whipping leaves and dirt into a blinding frenzy, carrying with it laughter, delight, the frightening sound of decided ignorance. Then it stopped. Sticks and stones rained down on the two shuddering boys.

"*Get out of here?*" The voice was now close by, at the bottom of the well. Strangely, it did not echo. "That's your answer?" Gabe searched every shadow for movement, but saw only the stillness of the black stone. "That's not something a winner would say. And that's what you are, right, Wraithen? A winner?" Seth grunted. Angry that he could not move. Could not fight. "*We won,*" said Mason, mimicking Seth. "Your words, Cousin." His laughter died, and he added. "I disagree though. We are only just beginning. Don't you think so, Meatpie?"

"N-no," Gabe said, remembering David's warning, wondering now if no was the only answer safe to give.

"What I think I have here," said Mason, "are a couple of *losers*. Losers at school. Losers with your little friends. Losers at *living*. 'Get out of here'?" He chuckled again. "If you want to win, you have to keep playing the game."

"Say no, Seth," Gabe whispered. "Tell him no."

"Ah-ah," said Mason. "No cheating. Everyone gets to decide for himself. Those are the rules."

"There *are* no rules," said Gabe, "and you know it. Even if there were, you'd probably break them anyway."

"Who told you that?" Mason asked, sounding amused. "Was it David?"

Gabe held his breath. Seth glanced up at him, confused.

"David told you about me breaking rules? Oh, I'm sure I interrupted some sort of private conversation back in your quaint little dungeon."

"What's he talking about?" Seth whispered.

"Oh, that's right," said Mason. "Wraithen's dead brother came to rescue Meatpie but didn't invite Wraithen to join."

"David's dead?" Seth's voice was high-pitched and shaky.

"And while you were sleeping, dear boy," Mason's voice dripped with venom, "your brother's ghost paid your friend a visit. They shared secrets. And why do you think that was?"

"It's not like that," Gabe blurted out. "Mason's twisting the truth."

"Doesn't he love his little brother?"

"David's dead?" Seth repeated. He managed to prop himself up against the stones at his back.

"I had some sort of . . . vision," said Gabe. "A dream. In it, I saw the past. David fell down here. Mason tricked him, made sure he never got back out. I was going to tell you about it, I swear."

Seth dug his fingers into the dirt beneath him, as if searching for bones. "I don't understand." He squeezed his eyes shut.

Laughter swirled around them, growing louder like a lasso tightening.

"I don't either," said Gabe. "In my dream, David told me that you were too far away. He said that Mason would come for us. That he'd ask us to join him. To play the game. He made me promise to say no. You too, Seth. If we don't, Mason will kill us. He'll be the Hunter, and we'll be the Robber Princes. Like, forever."

"When you put it like that, who would say yes?" Mason chortled. "No, no. David had it wrong. What I'm offering is much

more than that. An opportunity to start over. Think about it."
Mason sounded like an excited little boy. A Peter Pan. Unable to
grow up. "It only hurts a little. For that small price, you two can be
royalty. Heroes. When you're in Howler's Notch, you'll live in castles as big as you can imagine! You'll be free! No one will call you
names. No one will threaten you. Or hit you. Or lock you away. Or
burn everything you've ever loved . . . Well, no one besides *me*, of
course. Hee hee. We'll be worthy foes. Cats and mice. Hunters
and hunted. Just like before. Some days you'll win. Other days . . .
I'll eat you for supper." His voice lowered. The Hunter's growl
momentarily enveloped them, tasted their skin with a rough
tongue. "But the important thing is," Mason went on, a boy again,
"we can be friends. True friends. Admit it. Haven't the past few
months been the most exciting of your life?"

"No," said Gabe. "It hasn't been fun. It's been scary. You've
hurt people. Lots of people, in lots of different ways. You know,
after my grandmother told me your story, I felt bad for you.
Horrible, in fact." He spoke to the air, as if that was what Mason
was made of. "Because of what you'd been through, I didn't even
mind so much that you chopped off that rooster's head." Gabe
shuddered. "But you can't do this to us. To anyone." His voice
shook as it rose. "You obviously haven't known what it's like to feel
human for a very long time, but that still doesn't make you a monster, so stop acting like one. This isn't a game. We aren't your
puppets." He slapped the rock wall, making an exclamation point.
"You have to let us go! We said no!"

The well was silent. No sounds. Not even the ones they'd
heard earlier — the birds chirping, a trickle of water, the breeze
through the faraway branches of the crooked tree. Gabe released a
deep breath he hadn't even realized he'd been holding.

Mason was gone.

"Wait," said Seth. Wide-eyed, Gabe stared down at his friend.

When he tried to speak, nothing came out. He shook his head, begging Seth to stop talking, but Seth wasn't looking at him. With his eyes closed, he added, "I want to see my brother again." His tears welled, then rolled slowly down his cheeks. "So yes, Mason. I'll come with you."

The whole world seemed to sigh. Gabe felt the blood drain from his face. He reached for the wall. The stones were trembling. The earth began to shake. Gabe stared at Seth and shook his head.

"What did you do?" he asked.

"I'm sorry," Seth whispered, then opened his eyes

A great cracking sound erupted several feet above. Gabe watched as one huge stone slowly crept out from its ancient bed, rocking back and forth, back and forth. Farther and farther away from the wall. He imagined Mason's hands wrapped around it, pulling as hard as he could.

"David!" Gabe called out helplessly. "Don't let him do this!"

But the stone continued to move. And the pieces of the wall surrounding it began to follow. Several smaller rocks tumbled out, spilling onto Seth's face below. Gabe knelt beside him, struggling to pull him away from the spot where the wall was caving in. He grabbed at Seth's sweatshirt, but it slipped through his fingers. Seth seemed to be stuck in the mud and the leaves. Or maybe something else was holding him in place, something rising up from below, something with rotting skin and yellowed, split fingernails.

Another crack rang out. Gabe glanced up. An avalanche of rock poured down. He leapt forward, covering Seth's body with his own. He felt warm. Safe. Protected. But Seth squirmed, tried to cry out, his voice muffled by Gabe's torn coat.

Gabe didn't notice. He didn't care. For one brief moment, before the darkness behind his eyelids turned entirely to white, he realized something that made him wish he could laugh. Mason had been right. It only hurt a little.

Dead Boys

In the days that followed, a chill settled upon Slade. Those who woke before sunrise were greeted with lawns glazed in silver. Frost had come late this year. The leaves had begun to fall in earnest. By the end of the week, there would be few trees left able to hold on to their colorful, precarious gems. Yet, the ground itself still contained some of the warmth of the previous season.

The men who worked at Evergreen Cemetery were pleased about this. It was easier to dig holes.

Mazzy Lerman had never been to a funeral. Her grandfather had passed away when she was a baby, but that didn't really count. She remembered nothing of it. The Wednesday morning after Halloween, she stood with a large group at the side of a deep hole in Evergreen Cemetery. The air was brisk, the sky was perfectly clear. A priest was speaking, but Mazzy wasn't paying attention. She couldn't stop thinking that at any moment she'd wake up. Or the movie would end. Or she'd reach the last page in a book she'd been reading and find the final words: *The End*. Then she'd put the book back on the shelf, and call her friends and ask if they wanted to hang out. But this story just kept going and going all around her. And now they were putting a boy in the ground.

Returning from the emergency room that night, Mazzy and her mother found their phone ringing as soon as they had stepped into the house. Judging by the look on her mother's face when she answered, Mazzy could tell immediately that something even worse had happened. "I haven't seen them," Mrs. Lerman said to the person on the other end of the line. "We just got home. . . ." Mazzy reluctantly took the receiver. A voice on the other end introduced himself. A police officer. He asked if she'd seen Gabriel Ashe or Seth Hopper. "Not for a few hours. Not since we left the high school." He asked if she had any idea where they might be. Mazzy calmly answered, "The woods." She glanced at her mother, who glared back at her. She thought about everything the boys had shared with her, the game, their story, the Hunter, as well as the conclusion they'd reached about the need to find Mason Arngrim's body. Then it struck her. "There's a crooked tree," she added. "I'm not sure where exactly. I think they might have been searching for some sort of pile of rocks around there."

At Evergreen, she wiped wetness from her cheeks, then dried her palms on her black pants. Her mother tapped her shoulder, then shook her head. *Inappropriate*, she mouthed. Mazzy sighed, crossed her arms. Most of the other congregants were crying too, holding tissues, dabbing at their eyes. Across the way, Felicia stood with her parents. Her face was bone dry, apparently made of stone. Malcolm and Ingrid were beside her.

Felicia flicked her gaze toward Mazzy. The girls stared at each other expressionlessly, unwilling to concede to a display of emotion. To do so might hint at blame. Or guilt.

The Ashes were at the head of the casket, beside the priest. Gabe's parents stood frozen, staring into the hole in the ground, as if under a spell. His grandmother cradled Miri, who squirmed, unaware of the meaning of this gathering. Mazzy wished she might catch their attention, but she knew to do so would be to risk losing her already paper-thin composure.

Someone shifted to the side and revealed Seth Hopper standing several feet back. When he glimpsed Mazzy looking at him, he quickly ducked away again. So he'd finally gotten out of the hospital. Mrs. Hopper was beside him. She looked better than the last time Mazzy'd seen her — she stood up straight and the dark circles around her eyes had diminished.

People were saying that the Hoppers were holding a service for David tomorrow afternoon.

Mason Arngrim wouldn't be buried until the following weekend, a cost the town council decided to absorb since he had no immediate family. Mazzy could only pray that the hauntings, or whatever they'd been, were over for now. She'd feel a lot better once they put Mason in the ground. *Properly* this time. Whatever that meant.

In Memory Of . . .

THE LAST FEW DAYS OF NOVEMBER were disappearing like magic.

Sharon Hopper, as if having recently stumbled out of a thick fog, scoured the grime from her kitchen and bathroom and emptied the rest of her house of the clutter. Several times, as if in halfhearted apology, she commented to her son that she could not believe she'd allowed it to get so bad.

For Thanksgiving, she'd cooked an enormous turkey for the two of them, but Seth barely ate any of it. Later, he had a difficult time remembering the holiday at all. In fact, the weeks after Halloween were a blur. There'd been doctors' appointments. Crutches. Casts. Braces. Physical therapy. And pain. Lots and lots of pain. School for the time being was out of the question.

Though it was agonizing for Sharon to imagine what both of her sons had been through — were going through still — learning David's fate was like a salve that stung as it healed.

By mid-December, Sharon was worried that she and Seth had switched places, emotionally at least. While she'd found another restaurant job, her son had taken to sleeping half the day. He barely responded when she asked him questions about how he was feeling and never offered comments on his own. She had no idea what would happen if she forced him to be around others while in this state. But, according to Mr. Drover, Seth had already missed enough school that year. And unless she wished him to repeat the year, he needed to go back.

When Seth limped into homeroom on the first day back, his classmates greeted him with applause. He didn't know what to do.

All of these people who, for the past few years, had treated him like he was a monster were now cheering for him. He nearly turned around and ran down the hall, out the front entrance, and all the way home. Sensing his unease, the teacher took his arm, walked him to his desk, and helped him to his seat.

"Welcome back," she whispered in his ear. At that, Seth nearly threw up. How could he ever feel welcome here, when he wasn't the one who deserved to *be* back?

Lunch period was the most difficult. Seth tried to keep to himself — as he'd learned to do several years earlier — even though nearly all eyes followed him. Get up to throw away his brown bag? Knock over his juice box? Sneeze? Everything seemed to matter to these people. He didn't know whether they watched him because they were planning to somehow ruin him again. Or if they wanted to ask him what had really happened down in that hole in the woods. Neither choice was appealing.

He'd been purposely vague when the detectives had questioned him — and they'd had *so many questions*. He lied and claimed he didn't remember a thing. When he closed his eyes at night, he heard the conversation between Gabe and David that must have occurred in the dreamlike dungeon version of Castle Chicken Guts that Mason had mentioned down in the well. Listening to David's plea — *Tell my brother and my mom that I love them* — always woke him up, his chest tight with anxiety. He didn't know how he remembered this, or why, or even if the dream had simply come from his own imagination. He liked to think that maybe he hadn't been so far "gone" as David had said, that maybe he'd been right there with them.

Since he'd switched lunch periods over a month earlier, Felicia and her group were now in constant view from across the room. Once, she'd even waved him over. After that, he sat with his back to them.

Mazzy was a different story. When she approached in the hallways, inviting him to get together, to play catch, ride bikes, watch a video, Seth told her no, but secretly he was happy that she continued to ask.

In the evenings Seth threw himself into his homework. Every now and again, hunched over his desk, he thought he saw someone watching him from outside his bedroom window. Shaking off goose bumps, he'd reach for the curtains to block out the night and get back to work.

Life continued on in this way. By the end of the school year, the other kids seemed to have lost interest in him. He supposed that once they figured out he wasn't going to be sharing his secrets, he became less interesting again. Still, according to them, Seth Hopper was the Hero of Slade, a moniker that provided protection against any other sort of name-calling. That was enough for him.

The next summer, Seth found a job at a roadside vegetable stand. He rode his bike there every day. One afternoon Mrs. Ashe, Gabe's grandmother, approached the counter searching for fresh strawberries. Seth hid, emerging only after his coworker, a college student on break, completed the transaction. He'd managed to avoid the Ashes for months. They'd visited in the aftermath of the accident but hadn't been by in a long time. Seth had nothing against them — how could he? — Mrs. Ashe had insisted on paying for all his medical bills. But his secret guilt was like a heavy stone on his tongue.

That September, Seth moved up to the high school with the rest of the ninth-grade class. Whenever he passed Felicia Nielsen, she looked like she'd forgotten what had happened here the previous year. He couldn't help but wonder if walking these new halls was as difficult for her as it was for him. He'd heard that she'd joined the school newspaper, the Latin club, the Young Republicans group, and the homecoming committee. Sounded like she was trying to keep herself busy.

Leaves once again fell from the trees, and the events of the previous year replayed in his mind. With October's end swiftly approaching, Seth found himself waking in the night, his heart pounding. Bad memories lived in nearly every acre of the town — bus rides to and from school, the blackened ground where the old barn had once stood, the stone walls that wound through the woods. Slade had never before looked so threatening, but it was a date that he feared the most.

Seth had no idea how he'd get through this next Halloween. So when Mazzy asked him to spend it with her at her house handing out candy to the trick-or-treaters, he surprised himself by saying yes.

He asked his mother for a ride. Later, as he waited for Mazzy to answer her door, he felt dizzy. That feeling of guilt crept up on him again. But then the doorknob turned, and she greeted him with a warm smile. If only she knew the truth.

A steady stream of ghosts and ghouls, wizards and princesses knocked on the Lermans' front door. Over the next hour, he commented easily enough on the cuteness of one costume or the next. When the foot traffic slowed down, Mazzy gestured for him to follow her into the living room.

"I have a surprise," she said, plopping down on the couch. She picked up the remote and turned on the television. "I recorded this after school, but I didn't get a chance to watch yet. I hope you haven't seen it either."

"What is it?" Seth asked, sinking into a soft, deep chair.

On the screen, a strange animated clip began to play. Colors swirled, odd creatures grinned and danced, accompanied by music that was at once cheerful and sad. It seemed to be the opening to one of those weird, funny shows from that cable channel for kids. The title flashed as the music crested. *MONSTER TALK*. Seth had never heard of it. Then, like a sharp poke in the ribs, a coda appeared. *Created by Glen Ashe*. Seth released a small gasp.

They watched the show that Gabe's dad had been working on the year before. Milton Monster was the star — a fuzzy version of a late-night television host. And his first guest just happened to be the famous illustrator Elyse Ashe. She bantered with the puppet, laughing at his jokes, answering questions. She revealed that her latest project was designing a new production of *The Magic Flute*, which was opening in December at the Brooklyn Academy of Music in New York City.

When the program had ended, Mazzy asked, "What did you think?"

"I liked it," Seth said softly. "I thought it was good."

"We should try to get tickets for *The Magic Flute*," Mazzy suggested with enthusiasm. "Take a trip to New York." When Seth simply nodded, she added, "It was weird seeing Gabe's grandmother up there, wasn't it?"

"A little. But she looked . . . happy."

Mazzy was quiet for a moment. "I hope she is," she said seriously. Out on the street, some kids ran by, playfully shouting out, "Happy Halloween!"

"If *she* can be," Mazzy continued, "after everything that's happened, then maybe we can be too."

A few days later, Seth came home from the bus stop to find his house empty, his mother still at work. He made himself a snack of crackers and peanut butter, and decided right then to pay Mrs. Ashe a visit.

For the first time in a year, Seth wandered up the horse trail and into the woods between their houses. His heart raced as memories of Howler's Notch appeared all around him. But he pushed them away, concentrating on the path so that he wouldn't trip over a rock or a tree root. He emerged at the bottom of the grassy meadow that led up to the mansion. Hiking up it, he cringed, remembering the nighttime journeys he'd taken with his brother. He went around the side of the building to the front door, pulled the solid brass knocker, then let it go. It hit against the worn wood with a resounding crack. A few seconds later, he heard footsteps approaching.

The door swung open. "Seth," said Elyse, surprised. Seconds ticked by. He was about to turn and run when she added, "Come in. I just put on a kettle of water. Would you like some tea?"

With his shoulders hunched, he stepped across the threshold.

"The house is quiet now that Glen and Dolores moved to Boston to be closer to the studio," she said, leading him down the hallway toward the living room. "Did you see the show?"

Seth nodded. She directed him to sit. A few minutes later, she returned with a small tray and two steaming mugs. Before she could even place them on the coffee table, Seth blurted out, "Gabe saved my life." Elyse froze, and Seth blushed. "I'm sorry," he added.

Mrs. Ashe smiled. "What are you sorry for?" She handed him a mug and sat beside him.

"If it weren't for me . . . he'd still be here."

"Don't say that. There's nothing further from the truth."

"You don't understand."

"I understand perfectly well." She glared at him. "Don't do that to yourself. Trust me. It's not a good path to go down."

"I don't care if it's good or not," Seth answered. "I just needed you to know the truth."

"Okay, then," she said. "I suppose if it weren't for *me*, Gabe would still be here too. I'm the one who moved into this house. I'm the one who invited his parents to come when they needed a place to stay. Or better yet, if it weren't for Gabe's dad, Gabe would still be here. He was the one whose workshop caught on fire. Better yet, if he'd never built puppets, none of this would have ever happened. But wait, if it weren't for Jim Henson, Gabe would still be here. Mr. Henson gave my son the brilliant idea to become an artist. I guess we should blame him too."

Seth didn't know what to say. It seemed like she didn't want to hear the truth. It had been a mistake coming here. He sipped the hot drink and stared at the floor.

"If Gabriel saved your life, then he thought you were worth it. And you know what you can do for him in return?" She didn't wait for an answer. "You can be thankful."

Seth sat silently, considering her advice.

"Wait here," she said, and stood. "I have something for you." She disappeared through the doorway and down the hall. Half a minute later, she returned, clutching a small object in her hand. She placed it on the table in front of him. It was a figure carved from black stone — the one that David had stolen from her that first night. The one Gabe had noticed sitting in David's bedroom. "I want you to take this."

"Wh-why?"

"You *know* why," she said. Elyse stared into his eyes. Seth felt his heart stop. "Take it and go." She paused, then added, "But come back soon. It gets lonely on this hill. Bring your mother. I'll make cookies. What do you say?"

It was too dark now to go back through the woods, so Seth made his way down Temple House's long driveway. On the street, whenever a car's headlights approached, he stepped onto the curb. Patting the lump in his coat pocket, he thought about what Mrs. Ashe had said. *Be thankful.* He hadn't realized until now that he really was. In spite of everything, he was.

When he turned into his own driveway, he saw the porch light on, spilling its orange glow out into the yard. His mom was home. He climbed the front steps and opened the door. The smell of spaghetti sauce drifted toward him. "Hello?" he called out.

"Dinner's almost ready," his mom answered from the kitchen. "Go wash up."

He strolled down the hall toward his bedroom, but when he got to David's old bedroom door, he stopped. Reaching into his pocket, he stepped inside. Light from the hall spilled across the floor. He pulled out the figurine, felt the weight of it, then placed it on top of David's old bureau. He stared at it for a moment, imagining its incredible journey. "Mrs. Ashe gave this back to me," he said quietly, thinking of his brother. "I thought you might want it."

He almost expected a response, to see the figurine topple over, to feel a cold touch on the back of his neck. But nothing happened. He stood alone in his brother's bedroom for a moment more, then turned toward the hall and closed the door quietly behind him. In his own room, he took off his coat and hung it on the back of his desk chair.

He was so distracted by the aroma coming from the kitchen, that when he passed by David's door, he didn't notice it had opened again. Nor did he hear the hush of a whisper from the shadows just inside.

ACKNOWLEDGMENTS

Thank you to everyone who helped me work through this story. The team at Scholastic, including Rachael Hicks, Stacey Peltz, Jackie Hornberger, Chris Stengel, and Jana Haussmann, as always, has been fantastic. *Grazie* especially to Nick Eliopulos, David Levithan, Barry Goldblatt, Tricia Ready, Libba Bray, Robin Wasserman, Daniel Villela, Paul Sireci, Amanda Walsh, Bruce Roe. And of course to Maria Giella-Poblocki; my grandmother Wanda; my mom, Gail; my dad, John; my brother, Brendan; my sister, Emily; my friends at Red Horse; and especially to the bloggers, authors, and readers who continue to reach out and remind me why I like to do this crazy thing in the first place.

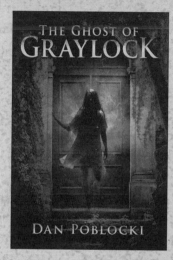

THE FERRY DEPARTED from Haggspoint Harbor into the still waters of the bay early Friday morning, two days before the wedding. A group of nine travelers huddled at the bow of the boat, wrapped in layers of cardigans and shawls and cotton scarves, clutching the iron railing as a salty breeze tousled their hair. Their luggage was piled on several wide wooden benches behind them. They sipped steaming cups of coffee, tea, and hot chocolate, though the fresh air was more bracing than the caffeine.

Despite the chill in the September air and the ocean spray that dampened their skin, it was a beautiful morning. The forecast had called for sunny skies — a perfect weekend for a wedding — so no one on the boat had any notion of the storm that would rise up later that evening. The ferry glided smoothly past the jagged rocks of the coastline. Tall pine trees stretched up from the land, packed tightly together. A bald eagle screeched. Several in the group oohed and aahed in surprise, pointing toward the bird's nest perched atop a tall barren trunk, unaware that by the next morning, the nest would be gone, taken out by the torrential rains and the gusts of wind that would also impede electricity, communication, and travel between the mainland and the many islands off the coast.

Behind the wheel, up on the bridge, the ferry captain stared into the peach haze of sunrise, setting a southeasterly course, steering as best as he could around the hundreds of lobster buoys that speckled the surface of the bay like colorful pieces of candy. The captain was a grizzled-looking but jovial man. His one crew member, his eighteen-year-old grandson, was hiding in the cabin below, reading a comic book, waiting to dock at the next wharf. The *Sea Witch* wasn't nearly as large as the ferries that delivered mail and sundries to the islands closest to the coast, but it was a good size for a private party like this one. Those other ships never journeyed out to the farther islands, especially islands with a single, extravagant home like the one on Stone's Throw Island, where he was now headed, completely unaware that the *Sea Witch* would be gone tomorrow, wrecked on a shoal off Haggspoint. If he'd suspected that a third of his current passengers would never set foot on the mainland again, he'd have turned the boat around immediately.

The wedding planner, a bubbly and bubble-shaped woman named Margo Lintel, had arranged this ride, as well as several more throughout the weekend. Margo stepped away from the small crowd and sat perched on the edge of a bench, disguising her clenched anxiety behind her businesslike face. She scanned her notebook, checking off completed tasks and writing down new ones. So far everything was going perfectly, but there was still a lot to do. She would not function half as well if not for her assistant — a young, bearded, and bespectacled man with narrow shoulders and a prominent gut — Gregory Elliott.

"The caterers confirmed the live lobster delivery for Sunday morning," Gregory whispered in Margo's ear while glancing at his cell phone. "Gagnon said he'd help me arrange the fire pit, and the seaweed planks tomorrow night. Everything according to plan. And the forecast is still clear."

"Good. Great." Margo nodded, jotting his words in her notebook. "Thank you, Gregory. Make sure everyone is comfortable, yes?" Gregory smiled and headed back toward the group.

Margo flipped through a few pages searching for the guest list, glancing up at the company at the bow, trying to place names with faces. There was nothing more embarrassing than calling the groom's mother by the name of the bride. Soon, she found what she was looking for:

The Sandovals
    Bruno, the groom
    Vivian, his mother
    Josie, his little sister
    Carlos, his father (arriving Saturday with the grandmother)

The Barkers
    Aimee, the bride
    Otis, her father
    Cynthia, her mother
    Elias (Eli), her little brother

The youngest two stood on opposite sides of the group, both staring into the distance. Josie and Eli. According to her notes, they were both starting seventh grade next week, in different schools, in different cities. They'd only just met on the wharf back at Haggspoint, and here they were already pretending that the other did not exist. Margo made a mental note to nudge the kids together once they reached the island. It was her job to make sure everyone had fun this weekend, not just the bride and groom.

She had no clue how quickly the coming storm would drag this idea away in a whirlpool of terror, spiraling it down into the depths of her memory, soon to be forgotten entirely.